A beautiful thief
steals what she
most desires—
the heart of a
Union officer.

Don't miss Lori Copeland's other
Sisters of Mercy Flats novels:
Promise Me Today
Promise Me Tomorrow

A thrill of frightened anticipation filled her at his nearness. "So," she taunted, "I suppose you're going to bully me again."

His smile was devilishly wicked. "Perhaps, or perhaps I'll only kiss you again."

"You do, and I'll scream my head off. I'll shout to the rooftops who you *really* are, *Captain* Kane."

His smile was nothing short of sinister. "I don't think so. You talk big, but you know that I'm your only hope of getting out of this one alive."

"You lay one finger on me and I'll scream," she vowed. "You'll die, too, you know."

Chuckling, he lowered his head, his breath fanning her lips. "Ahh, but what a sweet death."

PROMISE ME FOREVER

Lori Copeland

FAWCETT GOLD MEDAL • NEW YORK

A Fawcett Gold Medal Book
Published by Ballantine Books
Copyright © 1994 by Lori Copeland

All rights reserved under International and Pan-American Copyright Conventions. Published in the United States of America by Ballantine Books, a division of Random House, Inc., New York, and simultaneously in Canada by Random House of Canada Limited, Toronto.

Library of Congress Catalog Card Number: 93–90876

ISBN 0–449–14753–3

Manufactured in the United States of America

First Edition: May 1994

10 9 8 7 6 5 4 3 2 1

Author's Note

Well, we're down to the last McDougal sister. If you recall, in book one, Promise Me Today, Barrett was at the cemetery with Abigail trying to decide if he wanted a wife and son more than he wanted to hold on to the past. It's not an easy decision for a man who's declared rabid mules couldn't drag him to the altar again. In book two, Promise Me Tomorrow, Creed Walker had agreed to ride the last mile to the cemetery with Anne-Marie, knowing their parting is imminent, but reluctant to let her go. Creed, you'll remember, has given his word to Bold Eagle, his blood brother, to marry Bold Eagle's sister, Berry Woman. Of course, Creed knows that he's in love with Anne-Marie, but what's he to do? When a Crow gives his word, he keeps it. Now it's Amelia and Morgan's turn, the final book of The Sisters of Mercy Flats, Promise Me Forever. Good Lord, brace yourself.

PROMISE ME
FOREVER

Prologue

Five miles from Nacogdoches, Texas: March, 1865

Some people said they had it coming; others said it was a shame they hadn't gotten it sooner.

A March wind savagely whipped the jail wagon along the dusty road as three young women dressed in nuns' habits clung desperately to the bars, eyes clamped shut, praying for deliverance.

The driver, slumped over the front of the wagon could do little to console the screaming women, considering he had a Comanche arrow sticking through his back.

War whoops filled the air as four young braves chased the wagon, their black hair whipping wildly about their bronzed faces as they rode hard to overtake their prey.

"What do they want?" Amelia shouted, her voice nearly drowned out by the sound of thundering hooves.

Anne-Marie, eyes closed, gripped the beads of her rosary until her knuckles were white. "Hail, Mary, full of grace," she murmured, "the Lord is with thee—"

"They want the horses!" Abigail's heart pounded like the heathens' own war drums as the savages continued to gain on them.

"Tell them they can have them!"

"I hardly think they're listening, Amelia!"

"Holy Mary, Mother of God, pray for us sinners now and at the hour of our death—"

Oh, this is so typical, Abigail thought cynically. *Anne-Marie prays while Amelia falls apart at the slightest sign of adversity. Of course, this could turn out to be more than a slight turn of misfortune,* she conceded as her eyes darted back to the braves. But she wasn't worried. Lady Luck had always seen the McDougal sisters through the worst of times, and she wasn't likely to fail them now.

"If you'd listened to me and let Amy handle it," Anne-Marie put the blame where it belonged, "we wouldn't be in this pickle! I told you we shouldn't have tried to trick Ramsey McQuade!"

"How was I to know he had us figured out?" Abby shouted. "He was ripe for the kill. Posing as a wealthy Negress was brilliant—Amy could never have pulled it off!"

Amelia's eyebrows shot up. "And you did? Ramsey knew exactly what you were up to. Just because you think all men are stupid, doesn't mean they all are. If you ask me—"

"No one did, Amelia!"

"Ramsey McQuade looked brilliant standing by the sheriff on the outskirts of town when we rode out with his money," Amelia went on, determined to make her point.

Abby shot her a scathing look as the wagon lurched over a rut, pitching the vehicle into the air and Amelia to the bottom of the floor.

Clasping her hands over her face, Amelia began crying and wouldn't stop, even when Anne-Marie shot her a warning look.

When the visual reprimand had no effect, Anne-Marie diverted her litany long enough to give Amelia a swift kick with the toe of her boot.

"Good Lord, Amelia, control yourself!" Abigail snapped when Amelia bawled harder. You'd think she was the only one about to be scalped. Besides, nobody was going to be hurt. As far as Abigail was concerned, the braves could have the horses and the wagon, but if they laid one hand on her or her sisters, she'd personally see that they'd rue the day they were born!

As the jail wagon careened wildly along the road, three men, sitting on top of three separate hilltops, watched the scene playing out below them.

To the west, a dapper man riding a dark sorrel sawed back on the bridle reins as he caught sight of the spectacle.

He sat for a moment, absently removing his

spectacles to wipe away the thick layer of dust
coating the lenses.

The sight of four young braves in hot pursuit of
a wagon was of little concern to Hershall Earl
Digman. Hershall didn't go borrowing trouble,
thank you. He had quite enough of his own.

And it wasn't unusual for Comanche to be stirring up trouble. With the attraction of Mexican
horses drawing them south, they were raiding
deeper and deeper into Texas.

Since the wagon was of no value, the young
bucks were obviously in pursuit of the horses, and
there was little Hershall could do or planned to do
about it.

Flexing his sore shoulder muscles, he lifted his
face to the sun, momentarily dawdling as he
soaked up the warm rays.

To the east, Morgan Kane slowed his horse to a
walk. His first instinct when he spotted the wagon
was to ride to the women's aid. Even from this distance, he could see the wagon driver was dead or
gravely injured. The women were at the Indians'
mercy, and Morgan knew that with Comanche,
there would be none.

As much as he would like to help, Morgan felt
his sense of duty outweighing his sense of instinct.
Weather had already delayed him by several days;
he didn't need another interruption.

But as the women's cries shattered the peaceful
countryside, Morgan shifted uneasily in his saddle.

A gentleman by nature, he wasn't happy about the situation. The wagon was whipping down the road, the horses completely out of control now.

Whores on their way to jail, he argued when an inner voice nagged at him.

No one deserves a death like those women are about to face, the voice argued back.

Damn Comanche! Between the Comanche and the Kiowa, a man wasn't safe to travel the main roads.

Lifting his arm to wipe the sweat off his face, Morgan fixed his eyes on the braves as they drew closer to the wagon.

To the north, an Indian riding a large chestnut stallion topped the rise.

Tall and notably handsome, his piercing black eyes, straight brows, high cheekbones, lean cheeks, and prominent nose bespoke his Crow heritage.

The wind tossed his jet black hair as his dark eyes studied the scene below him.

Comanche.

Kneeing his horse forward, he rode closer, his eyes focused on the wagon.

The jail wagon bounced along, tossing the McDougal sisters around like rag dolls. The Indians were so close now that Abigail could see their dark eyes and youthful grins through the dust boiling up through the floor of the wagon. The boys couldn't be more than fifteen or sixteen, she thought.

Averting her gaze, she tried to block out the sound of thundering hooves. She had heard stories of women being captured by Indians and taken to live as their wives. Never in her wildest dreams could she, Abigail Margaret McDougal, imagine being a sixteen-year-old boy's squaw. She couldn't imagine being any man's squaw, and she'd fight until there wasn't a breath left in her if one of those heathens tried to make her one!

Her face puckered with resentment. She'd die before she'd let that happen. If they caught her, she would fight and fight dirty. She would pinch and spit and hit and bite, and if that didn't work she'd kick, and she knew where to kick because she had heard two men talking one day about getting kicked there, and presumably it wasn't where a man longed to get kicked.

And if that didn't work Anne-Marie would think of something to save them—Abigail's eyes darted back to the Indian drawing even with the wagon. She had to!

Jumping astride the lead horse, the brave tried to slow the team. The animals, wild-eyed from the harried chase, ran harder.

Hershall sat up straighter, watching as the ruckus neared a rowdy climax. By Jove, he suddenly realized, those weren't women; those were nuns in that jail wagon!

* * *

Amelia's throat was hoarse from screaming, but even her sisters couldn't stop her. The sounds of the Indians whooping and hollering as victory drew closer would terrify a saint!

Glancing frantically over her shoulder, Abigail groaned when she saw a bend coming up in the road. That's all they needed! They would be killed for certain now!

The horses galloped around the turn, and the wagon tilted sideways. Clutching the bars, Abby bit her lip until she tasted blood as the wagon tipped up to roll precariously on two wheels.

"Pray!" Anne-Marie demanded. "Pray!"

Morgan Kane edged his horse closer to the edge of the knoll. Either his eyes were playing tricks on him or those were nuns in that wagon, he thought. Damn. *Nuns.*

The wheels hit another pothole, and the wagon went airborne again as the horses thundered around a second bend in the road. The women screamed as they heard the right front wheel snap. Lurching to its side, the wagon skidded across the road toward a briar-infested ravine.

The Indians sent up a shout of victory as Hershall Digman spurred his horse into action. Holding onto his hat with his hand, he plunged his horse down the ravine.

Morgan Kane was already riding along the hillside as the Crow kneed his horse and sprang forward.

The wagon rolled end over end down the incline, violently tossing the McDougal sisters around inside the small cage. When the wagon finally came to rest on its side at the bottom of the ravine, two braves were already working to free the horses.

Blades glinted in the sunlight as a leather harness was slashed. Then, with another victorious shout, the youths mounted the two horses and rode them back up the steep incline.

Morgan Kane was riding hard as he approached, but the Indians whipped the horses into a hasty retreat. Yelping with triumph, the braves galloped off to rejoin the remainder of their raiding party, who by now were waiting a safe distance down the road. The braves cut their ponies across the open plains, their jubilant cries ringing over the hillsides.

Dropping from his horse, Morgan ran to peer down the steep slope, certain the women had been killed. A trail of dust marked the wagon's lightning descent, but the wagon was nowhere in sight.

Morgan whirled, reaching for his gun at the sound of approaching hoofbeats. An Indian riding a large chestnut stallion was moving in fast.

Morgan took aim, but stopped short when the Indian lifted his hand in a gesture of peace. As the horse came to a halt, the Indian slid off the animal's back and hurried to look over the side into the gulch.

A moment later, both men spun at the sound of Hershall's horse thundering toward them.

When Morgan saw that the approaching rider was having difficulty controlling his mount, he shouted at the Indian, and they both jumped out of the way as Hershall shot into the clearing.

Sawing back on the reins, the red-faced shoe salesman managed to stop his horse just short of plunging headlong over the ravine.

As the dust settled, Hershall calmly placed his bowler back on his head, then climbed awkwardly off his horse.

Shrugging his shoulders uncomfortably in the too-small jacket of his striped seersucker suit, he tipped his hat at the two men cordially.

"Afternoon, gentlemen."

Morgan nodded, slowly holstering his gun.

"My, my, my, my!" Hershall, round-eyed now, scurried to gape over the rim of the gulch. He fished a large handkerchief from his pocket and mopped anxiously at his perspiring forehead. "A most frightful turn of events," he fretted. "Are the women—?" Herhsall just couldn't bring himself to voice his fears. The thought of three nuns meeting such an untimely death was simply deplorable.

The three men edged closer to the ravine, their eyes trying to locate the wagon.

"Guess there's only one way to find out." Morgan glanced over his shoulder to make sure the braves hadn't decided to come back for their horses. "We'd better make it quick."

"Oh, my, my, my, my!" The thought of those savages returning just made Hershall sick. "Why ever do you suppose nuns would be riding in a jail wagon?"

Morgan shook his head. "I couldn't say."

The Indian was already making his way along the ravine. His moccasin-covered feet slid in the rocks and loose dirt as he worked his way down the incline.

Hershall cupped his hand to the side of his mouth and whispered, "Does the savage speak English?"

"I don't think so." Morgan started down the ravine, following behind the Indian.

Glancing anxiously at his carpetbag full of shoe samples, Hershall reluctantly joined the two men, who were halfway down the slope.

By the time the three men reached the bottom, they could see the jail wagon lying on its side. The back door was broken open, and the three nuns lay inside in a broken heap.

Wonderful, Hershall thought, setting his hat more firmly on his head. *Now I've got to bury three nuns.*

Morgan solemnly made the sign of the cross, then strode to the broken wreckage. "We better get them buried."

"Oh, my, my, my, my." Hershall thought he

might faint. "I'm developing a simply pounding headache from it all."

Shoving the broken door aside, the Indian ran his dark eyes over the crumpled heap of women. His fingers touched the side of Anne-Marie's wrist, feeling for a pulse.

Stirring, Anne-Marie opened her eyelids to encounter a pair of coal black eyes. Bolting upright, she screamed. The Indian, Morgan, and Hershall jumped as if they'd been shot.

Realizing that the good sister believed that the Crow was part of the band who had been chasing the wagon, Morgan attempted to calm her. "It's all right, Sister. You're safe now."

Anne-Marie stared back at the assortment of strange men, bewildered. She couldn't recall ever seeing such a mixed bag of masculinity.

She looked from the tall man with incredibly broad shoulders, to the dapper dandy in a puckered seersucker suit, whose main concern at the moment seemed to be preventing his hat from blowing off, to the splendid-looking savage whose dark eyes caused her to have the giddiest feeling when he centered his gaze upon her.

Amelia and Abigail were slowly coming around. Groaning, Abby tried to untangle her limbs from Amelia. "Sweet Mother of God, every bone in my body's broken!"

"*Sister* Abigail."

Abby winced at the sound of Anne-Marie's voice, groaning again.

"Your habit, Sister. It's askew."

Abby quelled the urge to shout back that her bowels were askew, let alone her habit! Pushing herself upright, she shook Amy, gradually becoming aware of the three men staring through the bars at her.

Great day in the morning! Hershall was nearly felled by the nuns' beauty. He had never seen three more beautiful women!

"Oh, dear Lord," Amy muttered, rolling to her back, glassy-eyed.

"Sister"—Abby punched her warningly—"are you hurt?"

"Are you crazy—I just had the shi—"

Abigail swiftly elbowed her again, quelling Amelia's obscene retort.

Amelia looked up. Upon seeing the men gaping at her, she pasted a serene smile on her lips and hastily made the sign of the cross. "Why, yes, Sister. I believe I've survived the fall quite nicely."

"God has smiled again," Anne-Marie said. "We must thank Him for His graciousness."

"Are you ladies all right?" Morgan asked, still finding it hard to believe that the women had no serious injuries.

Amy grunted, trying to sort her arms and legs from Abby's. Both women groaned as pain shot through their lower limbs.

"Sister, would you kindly get off me?"

"Certainly, Sister, if you will kindly get your foot out of my pocket."

"Well, nothing seems to be amiss," Anne-Marie assured the men brightly as she hastily straightened her veil.

Hershall bolted forward to assist Sister Abigail from the wagon. He removed his bowler and placed the hat over his heart, bowing from the waist. "Hershall E. Digman, at your service, ma'am."

Eyeing him sourly, Abby slid out of the wagon before he could touch her. But Hershall insisted on helping her to the nearest rock. After setting her down, he wrung his hands with despair as he noticed the beginnings of a dark bruise forming on her temple.

"You are most fortunate," he fussed, "most fortunate, my dear lady, that you weren't killed."

Pushing back the sleeve of her habit, Abby examined her skinned elbow. Was he serious? Fortunate? She didn't feel "fortunate." She had just eaten ten pounds of dust and nearly been scalped. If she got much luckier, she wouldn't live to tell about it.

Anne-Marie swayed with sudden light-headedness, and the Indian quietly stepped forward to assist her.

"Thank you," she managed. She got out of the wagon, her hand resting lightly on his bronzed forearm, an arm of such impressive width that it made her hand appear tiny.

His somber gaze met hers, and Anne-Marie felt the oddest quirk in the pit of her stomach. Shaken, she quickly severed the electrifying contact and stepped aside as Morgan reached to help Amelia down.

As Amy grabbed for Morgan's hand, she caught the look in Anne-Marie's eyes, silently urging her to maintain her best veneer of "sisterly" decorum. Well, Anne-Marie didn't have to worry about that! Amy knew how to act her part as well or better than her sisters.

Lifting her chin, she reached for Morgan's hand, but, drat it, the heel of her shoe caught in the hem of her habit and she pitched face-first out of the wagon.

Averting her eyes, Anne-Marie listened to the confusion as Amy stumbled from the wagon, knocking Morgan to the ground, then landing squarely on top of him.

"Oh, my!" Amelia gasped, attempting to regain what little composure she could under the circumstances. Scrambling to her feet, she tried to help Morgan up. "I'm ever so sorry, Mister . . . ?"

"Morgan Kane," Morgan supplied, momentarily dazed by the impact.

The Indian suddenly lifted his hand to command silence. As he nodded toward the road, his eyes mutely warned of impending trouble. Panic seized the small group as they listened to the sound of approaching horses.

"The remainder of the raiding party," Morgan guessed.

"Oh, my, my, my!"

"We'd better be on our way, gentlemen."

"Oh, yes, I think that would be most prudent of us," Hershall agreed. "Most prudent."

Pushing his glasses up on the bridge of his nose, Hershall extended the crook of his arm to Abigail. Surveying it glumly, Abby knew she had little choice but to let the simpleton help her.

Morgan took Amelia's hand and began pulling her toward the incline. "We don't have much time. If you can't make it up the hill, I'll carry you."

"I can make it," Amelia assured him, still so humiliated by her clumsiness that she could die.

"Wait," Anne-Marie murmured, closing her eyes as dizziness nearly overcame her again. The Indian paused, supporting her weight until the light-headedness passed.

Amelia was already scrambling up the hillside ahead of Morgan. Her feet slid in the loose dirt, but Morgan's hand boosted her onward. She turned, offering him an affronted glare. "Sorry, Sister—we have to keep moving." He meant no disrespect to this nun, but he wasn't thrilled about the prospect of his hair hanging from a Comanche's lodge pole tomorrow morning, either.

The Indian and Anne-Marie systematically made their way up the incline. When she occasionally lost her footing, the Crow's hand was there to steady her.

Hershall attempted to take Abby's hand, but she repeatedly brushed his efforts aside. If she'd ever seen a worthless man, this was it. A dapper dandy, with his hair slicked down and his spectacles sliding down the bridge of his nose.

Scrambling up the incline, she glanced over her shoulder, concerned about Amelia, who seemed disoriented. Of course, she conceded, with Amy, one could never be certain. Amy was in a daze most of the time.

Abby felt her feet slipping in the loose dirt, but Hershall's hand chivalrously shot out to support her backside. She irritably swatted it aside and muttered, *"Pervert."*

Pervert? Welll! Jerking his waistcoat back into place, Hershall made up his mind right then and there that it would be a cold day in Hades before he'd offer that woman his assistance again!

As the six scrambled over the gully, they spotted the dust of the returning Comanche raiding party.

"They're moving in fast," Morgan warned.

"We're going to have to make a run for it," Hershall shouted.

Whirling, he raced for his horse, leaving Sister Abigail standing, hands on her hips, glaring after him.

The Indian swung onto the stallion, pulling Anne-Marie on behind him.

Morgan caught Amy around the waist and lifted her into the saddle. Springing up behind her, he turned to the others. "We're going to have to split up!"

The Indian nodded, trying to control his prancing stallion.

Hershall's horse was side stepping nervously as he attempted to mount. Abby glanced anxiously at the approaching cloud of dust, then back at Hershall's bumbling attempts to get on the horse.

When it became clear that they were going to be scalped if he didn't get his foot in the stirrup soon, she smothered a curse and irritably marched over and hoisted him into the saddle with her shoulder.

"Why, thank you, my dear—"

"Just shut up, Hershall!"

Planting her foot atop his, she gathered her skirt around her thighs, grasped the tail of his coat, and hefted herself up behind him, forcing Hershall to grab frantically for the saddle horn to keep them both from hurtling to the ground.

Giving the horse a sound whack across the rump, Abby sent it bolting into a full gallop as Hershall held tightly to his hat.

"Abigail! Anne-Marie! Remember Church Rock!" Amelia shouted as the men turned their horses and galloped off.

Thus began an adventure few would ever forget.

Chapter 1

Sister Amelia was a nuisance.

Morgan Kane couldn't afford a nuisance right now. After narrowly escaping the Comanche, he needed to get on with his business. That delay, though small, had cost him valuable time, and for him time was running out.

Now that the imminent danger had passed, his thoughts shifted to the immediate problem—what to do with the sister.

Though the prospect was tempting, he couldn't just leave her by the roadside. It had become clear to him that Sister Amelia, whom he had snatched from a jail wagon hours earlier, had a penchant for nature that would result in even more delays.

Low-flying birds, blooming flowers, rolling clouds, blinding sunrises, glowing sunsets, and, it appeared, life in general enthralled this woman.

While Morgan could appreciate spontaneity, this nun's continual flights of fancy destroyed any semblance of a schedule and played havoc with his system of order. If these postponements continued, he could miss his Galveston contact. He had to rid himself of the sister and soon.

Sister Amelia viewed the day's events as unsettling, but far from alarming. At first, she had been perturbed when those awful ol' Comanche had swooped down on the jail wagon like a donkey with a pepper up its behind, but when this nice Union officer had ridden to her aid, her fears had flown right out the window.

Two other men had arrived to rescue Abigail and Anne-Marie, so there was nothing to be upset about. The Indians had been outwitted, and now everything was fine.

Sighing, Amelia again admired the considerable breadth of the Yankee's shoulders. The way he sat up so tall and straight in his saddle just made her feel all good inside. *He surely is an admirable sight,* she thought. Why, he must have at least a hundred women in love with him—that, or Texas women were just plain blind.

They had been together for over a day now, and he had seemed so cordial to her and so capable. In fact, he was the most organized, masterful man she'd ever met. He had escaped those Indians with hardly any effort at all.

When this was over, she wanted to introduce him to Abigail and Anne-Marie. Meeting such a fine, manly specimen might change her sisters' less-than-charitable feelings for the opposite sex.

They'd like this man. Though the officer had
seemed pensive throughout the ordeal, he had
treated her with the utmost respect, seeing to her
every need as if she were a welcome guest instead
of just some ol' bother.

And, although they had just met, Amelia had a
hunch that this handsome Yankee had taken a
fancy to her. Her intuition hadn't been inspired by
anything he had said or done: she just saw a glint
of interest every time he looked at her with those
remarkable steel gray eyes.

Odd how two people seemed to gravitate to each
other, she mused as she rode in the saddle behind
him, admiring a scenic fence post.

Although her knowledge of men could fit inside
a thimble, she was positive this particular man
thought her attractive. No telling how she knew;
she just knew.

"Oh, this is just perfect!" Amelia twirled around
the clearing that evening, arms flung wide as she
admired the setting. It was uncanny how the captain always knew just the right thing to do. How
could he have known that she absolutely adored
clearings beside wooded streams?

Morgan quietly side stepped her, then side
stepped her again as he tried to make camp.

"Oh, look! A squirrel!" Running to the trunk of
a fallen oak, she crouched down low, making
small, clucking noises with her tongue. When the
animal bolted and ran off, Morgan envied him.

More than once this afternoon he had considered
doing the same. But his conscience wouldn't allow
him to leave a woman in the wilds, particularly a
nun.

"Oh, here, let me do that," the sister scolded
when she saw that he was doing all the work.

"No, if you'll just step aside—"

"I insist," she protested. Taking the branches
from his arms, she smiled. "Now, you just go on
and do whatever you need to do. I'll gather the
wood."

Side stepping her a third time, Morgan returned
to the horse for the saddlebags. "Hope you don't
mind hardtack and jerky."

"Oh ... well ... don't you have any bacon?"

"No, no bacon. Just hardtack and jerky."

"Then just go on and eat without me," she said
cheerily. "I only eat bacon."

Morgan looked up. "*Only* bacon?"

"Well, just about. Sometimes, if I get hungry
enough, I'll eat ham or something, but mostly I
just eat bacon." Humming beneath her breath, she
scurried around the clearing gathering small
branches and twigs to feed a fire.

Morgan watched, trying to temper his impatience.

"We should be safe here tonight," he told her as
he shouldered the heavy leather bags. The area was
crawling with Confederate troops. He'd passed
three contingents on the road in the past two days,

moving in this direction. "We'll keep the fire low in case we're detected—"

"Oh, no!" she burst out.

The hair on Morgan's neck bristled as his hand whipped to his holster, his eyes searching for the intruder. When there was none, he glanced at her.

"Over there!" she enthused. "I could swear that was a yellowthroat warbler! No, it could have been a wood warbler—oh, shoot! I can't be certain because it flew in and flew out so fast I barely caught a glimpse of it. Did you see it?"

Morgan felt heat suffusing his neck. "A warbler?" The woman had just scared five years off his life for a blasted bird!

"Yes! Didn't you see it?"

"No," he said shortly.

"Well, what a shame. It was there, I'm almost positive!"

She tripped, nearly dropping the armload of wood in her excitement. "Oh, dear," she murmured, taking care not to step on her shoelace, which had come untied. She looked up. "I hate to be an ol' bother, but my shoe's untied, and, as you can see, my arms are full." She smiled apologetically. "Could you tie it for me?"

Retaining his calm, Morgan holstered his gun. After he tied her shoe, he straightened to take the wood from her.

"Will that be enough?"

"As I said, we'll keep the fire low."

"Oh, yes, I remember hearing you say that," she agreed. "I guess it's kind of dangerous out here."

"I think we can safely assume that it is."

While he started a fire, she fussed with her headdress, loosening and unloosening the veil, trying to get comfortable, which was nearly impossible. That was the thing about a tight headdress and veil, she didn't know how real nuns stood them. Maybe it had something to do with self-sacrifice and being kind and tolerant. Then again, maybe it was because somebody made them wear the blasted things.

Freeing the hook on her collar, she released a deep, audible breath. There, that was definitely better.

"Tomorrow we'll proceed to the nearest port," the handsome captain told her as they finished their evening meal. He had talked her into eating some of the jerky. It wasn't as good as bacon, but it was nourishing. Or so he told her.

The night was clear under a starry sky, but the cold wind had a bite to it. Amelia thought it felt like snow.

"Where is the nearest port?" she asked as she huddled closer to the warmth. She'd never been good at directions. All day long, she hadn't known east from west.

"Galveston." He pitched the remainder of his coffee, watching as steam rose from the frozen ground. "I was on my way there when I encountered the jail wagon. You are welcome to accompany me there in the morning."

"Oh?" She tilted her head to look up at him. He was over six feet tall, she decided. "Why are you going to Galveston?"

"I have business there."

"What kind of business?"

"I'm not at liberty to say."

"Oh." She was silent for a moment. "Secretive business, maybe?"

"I'm sorry, Sister. I'm not at liberty to say."

Must be something to do with the war, she thought. "But you did say you didn't care if I come with you?"

"No, that is the only logical choice at this point." He would prefer to cover the remaining distance alone, but he could hardly leave the sister without protection.

Tipping her head up to gaze at the sky, she sighed. "Isn't it a heavenly night?"

He huddled deeper into his frock coat. "I find it unseasonably cold for this time of year."

"Yes, but just look at those stars. Have you ever seen anything more lovely?" It was worth a little cold for a vision as pretty as this one.

They sat in silence a moment, she studying the sky, he drinking his coffee and reflecting on the day's troubling delays. He savored the blessed silence. It was the quietest she'd been all day.

"Captain?"

"Yes, Sister."

"My veil is caught on the hook of my collar. I can't lower my head."

Resignedly he set his cup aside and moved over to free her veil from her collar.

"Thank you ever so much. I don't know how that happened." Amelia gazed up at him warmly, marveling over the way her stomach felt all jittery every time he looked at her.

Yes, he did find her attractive, even though he should be ashamed of himself. After all, he believed her to be a woman of the cloth.

Still, she smiled, finding pleasure at the thought. "Now, about us traveling together. It's very kind of you, but I have no funds—"

"Please, Sister." He lifted his hand in protest. "It would be my honor to provide for your meals and safe return to Mercy Flats."

Staring into the fire, Amelia measured his generous offer. Actually, she did have little choice in the matter. She was penniless, and traveling alone didn't interest her. She felt safe with this man, safe and protected. She couldn't have a more honorable escort, cool in the face of adversity, reserved, competent. And he had been enough of a gentleman not to question her reason for being in the jail wagon.

"Are you from around here?" She asked.

"No, I'm from Washington."

"Oh, really? Have you ever met a President?"

"Washington Territory," he corrected.

"Oh. Well, that's nice, too. I've never been to

Washington Territory, but I'd like to go there
someday—is it far?"

"It's a good distance from here."

She let her eyes travel the width of his shoulders
beneath his impeccable double-breasted frock coat
as she heaved another mental sigh. The North
surely must be bursting with pride to have a man
like him on its side.

Over the years she'd watched the Union troops
going about their business, and she'd developed a
certain admiration for them.

To be fair, the Confederacy had its share of no-
table specimens, but she was drawn to the handsome Northerners. Oh, her feelings had little to do
with the causes of the war because she had never
understood why everyone was so mad. Whatever
the reasons, she knew that the quarrel had turned
ugly.

Her fondness for this uniform also evolved from
her interest in the man wearing it. He was so powerful, so decisive, just as a man ought to be.

Abigail and Anne-Marie would say she was
foolish for thinking any man worthy of second notice, but Amelia didn't think so. She'd met men
who weren't all that disagreeable. And besides, she
almost liked men.

Her eyes returned to his tall form as he stood,
warming his backside at the fire.

"I live here in Texas."

"Yes, I believed you mentioned that. Mercy
Flats?"

"Yes, it's a small border town ... mmm ... somewhere here in Texas ... I'm not sure how far away ... not as far as Washington Territory, I'm sure, but pretty far, I think." She was never a good judge of distance. "There's not a whole lot there except the mission where I was raised."

Morgan wondered how a young woman who'd led such a sheltered life had ended up in a jail wagon, but he declined to ask. If she wanted to explain, she would. She was anything but timid.

"You were orphaned at a young age?"

"Yes, my two sisters and I."

"That must have been hard on the three of you."

"I was very young," she admitted. "The only thing I remember about my parents was my mother's eyes. I remember they were as gentle as a fawn's."

He was being so nice to her that her conscience began to hurt. So nice, in fact, she felt compelled to be truthful with him. She knew that he might find her admission startling, at best somewhat annoying, but considering the pleasant way he was acting she couldn't let him go on thinking that she really was a nun. It just wouldn't be right.

"You eat nothing but bacon?" he asked again, as if the subject still troubled him. "No fruit?"

"Maybe a peach once in a while."

"What about apples?"

"I don't like apples."

"Oh."

The moments stretched into even longer minutes before they spoke again.

"Captain?" She realized she didn't remember his name.

Covering a yawn, he stood up to stretch his long torso. Twelve hours in the saddle had taken its toll. "Yes, Sister?"

"There's something I must confess."

From the look on his face, she gathered that the prospect of listening to a long, dreary confession didn't intrigue him.

"Perhaps it could wait until morning, Sister? I am unusually weary tonight."

"No," she replied, her mind firmly made up now. "It's important that I tell you tonight." If she waited until morning, she might have second thoughts. She was bad about that.

"Very well," he conceded.

"Promise you won't get mad?"

What is it now? he wondered. Had she spotted a great horned owl she'd neglected to mention?

"Promise you won't get mad."

"I don't anger easily, Sister." The past twelve hours had been mute testimony to that.

Getting slowly to her feet, Amelia lifted her hands to her head and peeled off the tight head-dress and veil, freeing a mass of luxuriant auburn hair that tumbled over her shoulders.

Afraid to look at him now, she quickly removed her collar and awaited his response. Would he be angry? The last thing she wanted was to make him angry.

As his silence grew more palpable, she mentally braced herself for his reaction, fearing that she had misjudged his character. Was it possible that he would be so furious with her that he would order her to find her way back to Mercy Flats alone?

Oh, he was angry, she agonized. She didn't blame him—he should be furious with her. He had unselfishly risked his life to rescue her because he'd believed that she was a woman of exemplary virtue. Now he could see that she wasn't righteous, that she'd only been pretending—not that she wasn't righteous. She could be when she wanted to be, but she wasn't nun-righteous. None of the McDougal sisters were nun-righteous.

"You're furious," she murmured when she couldn't bear the damnable silence a moment longer.

The captain stared at her.

"Oh, you hate me, don't you?"

Very little surprised Morgan Kane anymore, but she had. Why would a woman parade around the countryside in a nun's habit when she wasn't a nun? That was blasphemous!

"All right." He would handle this calmly. Blowing up would gain him nothing more than another costly delay. He had endured twelve hours; he could endure another few. "Do you care to explain your disguise?"

"I'm a thief," she concluded grimly.

His brows knit in a tight frown. "What?"

"Not a mean thief," she clarified. "But, nevertheless, a thief." She felt just awful having to tell
him, but in view of the circumstances he needed to
know.

"A thief." His shifted his stance irritably.

"Yes. I thought you should know."

"Thank you."

"You're welcome." A strained smile touched her
lips. There, that hadn't been so bad. He had taken
it quite well, actually.

"So are my sisters. They really are my flesh-
and-blood sisters—the ones who were in the jail
wagon with me."

"They're thieves."

"Yes." She smiled tightly.

"That's why you were in the jail wagon? Because you're three sister thieves dressed in nuns'
clothing?"

"That's right."

He stood for a moment, color building in his
face. He had squandered thirty-six hours and risked
his mission for a bunch of thieving women!

"Now, you promised you wouldn't get mad."
His face had become rather mottled.

He strode around the fire and jerked open the
straps on the saddlebags. After fishing inside, he
produced a pair of wrinkled overalls and a plaid
shirt.

"What are you doing?"

"Getting a change of clothing," he snapped.

"Why?"

"I consider that to be my business." The gloves were off. She heard it clearly in his tone.

"Oh." She took a hesitant step toward him, then paused. "You are angry, aren't you?"

"It matters little how I feel, Miss—"

"McDougal. Amelia McDougal," she supplied as she reached out to shake his hand.

For a moment, he stared at her extended hand. Finally, with an impatient sigh, he took her hand and gave it a perfunctory shake.

"Captain Morgan Kane."

"Amelia—McDougal," she shared again. "I'm sorry about the fib."

He didn't say that he'd accept her apology, but he didn't say he wouldn't.

"I can still ride to Galveston with you tomorrow, can't I?" He couldn't just leave her out here alone, no matter how angry he was with her.

Morgan would have liked nothing better than to retract his offer. He should feel no further responsibility for her, now that he knew she was nothing more than a common thief, but he did. She was a woman, thief or no thief, and a woman had no business traveling alone.

"To Galveston," he said, turning away, grim resignation in his voice, "and not a mile farther."

"Oh, I won't be a bother," she assured him. "You'll hardly know I'm around."

"Make certain that I don't."

His words stung her. She'd braced herself for a

wave of indignation, perhaps fury, but not cold indifference. He'd been so kind to her that she'd expected him to forgive her for the tiny iniquity.

Perplexed, she sank to the log. Cold dismissal was something she hadn't been prepared for, especially from a man. Her head dropped into her hands, regret assailing her. The truth was she hadn't really anticipated his reaction to her impulsive confession. She'd leaped again without looking. She had a bad habit of going on instinct instead of logic, of rushing headlong with a heart full of good intentions only to stumble into trouble. It had happened again, only this time it was worse.

Morgan Kane didn't know her; worse yet, now he didn't want to know her. She'd seen the shock in his eyes, watched it turn to disillusionment. If she'd only thought things through, she'd still be basking in his warmth.

When would she learn? she wondered as she glanced up to see him disappear into the brush.

When he reappeared, he was wearing the wrinkled plaid shirt and the faded overalls he'd dug out of his saddlebag. His military uniform draped over his arm, he brushed past her with only a brief, slanted glance.

He no longer looked like her dashing captain. Watching his back as he spread his bedroll, she thought he looked like a poor dirt farmer. But when he rose to his full height and turned to face her, she recognized the pride in his military bearing, the lean muscle beneath the thin fabric.

He was still the captain, but not her captain. The chill in his gaze exposed the degree of his disappointment.

She tried to swallow around the lump in her throat. His icy regard was difficult to endure.

He tossed a bedroll at her feet. "Turn in. We ride at daybreak." His cool response cut her deeply. A spark of resentment flickered to life. After all, she'd only told him the truth. He could give her credit for that. She could have fooled him for days with her nun's charade. She'd trusted him with the truth, and this was the thanks she got.

Her chin lifted, and she brushed the bedroll aside. "You may be accustomed to people jumping when you give orders, but I don't jump—"

"Unless it's from a jail wagon," he muttered as he stretched out.

Her jaw dropped open. "I'll have you know, Captain Kane, that I—"

He rolled over and sat up so suddenly that she strangled a cry when his face came perilously close to hers. As his eyes bore into hers, her breath froze in her throat.

"The rules have changed, Sister," he said in a tight voice.

He was so close she could see the dark flecks in his eyes, feel his warm breath on her face. Her gaze dropped to the firm lips that hovered above hers.

"What?" she whispered as she swayed toward

him. She could feel the heat of his anger, but she felt irresistibly drawn to him.

His eyes narrowed ruthlessly. A man would have recognized the danger in his look. An instant later his lips ground down upon hers. Without touching her, he relentlessly plundered her mouth, searching, thrusting, driving her backward until she found herself on her back, his body arched above her.

She was sinking into a swirl of needs she hadn't known existed. Primitive needs she'd never experienced drummed in her pulse. What was he doing to her?

Her head was spinning and her heart pounding in desperation. Nothing her sisters had told her had prepared her for anything like this.

All Morgan intended to do was punish her. Punish her for the most miserable hours of his life!

Bells were going off in Amelia's head, but she felt powerless to resist. Everything was happening so fast, too fast. The sensations racing through her were too sudden to comprehend.

Terrified, she shoved him back. "Stop!"

He jerked back, his breathing ragged as his mouth left hers.

Wiping her hand across her mouth, she spat on the ground contemptuously. "Poophhhph! How dare you!"

With a lunge, he shoved away from her and rolled to his feet. "Little girls who play dangerous games should expect dangerous consequences."

Amelia watched dumbfoundedly as he stalked off into the thick underbrush.

Drawing her knees to her chest, she wrapped her arms around them tightly. Rejection and humiliation bloomed on her cheeks. How could she ever look him in the eye again? She couldn't; not tonight. She'd take the coward's way out and feign sleep even though she couldn't possibly sleep. Not now—not after this.

Why, he was dangerous.

She quickly spread her bedroll and curled up, her back to the fire, her face hidden under the blanket she drew tightly around herself.

The beast.

Chapter 2

Exactly why had he changed his clothes? Just what sort of man was this Morgan Kane?

Amelia lay listening for his return, her body so tense she ached. It seemed like hours before she heard him return, his footsteps stealthy. She listened intently as he stretched out beside the fire on his blanket. Hours dragged by, but she never heard the even breathing of slumber. She wondered if he was a silent sleeper, but she dare not risk a glance. She lay silent and unmoving all night.

She didn't realize she'd fallen asleep until the slanting rays of dawn pierced her eyelids. She rose with a shiver and glanced over her shoulder. The fire was out and the camp was deserted.

Gone was his bedroll, his coffeepot, even his saddle. Her gaze darted to the tree where he'd tethered his horse the night before. No horse.

Gone without a trace, without a shred of evidence to prove he'd ever been there except for the army blanket wrapped around her.

Perhaps he'd never existed. Perhaps her entire encounter with him had only been a dream. She touched her fingertips to her swollen lips. His kiss hadn't been a dream. She couldn't have imagined anything that startling.

"Now what?" she moaned. She'd always had someone to fall back on. Here she was in the middle of nowhere with no one. She sat cross-legged in the center of the blanket, her mouth agape, her fingertips lightly testing her lips, her thoughts in a blur.

She sat up straighter when she heard muffled hoofbeats.

"On your feet, Sister."

Her head spun around and she looked up into the blinding rays of the sun. It was only when she raised her hands to shield her eyes that she saw the captain, sitting astride his horse, watching her with a grim expression.

This was no dream. Harsh reality had returned.

He took in the vision of her, sitting on the blanket, her sleep-tossed hair cascading over her shoulders, her fingertips tapping her swollen lips. Something flickered in his gaze before his eyes narrowed.

"Where have you been?" she blurted.

"Shopping."

"Shopping?" If she weren't so relieved to see him she would give him a piece of her mind!

"Corral that mane of yours under your veil, Sister. It's time to climb aboard your new friend here."

Her eyes followed his gesture to the scrawny mule standing behind his horse. "What's that?"

"Your transportation."

"That ol' thing!"

Turning his horse, he started to ride off. "Take it or leave it."

Scrambling to her feet, she quickly tucked her hair beneath her veil. "Where did you get him?"

The mule was so skinny that his backbone protruded noticeably under the woven cloth on his back. His coat was long and matted, and beneath his long lashes he seemed to regard her as mournfully as she regarded him.

"You ask too many questions," Morgan said shortly. He rode back to give her a leg up. Before she could think of a delay, she felt her backside land on the mule's sharp spine. She was about to voice a protest when she thought better of it. She wouldn't give him the satisfaction, nor did she want to face the prospect of being left behind again.

"Here are the new rules, Sister."

Her eyes widened momentarily as his words from the night before echoed back to her. The rules have changed, he'd said to her before he'd delivered that punishing kiss.

He saw the surprise on her face as his eyes traveled over her kiss-swollen lips. "You will not, at any time, address me as captain. In fact, the less you say the better." He raked her with a look of disdain. "Keep your costume in place and play the role of the good sister. The moment we reach Galveston you will book passage on the first vessel sailing for Mercy Flats. Understood?"

"Why? Are you trying to hide something?" That must be it. He was up to something sneaky.

Before she could ask again, he turned the animals and moved out in the lead.

A cold wind rolled in from the water as the odd couple rode into Galveston late the following day. A wintry sun glittered off the Gulf of Mexico as Morgan and Amelia guided their horses into town. Threading their animals through the crowded streets, their eyes quietly appraised the situation. The town was teaming with Confederate soldiers.

Glancing warily at the captain, Amelia wondered if he was aware that Glaveston was a Confederate naval center. Even she knew that, and she didn't know hardly anything.

If Morgan found the atmosphere threatening, he didn't show it. His features fixed dispassionately as they rode through town.

"For Heaven's sake don't call him captain," Amelia reminded herself under her breath, recalling his earlier warning. It would only set him off again, and he had been sullen ever since she'd told him the truth about her.

The dirt-poor farmer and the sister in a threadbare habit casually wove their way past rows of weather-beaten storefronts, trying to blend with the crowd.

The streets were filled with boisterous Confederate naval soldiers. Ship boys and officers alike had set out to get roaring drunk, seeking a few hours' reprieve from sea duty with its steamy, salt air, heaving decks, and stench of gunpowder.

Amelia's eyes anxiously scanned the area. Swallowing dryly, her thoughts wandered to Anne-Marie and Abigail, wondering what they were doing now. It hadn't occurred to her to be concerned about the fate of her sisters. Bad things happened to other people, never to the McDougal sisters. Sister Agnes had said that they were all blessed, and Amelia believed her. People were always blessing the McDougal sisters up one side and down the other.

Her eyes darted to the various signs tacked to storefront windows, offering a reward for the notorious "Lanigan," a daring privateer who was barbarously good with a knife.

Spying a vacancy at a nearby hitching post, the farmer and the nun maneuvered their horses toward the rail and dismounted. Securing the reins, they stood for a moment, anticipating their next move.

Amelia edged closer to the captain and murmured from the corner of her mouth, "Better watch it. The enemy is everywhere."

Morgan glanced down at her. "What?"

"They're all around us," she repeated, motioning with her eyes to their treacherous surroundings. "The enemy—everywhere."

Her voice carried like a feather in a hurricane.

She stepped closer, working her words through stiff lips. "Did you hear what I said?" If he were up to something sneaky, he was in a nest of hornets now.

He gave her a glare that would blister paint off a ship.

"What?" she asked, annoyed by his look. She couldn't do anything to please him.

"Lower your voice."

"What?"

"Lower your voice!"

Color suffused her cheeks. Was he implying she talked too loud!

"Lower your voice," he demanded tautly.

"I wasn't talking loud," she argued, appalled that he thought she was. Wasn't that just like a man? Try to look out for him, and all he can do is criticize. "I was only trying to warn you that you'd better be careful because this town is crawling—"

Her eyes widened as his hand clamped over her mouth.

"Shut up!"

"Shut up?" she spat in a garbled indignation. Her reaction was starting to draw a crowd.

Well, that did it! Now he had hurt her feelings! He'd been sore ever since he'd found out she wasn't a nun, and now he'd done it! Never, in her entire life, had anyone but her sisters ever told her to shut up. Tears smarted in her eyes. How dare he tell her to shut up! Who did he think he was? The President of the Union, Abraham—Abraham Whatever-his-name-is!

When Morgan saw her eyes flare with teary anger, he swore under his breath. A crying female— one more thing he didn't need.

"Quiet down," he whispered, his tone losing its harshness now in an effort to appease her. "Your voice carries. I don't want to be noticed."

"My voice carries?" Her tears grew brighter. "My voice carries!"

"Dammit," Morgan snapped, realizing that anything he said now would only make matters worse.

"Well, for your information, Captain Rude," she barked, as if they were alone in the desert instead of the midst of the Confederate Navy. "I was only trying to help."

Help . . . help . . . help, her voice echoed.

Turning his back to her, Morgan nervously busied himself adjusting the horse's bit in a effort to divert attention. "I told you not to refer to me as captain. I know what you're trying to do, but if you want to help, lower your voice."

She glared at his back, appalled by the lightning turn of his personality. Where was the formal, courteous Yankee officer she had found so attractive? Gone, that's where. Gone.

"I am aware of the danger." He assured quietly in an effort to calm her, but it wasn't working.

"Well," she said, unwilling to overlook his burst of ill temper. Some women might, but not her. Had she ever misjudged him! "Since I'm such a loud-mouth, you'll want to be rid of me as quickly as possible."

It was a good thing he'd shown his true colors. To think she'd actually been dreading to leave him!

Unbuckling the strap on his saddlebag, Morgan removed a roll of currency. He peeled off three bills and handed them to her. "Two blocks down the street is the ship's office. Tell the clerk you want to buy passage on a vessel sailing near the vicinity of Mercy Flats on the morning tide."

"I'm perfectly capable of taking care of myself," she assured him loftily.

His look conveyed that he thought otherwise, but, thank God, she was no longer his problem. "Just do as you're told."

She listened with crossed arms, tapping her foot impatiently as he went on to warn her not to talk to anyone, to keep to herself. He was treating her as if she were an infant and it burned her to the core.

"With any luck," he told her, "you'll be enjoying a hot meal aboard ship within the hour. Are you listening?" he demanded when he saw her glaring into space.

"Yes!"

"Lower your voice!"

She whirled and marched off. She didn't have to

take this. She didn't want his ol' money. He could just take it and stick it up his ol' butt! She would *crawl* to Mercy Flats on her hands and knees before she'd accept his *help*.

"Amelia!" All patience left his voice as he watched her trounce off in the opposite direction.

"I can take care of myself, Cap— Mr. Rude! You don't bother your head about me one more minute!"

"Amelia," Morgan repeated tightly. "Get back here."

"Go fly a kite."

In a few long strides, Morgan overtook her. Grasping her firmly by the arm, he halted her flight.

"Take your hand off my arm or I'll scream," she threatened, and he had no reason to doubt her.

His hand dropped away, his hasty compliance assuring her he was striving to keep this friendly.

Allowing her a moment to cool off, he smiled at the small crowd that had started to assemble. Their faces were puzzled as they watched the vocal dispute taking place between the farmer and the nun.

"Just a minor disagreement," he assured them in a strained voice, motioning for them to move on.

A young, sturdy chap suddenly stepped forth, doffing his sailor's hat respectfully. "Is this man bothering you, Sister?"

Amelia refused to meet the eyes of her youthful protector, aware she was causing a scene. "No, he's trying to buy my silence!"

The crowd drew back, stunned.

When Amelia realized what she'd implied, she exhaled a disgusted ooohft, spun around, snatched Morgan Kane's money out of his hand, and stalked off.

Oh, he made her so mad! She'd show him! She didn't need him to get back to Mercy Flats! And he could bet his ol' stuffy, spit-shined boots he'd seen the last of her!

"And you'd damn well better start eating something other than bacon!" he shouted after her.

Eating only bacon and peaches. That was disgusting.

Chapter 3

She didn't go straight to the shipping office. That would be too much like doing what the captain had told her, and she was determined to avoid that. Besides, she loved adventure and this certainly had the earmarks of a whopping good one.

Instead, she wandered around for a while, peering into storefront windows, perusing the meager merchandise displays as if she had enough money to buy anything more than food and passage on an ol' ship.

She was dawdling in front of the bakery window, staring at the crusty brown delicacies the baker was removing from the steaming oven, when the sun gradually slid below the gulf waters. The little rolls being set out to cool looked and smelled so good she could just die.

The captain had provided ample funds to purchase food, but common sense warned her not to squander it on cinnamon rolls.

She thought about his shouted warning about eating something other than bacon. Her eyes moved back to the rolls as her teeth worried her bottom lip. How badly did she want one of the tasty-looking rolls? What if she purchased one, then discovered bacon two blocks away? Then what would she do? She would have spent a portion of her money and be stuck with a roll that she might not have wanted as badly as she wanted the bacon she might just find two blocks away.

Shoot. Why did life have to be so complicated? She wandered on down the sidewalk.

It was really cold now. Her habit was hardly any protection at all from the icy wind blowing off the water. It was the coldest spring she could ever remember.

Spotting a millinery, she crossed the street and hurried up the wooden steps. A bell over the door greeted her warmly.

Hurrying quickly to the pot-bellied stove stationed in the middle of the room, she warmed her hands. As feeling gradually returned to her fingers, she began to browse through the store, taking care to keep her answers to the clerk brief and to the point. She supposed a woman traveling alone should exercise caution.

The clerk, a stout, vocal woman, appeared to have nothing better to do than visit. It was late, and the store was void of customers.

Amelia half listened as the woman took on about the weather and how her husband was down in his back again. Lumbago. Worse than usual this year. She still had a long walk home in the cold once she closed up here, she complained, and Amelia sympathized; it was uncommonly cold for these parts.

When Amelia had browsed long enough to wear her welcome out, the clerk grew more talkative.

"Is there anything you're looking for in particular?" she asked. She had eight mouths to feed once she got home—if she ever got home.

Glancing out the storefront window, Amelia saw that it was dark now. Lanterns flickered on, and an occasional drunken laugh drifted in from the sidewalks. She suddenly felt very alone.

She had nowhere to go until the ship left in the morning— She frowned. Oh, dear. She had frittered away the past two hours and still hadn't bought ship's passage.

After hurriedly selecting a warm black woolen shawl, Amelia carried the garment to the counter. The captain hadn't said anything about buying clothing, but he should have. He'd prided himself on begin so organized, and he hadn't even thought about her comfort. The habit she was wearing was completely unsuitable for this kind of weather.

"That be all for you?" the clerk asked cheerfully.

"That will be all." Amelia handed her a bill and waited as the woman counted out her change. Even with this impulsive purchase, she still had enough money for ship's fare. She'd just have to eat lightly.

"Can you tell me what time the ship's office closes?"

The clerk turned to glance at the clock hanging behind the register. "Closed about ten minutes ago."

Amelia gasped. "It's closed already?"

"Closes five on the dot." She handed Amelia her change. "Most everything around here closes early, except the saloons. With all them sailors in town, they carry on most of the night."

Shoot! Now she had done it. Well, at least she would be warm, should she be forced to sleep in the livery tonight because of her dawdling. She'd probably have to share her bed with a horse. She squared her shoulders resolutely. At least she'd be in better company than she'd been the night before.

When she saw the clerk was about to wrap the purchase, she quickly waved the effort aside. "That won't be necessary. I'll be wearing it."

"Whatever you say."

Amelia removed her headdress, veil and collar, then settled the warm cloak around her shoulders. Handing the discarded articles to the clerk, she asked her to dispose of them. She wouldn't be needing the disguise any more, and, besides, it was just an uncomfortable nuisance.

Her request didn't phase Nellie Benson. She was accustomed to peculiar people. Galveston had attracted more than its share since the war had started. She disposed of the collar and veil, then ushered Amelia toward the door.

"You take care now," she called.

A blast of frigid air nearly bowled Amelia off her feet as she heard the bolt slip firmly in place behind her.

Well, now what? she thought.

Lifting the hood of the cloak, she shielded her hair from the stiff wind. *I really should have bought ship's passage first thing,* she thought, even though it would seem that she was letting a man tell her what to do.

The barren feeling in the pit of her stomach reminded her she hadn't eaten in hours. A hurried glance told her that the two eating establishments she had spotted earlier were dark and deserted now.

Drat, she hadn't been thinking again. Her sisters had often accused her of not using her head. Without their guidance, she had let it happen again.

Stuffing her hands into the pockets of her new cloak, she meandered down the sidewalk. She didn't know where she was going, but she couldn't just stand in front of the millinery all night. That would surely draw attention.

There wasn't much activity on the streets now. The sailors had moved their horseplay into the warmth of the saloons.

Her pulse quickened as she saw a tall, sinister-looking outline suddenly emerge from the shadows. Her footsteps slowed as she watched the menacing figure walk toward her.

Heart hammering now, she told herself she

shouldn't just stand there and stare. She should run! She was a woman, alone and unprotected. Her sense of outrage stung when she thought of Captain Kane. What sort of man would leave a woman as scatterbrained as her to look after herself? A louse. That's what kind a man he was. A big ol' uncaring louse.

The form drew closer, and she released a sigh of relief when she saw that it wasn't as menacing as she'd first thought.

Actually, the man looked almost congenial— clean shaven, impeccably dressed in a morning coat, stiff collar with an immaculate cravat, and pin-striped trousers. Nothing at all seemed threatening in his manner, she assured herself as he courteously stepped aside to allow her room to pass on the narrow walkway.

He smiled as he tipped his colored beaver top hat, and she hesitantly smiled back.

"A touch of chill in the air this evening," he observed amicably.

"Yes, quite chilly." She stared straight ahead, afraid to look directly at him. He might look innocent enough, but perhaps he was one of those friendly but depraved souls Anne-Marie had warned her about.

"You bundle up real good now," he warned, and started on.

Her teeth scraped her bottom lip as she deliberated. She knew better, but his was the first friendly face she'd seen all day, and she needed a friendly face right now. And truly depraved souls were never as polite as he'd just been—were they?

Lowering his walking stick, the man suddenly turned again, his gaze prudently assessing the young woman.

"Is it not late for one so lovely to be out without the protection of an escort?" he observed with a note of fatherly concern.

Amelia felt herself instantly warming to his kind eyes. He looked so benevolent—so trustworthy.

Could she dare trust a complete stranger? Anne-Marie was always adamant about such things—never trust anyone, especially a man, she'd always said.

But Amelia felt so alone, so uncertain. It was cold and dark, and there was no one to tell her what to do.

"Yes ... it is rather late." She glanced away, hoping that he would see her distress and feel compelled to offer his help without her having to ask.

He lifted a blonde brow. "Forgive me if I'm intruding or if I'm overstepping my bounds, but I sense that something is troubling you. Is something amiss?"

"Well ... sort of," she conceded.

Sweeping his hat from his head, he bowed from the waist. "Théodore Austin Brown, at your disposal. That's Théodore with an accent over the first e," he clarified. "Might I be of assistance?"

Concern was so evident in his voice that Amelia didn't see how she could resist his generous offer.

After all, he had said that he might be overstepping his bounds, and what man would bother to say that if he had anything other than her welfare in mind?

"Well . . ."

Austin was taken with the young woman's remarkable beauty: her delicate features, her small-boned frame, her thick mass of auburn hair. An exquisite commodity, to be sure.

Noting her continuing reticence, he sought to erase her fears. "The wind is biting. Please, allow me to buy you something warm to drink to ward off the chill."

Before Amelia could decide if she should let him take such liberties, he had taken her arm and was steering her into a nearby hostelry.

"Well," she murmured. "I suppose it couldn't hurt. . . ." After all, she would be in plain sight if he turned out to be something of a scoundrel.

The hotel lobby was vacant as Austin guided her behind a curtain into a small side room where four tables were set for dinner.

The waiter looked up, surprised by the unexpected arrivals. "Mr. Brown! How nice you could join us." He paused, his eyes focusing on Austin's lovely guest. "Two for dinner?"

Austin glanced at Amelia expectantly. "I had thought something warm to drink—but if the young lady would agree to dine with me?"

Flushed, Amelia quickly nodded her acceptance of his offer. If she went much longer without eating, she would faint dead away.

Austin helped her out of the cloak, then held the red velour seat out for her. Closing her eyes, Amelia sank into the plush softness, savoring the heavenly aromas drifting from the kitchen.

When Austin was seated, the waiter opened a menu and presented it to Amelia.

Her eyes widened when she saw the prices. One meal would deplete her entire food allowance!

Austin leaned forward and whispered, "Order whatever you wish. You're my guest, my dear."

"Oh, I couldn't," she protested. Two dollars for a steak dinner! Highway robbery! And bacon wasn't even on the menu.

Laying his hand over hers, he smiled. "Then permit me to order for you." Lifting the menu, he perused the selections, then ordered two of the most expensive dinners, complete with red wine. Handing the menu to the waiter, he turned back to Amelia. "Now, tell me. What is one so lovely doing on the streets of Galveston at this hour?"

While the waiter poured their wine, Amelia warmed to Austin Brown. Before she knew it, she was telling him the whole confusing story of how she and her sisters had been rescued by three complete strangers from a band of marauding Comanche. She omitted the part about the men thinking the sisters were nuns, and about how they were in the jail wagon. It wasn't relevant to the story, and, besides, it was embarrassing. What would this good, upstanding man think if she told him she and her sisters had been running con games—however

worthy the cause—across all of Texas for the past
few years? Well, he would just be disillusioned by
her, that's what. And she didn't want that, not
again. Her honest admission had certainly ruined
things with the last man she'd met.

Austin listened to her unfolding story, sipping
his wine and contributing an occasional sympa-
thetic comment. She and her sisters had indeed
been fortunate to escape unharmed, he agreed. Indeed, quite lucky.

"But I've been irresponsible," Amelia admitted,
still smarting from the way Morgan Kane had
dumped her like a sack of garbage. Reaching for
her wine, she took a long drink to soothe her
parched throat.

"And how is that?"

"I was supposed to—well, actually, I should
have purchased passage on a ship that would take
me back to Mercy Flats, but by the time I'd finished shopping, the ship's office had closed."

"How unfortunate." Leaning back in his chair,
Austin took out a pipe and small pouch from his
vest pocket.

"Now I don't know what to do." Amelia realized that she was being terribly straightforward,
but Théodore Austin—with an accent over the
e—Brown, was the nicest man she'd ever met.

"Are you married, Mr. Brown?"

"No, I'm afraid I've never had the pleasure."

"What a shame. You'd make such a nice husband."

Austin filled the bowl of his pipe, then absently brought it to his mouth. Belatedly recalling his manners, he paused. "Would my smoking offend you?"

"Oh, no," she assured him. He was being so kind that if he wanted he could set his hair on fire, and she wouldn't mention it.

The rich tobacco aroma filtered pleasantly through the air as Austin settled back on his chair, drawing deeply on the stem. He dropped into deep thought momentarily as she sipped her wine. The drink made her feel slightly giddy, but she liked it. Kind of.

Finally, he looked up and bestowed another benevolent smile. "This must indeed be your lucky day. Quite by coincidence, I think I can be of assistance to you."

"You can?" Amelia sat up straighter, her eyes bright and her cheeks flushed from the wine.

"Yes, through a quirk of fate, an acquaintance of mine has a vessel residing in the harbor, as we speak."

"Really?" This must indeed be her lucky day! To be honest, she didn't know what she would have done if Austin Brown hadn't happened along to help her.

"My friend is captain of an older, but highly seaworthy, clipper," he assured her.

"And your acquaintance is leaving in the morning? Sailing in the vicinity of Mercy Flats?" It seemed too good to be true!

"His original destination was New Orleans, but a storm blew his vessel off course, and he was forced to make port here in Galveston," Austin mused. "But I'm sure when I tell him of your plight, he will be persuaded to leave on high tide. This Mercy Flats—is it far?"

She frowned. "I don't know—maybe not too far." She had no idea how far it was, but surely the good captain would know.

"Well"—leaning forward, Austin patted her hand consolingly—"I'm sure something suitable can be arranged."

Clasping her hands together, Amelia beamed. "Oh, that's wonderful!" She suddenly frowned again. "Of course, I'll purchase your friend's services."

"There's no need," Austin protested mildly. "I'd be most happy to see to your safe return—"

"No, I must insist on paying my own way," she contended. This man had been too kind as it was. She fished inside her cloak pocket and pulled out the remaining money Morgan Kane had given her. She pressed the roll of bills into Austin's hand. "If that isn't enough, I can get more when I return to Mercy Flats."

Austin reluctantly took the money.

"It would be my pleasure to secure your passage, my dear . . . but if you insist." His expression told her that he would accept her money rather than insult her pride. What a thoughtful man! Why couldn't all men be so considerate, she thought as he discreetly tucked her money into his vest pocket and refilled her wine glass.

Lifting her glass, Amelia relaxed, relieved to have that weighty matter settled. She had finally done something right. For a short while it had looked as if she might be forced to go back to Morgan Kane for his ol' help. Well, she smiled. She wouldn't have to go to him now. She had arranged for safe passage on the morning tide without his rude interference, thank you.

"Yes," Austin pondered. "I'm certain Captain Garrison will be delighted to be of service. When we're finished here, I'll escort you to my friend's ship. You can settle in there tonight, and be fresh for the early morning departure."

"This is just so kind of you." Amelia glowed.

"My pleasure, dear." Lifting his glass higher, he toasted her rare beauty. "It is, indeed, my deepest pleasure."

Chapter 4

The two figures sank deeper into the shadow between the buildings.

"I was beginning to worry; I thought we'd missed connections."

"Sorry, I was unavoidably delayed."

The figures pressed closer together, conversing in hushed undertones.

"Do you have the information?"

"Lanigan has been detained. Some sort of accident—details are sketchy."

The taller figure swore, casting a wary glance to the entrance of the alleyway. "How long?"

"I'm not sure. Four, maybe five, days."

Nearly a week's delay. The lag could prove costly.

"But will he come?"

"He'll show up. His type always does."

A rowdy group of sailors crossed the alley, their boisterous laughter sending the figures deeper into the shadows. When the men had passed, they spoke again.

"Do we stay?"

Silence, then: "We don't have a choice."

"I agree."

Laughter rang out again as another bevy of drunken men crossed the alleyway.

Concern dominated one of the voices now. "Keep off the streets. There could be trouble."

"Don't worry. I don't care for the looks of things either."

"Stay in touch."

"You do the same."

A moment later the two figures parted at the entrance of the alley, walking in opposite directions.

It was late when Morgan entered a local pub. Taking a table in a dark corner, he ordered a hot buttered rum. As he waited for the drink, his attention was drawn to the center of the room where a group of men was gathered around a large table. Their voices were loud and demonstrative, dominating the noisy pub.

The bar was in chaos. Morgan planned to stay just long enough to eat and enjoy a rum before retiring.

His mind drifted briefly back to Amelia, whom he assumed was safely aboard a ship by now. That woman was an odd package. Jabbering incessantly, she could not keep a secret if her life depended upon it.

Morgan ducked as a chair went sailing over his head, shattering a row of liquor bottles behind the counter. A fight had broken out, sending the occupants of the bar scattering until the ruckus could be brought under control.

When order was restored, Morgan moved to a dark corner of the room. After a few moments, his attention was drawn back to the group of men seated at the center table.

"I'm telling you, I've never seen anything like it," a well-dressed man was saying.

"Nay, guv'ner, you're puttin' us on," another scoffed.

"I swear on my mother's grave, it happened exactly as I said." The man threw back his head and laughed uproariously. "The silly little twit paid me!"

The pub vibrated with male merriment.

"You actually mean she *paid* you to book her passage on *The Black Widow*?" another hooted.

"I swear on your mother's grave, mate!"

That was too much. The men rocked back in their chairs, holding their sides.

The buttered rum arrived, momentarily distracting Morgan.

"It is a stroke of luck, to be sure," the well-dressed man mused as his laughter subsided. "I usually have to knock them senseless, tie them up, and drag them to the ship, but this one just up and insisted that she pay for the privilege. Wouldn't have it any other way."

With a snort, he burst into laughter again.

"Must be ugly as sin," a man sitting to his right surmised in a droll tone.

"On the contrary." Austin Brown's smile faded as he recalled the comely young beauty lying at this very moment in her lonely bunk aboard *The Black Widow*. "She's really quite lovely."

"Is she securely snared?"

"Ah yes. The lovely nightingale is safely in her nest, and I can assure you, gentlemen, that she, fairest of the fair, will bring top price from Lanigan in New Orleans.

"Heard this Lanigan likes them young and impressionable as new fallen snow," one observed.

"That he does." Austin leaned back to light his pipe. And that she was.

"You know Lanigan personally?"

"I've never met him, but I've heard of his preferences—only wise to know the market one's selling to, wouldn't you say, gents?"

The men all agreed.

"This Lanigan—is he as good as his reputation?"

"None better," Austin confirmed.

Talk continued about Dov Lanigan's expertise with a knife and a woman. That ruggedly handsome privateer with an exorbitant price on his head was rumored to be unrivaled in his field.

"How do we know we can trust him?" piped up one of the men. "None of us has ever seen him. How can we be sure he won't cheat us?"

Exhaling smoke from his pipe, Austin smiled. "I'll take care of Lanigan. His reputation doesn't intimidate me. He's a man, same as us, making a living best as he can. You don't run blockades and sell contraband for as many years as I have without risking your neck and sullying your reputation. But those days are over, gentlemen. Dealing stolen women is a lot easier and a lot less risky. Hauling their whining carcasses across the sea is a bothersome task, but not without rewards, my friends." His smile grew sly. "Not without a few rewards. Some have been known to show their appreciation for little treats," he reminded them.

Morgan tossed the last of the rum down, imagining what these thugs would consider little treats for their stolen women—food and water, more than likely.

For a moment, the wanted poster he'd seen of Dov Lanigan surfaced in his mind. The picture had portrayed a dark-haired man, tall, about his own age, without distinguishing features or scars.

"I'm for selling the woman here," one of the men challenged. "If this one is as beautiful as you say, she'll bring top price right here in Galveston."

"No!" Austin snapped. "The McDougal woman will bring more than that once Lanigan sees her."

Morgan's head shot up at the mention of Amelia's name.

"I say a bird in the hand is worth two in the bush," another man interjected. "I say we sell her right here, right now, tonight!"

The other men added their impassioned, rowdy agreements.

"Gentlemen, gentlemen, keep your heads. From what I've seen of our other women, they'll bring a mere pittance compared to what this woman will, if what Austin says is true," a man argued.

A vision of Amelia—starved, beaten, and abused—flashed through Morgan's mind. An evil smile lifted the corners of his mouth. It would serve her right.

Once that delicious thought faded, reality took over. How in the *hell*, in the brief time since he had left her, less than four hours ago, had she managed to fall into the clutches of men as unscrupulous as these?

"I'm still running things, and we'll do as I say!" Austin snapped. "A deal is a deal. Lanigan's brother has assured me Lanigan will pay top price for any woman I bring him of exceptional beauty. Now, gentlemen, you would not have me go back on my word? There is, after all, honor to consider, even among thieves."

"I'm relieved to hear it. I was beginning to wonder," a deep voice rumbled from the darkest corner of the pub.

Swiveling in their seats, the men scanned the shadows for signs of an intruder.

"Who's there? Show yourself," Austin commanded. The others strained their eyes to make out the sizable outline behind the table.

Morgan calmly slid his hand inside his boot, touching the butt of his dagger.

A burly man, eyes narrowed, saw the gesture and went for his pistol. "I know how to rid us of nosy rats!"

Coming to his feet, Morgan set the dagger on its course. In the wink of an eye, the knife pinned the sleeve of the man's shirt solidly to the post. The man's pistol discharged harmlessly into the air before clattering to the floor.

Pushing back from his table, Austin rose to face the mysterious marksman. There was only one person that good with a dagger, only one: Dov Lanigan himself.

Emerging from the shadows, Morgan casually strolled over to retrieve his knife. The owner of the pistol, mumbling and rubbing his shoulders, turned away from Morgan's cold, measuring eyes.

"Dov Lanigan?" Austin asked softly. The man was dressed like a impoverished farmer, but then Lanigan would not want to be noticeable.

"If I were you, Mr. Brown, I'd be more careful about my public conversations."

Austin hurried to set things right. "I'm sorry, Mr. Lanigan . . ." He winced, realizing his blunder. "I wasn't thinking . . ." Reaching for a chair, Austin offered it to the living legend.

When Morgan was comfortably seated, Austin nervously signaled the bartender for a round of drinks.

"You took me by surprise," Austin admitted as

he pulled his chair up to the table. "I understood you were in New Orleans."

"I was, but unexpected business brought me here tonight." Morgan didn't know what the hell he was doing, but on an impulse he'd decided to run a bluff until he could figure out what to do about the blasted McDougal woman. Her safety should no longer be his concern, yet he could hardly stand by and knowingly let her be sold into prostitution.

Austin couldn't believe his latest stroke of luck. Now he could get top price for the girl, and still remain in good standing with his men.

After the drinks arrived, Morgan methodically drained his glass, stalling for time.

Austin and the others followed suit, wiping their hands across their lips when they finished.

"Where's the woman?" Morgan asked casually.

"Safely aboard *The Black Widow*," Austin assured him.

"She's uncommonly beautiful, you say?"

"Ah, uncommonly so. Eyes the color of spring grass, rich carmine hair, and a figure men would surely go to their graves for. She'll bring twice what you pay for her."

"An amount which I assume will be considerable?"

Austin's smile grew sheepish. "Well, you pay for quality, isn't that what they say?"

"I'm curious about one thing. If she's so lovely, why not keep her for your own pleasure?"

Austin chuckled. The man wasn't a fool. "There isn't anything I own that isn't for sale—at the right price. She is yours—if you want her. It is your good fortune that one so exceptionally lovely should happen into my hands."

When Morgan had asked every pertinent question he could think of, he was afraid to stall any longer.

With a cool smile, he finally said quietly, "Take me to this most lovely one."

"Certainly." Shoving back from the table, Austin stood up. "If you'll follow me?"

Morgan nodded to the others. "You will excuse us, gentlemen?"

A moment later, the two men left the bar to view the spoils of the trade.

Chapter 5

There was something fishy, and it wasn't just the revolting smell permeating the old clipper. Amelia couldn't say what, but something was terribly wrong. She'd felt it the moment Austin had brought her aboard.

Rolling off the narrow bunk, she tiptoed to the door, listening. The old vessel creaked under the weight of the heavy timber as it rocked back and forth in the water. The ship was large, with heavy masts and yards.

Straining closer to the door, she listened more intently. She was certain she'd heard someone crying.

She scurried back to the bunk and sat down to think. She glumly inspected the tiny quarters. She didn't know anything about ships, but common sense told her she had overpaid to travel on this one. The quarters were plain and cramped. And smelly. Even Mr. Brown's captain friend had smelled as if he hadn't seen soap and water in months.

She suddenly sat up straighter as the sound came to her again. A low, despairing wail amid creaking timbers.

Slipping from the bunk, she opened the door a crack and peeked out. The narrow passageway was deserted. A whale oil lantern burned low, barely illuminating the narrow corridor.

As she listened, the sound grew more distinct.

Glancing behind her, she spotted a candle sitting on the washstand. She reached over and grasped it, allowing the door to open wider.

Moving cautiously out into the hallway, she paused to listen again. The ship's atmosphere made her uneasy. Something seemed evil about it—a premonition she was powerless to explain. She wished she had waited until morning, and then bought a ticket to Mercy Flats on the stage. It might have taken her longer to get there, but it would have been worth it.

Feeling her way down the corridor, she followed the sound of weeping. The lamplight was barely adequate, casting elongated shadows through the passageway.

At the end of the hall, a door stood slightly ajar. Amelia could barely make out the silhouette of a young girl sitting alone on a narrow cot, sobbing. She felt a flood of pity for this girl, who was probably traveling alone and feeling frightened.

Amelia moved closer, tapping softly on the door.

When she received no invitation to enter, she peeked around the door into the cramped quarters that were larger but just as unpleasant as her own.

The ship's owners should be ashamed to operate such a disorderly establishment, Amelia thought. She didn't see how they could hope to maintain a thriving business when they apparently cared so little for their customer's comfort.

"Hello." Amelia summoned a pleasant smile for the girl, who appeared to be very young.

The girl's head shot up, and Amelia saw that she was not only crying, she looked frightened.

"Don't be afraid," Amelia began. "I heard you crying, and I wondered if there was anything I could do . . ." Her words faltered when she noticed the young girl wasn't alone. Squatting along the walls of the cramped room were nine other young women, all of varying ages, all looking at her with equally desperate expressions.

For a moment, no one spoke. Finally, the girl on the cot choked out in raspy whisper, "What do you want?"

"I heard you crying. Is there something I can do to help?"

"Help?" The girl looked at her as if she didn't understand.

"Yes . . . you're crying. Are the accommodations not to your liking?" Amelia could see why. In fact, if she had it to do over, she would just tell Mr. Brown thank you but no thank you for his offer of assistance. The accommodations were horrible, and she'd venture that the food was even worse!

A slender, young girl in the far corner spoke up. "Who are you?"

'A passenger. I, too, find the accommodations deplorable," Amelia confided, wondering why the women had congregated in such tiny quarters.

"A passenger?" an older, dark-haired girl in the opposite corner mocked.

Amelia smiled. "Yes, I came aboard about an hour ago." She glanced around the narrow quarters. "Why are all of you in the same room? Are you traveling together?"

This might be fun, Amelia decided. She was ready for a little fun for a change. Companionship with other women her own age could be just the thing she needed to boost her sagging spirits during her return to Mercy Flats.

If Morgan Kane could see her now, he'd know he'd been sadly mistaken when he implied that she was a child and didn't have enough sense to come in out of the rain.

A young woman with incredibly unkempt blonde hair suddenly got up. "Oh, really now. You're a 'passenger'?"

Amelia's smile brightened. "Yes. Where are you all going?"

"To hell," the dark-haired girl returned in a listless tone. "In case no one's told you, we're all on our way to hell."

To hell! Well that was ludicrous. She'd paid for a ticket to Mercy Flats!

"Hell? Is there a Hell, Texas?" Amelia asked, still not comprehending the situation.

A hard-edged woman rose from her bunk. "Try again, lovey."

Realization slowly dawned on Amelia. "You don't mean hell . . . as in blazing inferno?"

"You have it."

Amelia sank to a bunk, the woman's words ringing in her ears. Hell? Not Texas? What were they talking about?

Lifting her eyes, Amelia confronted the woman. "You're not making a lick of sense."

"Maybe she really doesn't know, Elizabeth," the dirty blonde-haired girl said softly.

"Not know? Does she think she's on a cruise?"

Amelia nodded. "Yes . . . to Mercy Flats."

Elizabeth turned away with contempt.

A thin girl stood unsteadily and came over to kneel beside Amelia. "You really don't know what's going on, do you?"

Amelia was grateful for the kindness she saw in the girl's large eyes. The others seemed so cold and hostile. "I'm confused," Amelia admitted.

"You're more than confused," Elizabeth said. "You're a prisoner, dearie."

As Amelia bolted to her feet, she struck her head on an overhead bunk. Rubbing the rising welt, she bit her lip to keep from crying. "A prisoner! There are no bolts or bars on the doors! What are you talking about?"

"It's true," one of the others whispered. "There may be no bars on the doors, but we are watched day and night. If we were to try and escape, we would be shot on sight."

"Prisoners?" Their words made no sense to Amelia. Nothing had made any sense for hours now!

The girl on the bunk nodded. "We're all prisoners."

"Of whom?" Amelia demanded to know.

"Prisoners of an evil man by the name of Austin Brown," another supplied.

"Théodore Austin Brown?" Amelia asked.

"I see you've met him," Elizabeth snapped.

There was something about Elizabeth that Amelia immediately didn't like. She'd sensed it the moment she'd stepped into the room. She didn't know what it was. Perhaps it was the coldness in her eyes or the razor-sharp edge to her voice. One thing was certain; they would never be friends.

"What would Austin Brown want with me?" Amelia asked. "I don't even know him."

Elizabeth laughed harshly. "Undoubtedly you do."

"We've met, but only a couple of hours ago. He ... befriended me," she said lamely.

"He hood-winked you, you little twit, the same as he did all of us."

"I don't believe it!" Amelia cried.

"Believe it."

This was terrible. Horrible! Amelia began pacing the cramped quarters. Had she fallen out of the frying pan into the fire? "What does he plan to do with us?"

The girls exchanged hesitant looks, but Elizabeth had no qualms about telling her. "He plans to sell us."

"Sell us? Into slavery?" Amelia thought only blacks were sold into slavery. Wasn't that part of what the war was about?

"Prostitution."

Elizabeth's words hung heavily in the air.

"Prostitution?" Amelia whispered. *Prostitution?* She'd heard of such wicked things, but that was for worldly, tainted women, not women as young as these. Why, one of them didn't look to be any older than twelve or thirteen.

The girl on the cot started sobbing again. "It's so awful. I'd rather die than be sold for a man's pleasure!"

Another started weeping, and before long they were all sobbing. All except Elizabeth. She simply stared at Amelia.

"Now listen. I don't know what is going on, but I know one thing. I do not intend to be sold," Amelia stated flatly. Now that the shock was wearing off she could think again. Prostitution indeed! Over her dead body!

Leaning back on a bunk, Elizabeth casually rolled a cigarette. Amelia watched with fascination as she struck a match with her thumbnail, lit the cigarette, and began to blow lazy smoke rings at the ceiling.

Elizabeth sent Amelia a snide glance. "Tell us what you plan to do, lovey, so we can all 'refuse' to go along with Théodore—with the accent over the first e—Austin Brown's plans." She sailed a series of little round *o*'s toward the ceiling.

"Well, I'm not sure what I'll do . . . but I'll do something. I'll escape. I won't stand by and let this happen to me!" Oh, she should have known not to trust Austin Brown! He had tricked her! He had wined and dined her then sold her down the Prostitution River!

Elizabeth casually extended the cigarette to her. "Smoke?"

Amelia shook her head. "I don't smoke." In fact, Elizabeth was the first woman she'd ever met who did.

The youngest of the girls slipped to Amelia's side. "What do you think we should do?" Her eyes focused on Amelia trustingly.

"Do you know where they're taking us?" Amelia asked.

"I overheard one of the men say something about New Orleans," one of the women ventured.

"New Orleans?" Amelia's heart sank. A decadent city to be sure—she'd heard of the red-light district there and of the music houses where women danced as they took off all their clothes before men.

Until now, she'd been sure that such rumors about the French Quarter had been wildly exaggerated. Perhaps not, she conceded. Discovering that she was aboard a ship of women bound for the worst kind of slavery suddenly made all other evils more believable.

"Well, we'll all just have to escape," Amelia said firmly. "Since they haven't locked us in our rooms we can manage it. They can't watch all of us every hour of the day."

Elizabeth boldly sent another series of smoke rings spiraling toward the ceiling. "Are you willing to wager your life on it?"

"She's right," another girl said. "There are dozens of men aboard ship, and they're watching us like hawks." Her eyes focused on the dark-skinned girl. "Ask her; she tried to escape, but they caught her."

The dark-skinned girl's eyes burned with shame when she thought of what they'd done to her.

The horror of their predicament slowly seeped into Amelia's consciousness. "How long have you been here?"

The women gave varying accounts of their captivity, ranging from hours to weeks. Some had been captured far away, and some as near as Galveston.

Elizabeth's eyes narrowed as she gazed at Amelia with a mixture of contempt and resignation. "You know, if the storm hadn't blown this clipper off course, we would be in New Orleans by now. And you, Miss Innocent, where would you have been?"

Amelia looked away as she felt the prick of tears behind her eyes. Mercy Flats—the answer rose within her quickly, and with it came a knot of longing and desperation.

Mercy Flats. A wave of despair beset her as she sank to the soiled mattress on a bunk. Now she wondered if she would ever see it or her sisters again.

Chapter 6

The Black Widow lay in the water beneath a full moon. The wind gently rocked the old clipper back and forth as the moon dipped lower in the sky.

Two men approached the gangplank, their shoulders hunched against the damp gusts.

A shout rang out. "Who goes there?"

"Permission to board," a man called back.

"That you, Brown?"

"It's me."

"Come aboard, mate!"

The two men quickly crossed the gangplank and stepped aboard the ship.

Austin addressed a burly Welsh packet rat as they stepped aboard. "The captain in his quarters?"

"He is, but he don't want to be disturbed." The packet rats were a breed of their own. They were wild, rough men, commonly of English, Irish, or Welsh origin, who understood no law but force. Dirty, uncouth, ignorant bullies, they nonetheless were superb sailors and feared neither man nor weather.

"He'll see me," Brown said.

The smell of Stockholm tar from the rigging hung heavily in the air as Morgan followed Austin to the lee side of the poop deck. The captain's quarters was forbidden territory to all except those invited.

The two men made their way below deck. The ship reeked of bilge water and rotting timber. As he walked down the dimly lit, narrow corridors, Morgan saw several doors ajar. Muffled cries drifted from beneath the doors.

Pausing before a door at the end of the corridor, Austin rapped softly. "You in there, Elliot?"

A gruff voice returned. "That you again, Brown?"

"Yes. Open up. I've got someone with me."

The door opened a crack and a pair of rum-sodden eyes looked out. "You bring another woman?"

"No, I have important business to discuss. Let me in, Elliot."

"Business? Now?"

"Just open the door, Elliot."

The door swung open to reveal a disheveled, dirty captain who was well into his cups. Pushing past him, Austin entered the stinking cabin, motioning Lanigan to follow.

"Who do you have with you?" Elliot viewed the intruder warily.

"This is Mr. Dov Lanigan."

"Dov Lanigan." Elliot's eyes narrowed as he lifted a shoulder to wipe his runny nose. "What's going on? I thought we were supposed to meet Lanigan in New Orleans."

"We were, but a stroke of good fortune has brought Mr. Lanigan to Galveston this evening."

Raising a bottle of rum to his lips, the captain eyed Lanigan briefly before he took a hearty swill. He grunted when he noted the men staring at him. "State your business, Brown." Wiping the back of his hand across his mouth, he wove his way toward his bed.

"We've come for the woman."

Lying back on his bunk, Elliot raised his hand to block the light from the one small candle. He squinted at the tall, broad-shouldered stranger. "Dov Lanigan, huh?"

Brown heaved an impatient sigh. "I believe I've made the proper introductions."

"Funny, don't you think, Lanigan showing up here?" The captain hiccuped loudly.

Brown shrugged. "I'll admit it was a bit of a surprise to me, too, but here he is."

"How can you be so sure he's who he says he is? I hear Lanigan sticks real close to New Orleans. A price on his head and all."

"My dear captain," Brown replied condescendingly, "may I remind you that we all have a price on our heads."

The captain leaned on one elbow unsteadily. "Yeah, well, the reason no man has had the good

fortune to claim the reward for my dead body is
because I'm just a wee bit on the cautious side."
The captain slapped the lumpy mattress beneath
him to make his point.

A puff of dust rose from the filthy coverlet, and
a large cockroach sprang to the floor and darted in
Brown's direction. The roach had scurried several
inches before a dagger sliced the air and split its
back, nailing it to the wooden floor.

Brown and the captain watched in stupefied silence as the roach's legs pumped furiously for an
instant, going nowhere. The legs halted abruptly,
then slumped.

Lanigan's expression remained unchanged as he
pulled his dagger out of the plank and leaned toward the bed. Instinctively, the captain drew his
legs up as Lanigan lay the dagger against the coverlet at the foot of the bed. He slowly wiped both
sides of the blade before inspecting it. The candle-
light glinted off the beveled blade but didn't pene-
trate the shadowed eyes of the man who turned it
slowly, lovingly with nimble fingers.

Lanigan silently slipped his dagger into its
sheath, and Austin Brown cleared his throat. "Mr.
Lanigan, you're quite handy with that thing."
Brown glanced at the captain. "Well, I hope the
matter of his identity is settled to your satisfaction."

The captain grunted as he swung his feet to the
floor. "We'll see." It seemed apparent that his
pride was injured. "What do you want with me?"

He pushed himself to his feet, looking more alert and wary.

"I want to see the woman." Lanigan's voice was demanding and his gaze uncompromising.

Austin Brown became the diplomat. "I'm sure Dov here wants to see for himself if the lady is as beautiful as I've claimed her to be."

The captain seemed to be taking measure of this man Lanigan. "No harm in lookin'," he said finally, gesturing toward the door, "long as you remember not to touch till she's paid for."

Brown turned to lead the way back to the deck. "I think Mr. Lanigan knows those rules better than we, Captain."

Moments later, two burly seamen appeared on deck, dragging between them a fighting, spitting Amelia.

"Let me go, you miserable, stinking brutes!" She bit the hand of one of the men restraining her, inciting a string of oaths that fouled the already putrid air.

The man with the bleeding hand looked at Austin pleadingly. "Let me teach this one a lesson. She's a bloody handful, she is! My pay ain't worth puttin' up with this blooming persecution!"

Jerking the bodice of her dress back into place, Amelia glared at the beast threatening her. Why, oh, why had she discarded the veil and headdress at the mercantile earlier? The plain dark dress gave her no particular distinction now. With a toss of her head, she turned her attention to Austin Brown.

She was preparing to tell him what a blackguard he was when she recognized the man standing beside him.

Her jaw dropped "You—!" she sputtered. What was Morgan Kane doing here?

Austin smiled. "Watch your language, dear. My friend, Lanigan, will think you're a hooligan."

"Lanigan!" she spat. Lanigan, the privateer who was reputed to be merciless with a knife? Her Captain Kane was the notorious Lanigan. She shook her head in shock. How bad could her luck be?

"Ah, this one seems to have spirit," Lanigan observed as he watched her struggling to free herself.

Amelia twisted and pulled until her breath heaved in gasps. With exasperated oaths, the men on either side hauled her arms behind her to force her cooperation. The sleeves of her gown tore at the seams and the small buttons at her throat gave way, popping off in all directions. Her dress gaped open, revealing the swell of her rounded breasts beneath her thin chemise. She stifled a small cry as she glanced down in dismay. For an instant, she stood perfectly still.

"Indeed, she will bring a handsome price," Austin breathed softly. "Not only does she have uncommon beauty, she has fire to match it."

"You low-down, dirty, thieving snake-in-the-grass!" Amelia screeched. "How dare you take advantage of me this way!" Whirling, she leveled her rage on Morgan or Lanigan or whoever he was. "And you! How dare you—"

A slow smile spread across Lanigan's features. "Yes, she does have fire, doesn't she."

"You bastard."

Turning away, Lanigan said in a bored tone, "Can someone cease her tiresome prattle?"

"Listen, you!" Amelia's eyes shot fire as she stamped her foot. "You get me off this ship, and you get me off here now!"

"I don't know about this one. Perhaps she's touched with madness." Lanigan pondered.

"And while you're at it, you get the other women off here, too! You men can't just truss us up like a bunch of brood hens and sell us!"

"Ah, but it appears we have," Lanigan reminded her.

With helpless rage, she pooled a mouthful of spit and hurled it at him.

Stiffening, Morgan reined his anger. Dammit, he had a weak stomach, and she was testing his patience again! Didn't she have enough sense to realize that he was here to rescue her?

She spat at him. "You no-good rat." She spat again.

"Stop spitting on me."

She spat again.

Austin rushed over to wipe the spittle off Lanigan's coat, and she spat on him, too.

"See here! You stop this!" Austin demanded. "Do you know who you're spitting on?"

"As a matter of fact, I don't! Who am I spitting

on?" Her eyes fixed accusingly on Morgan. Was he Lanigan, or was he Morgan Kane?

"The woman is a lunatic," Morgan said.

"You louse!"

Morgan stepped back as she spat at him again.

Austin snapped his fingers, and the two seamen stepped forward to stuff a dirty rag into her mouth.

Amelia kicked and clawed, trying to dislodge the vile-tasting cloth. The men bound her tightly with a rope, laughing at her useless struggle.

Lanigan circled her slowly, appraising her. Up and down, her eyes followed his, promising revenge.

"She is a virgin?" he asked casually.

Brown nodded assuringly. "Of course, of course."

"Is there a doctor aboard?"

"Certainly," Brown replied. "Of course, there's the little matter of his license being revoked, but when he's sober, he knows his business well enough."

"I will expect her maidenhead to be intact," Morgan warned him. "I want her examined, and a certificate of verification issued."

"She will be examined immediately, but I can assure you this one's pure as the driven snow."

Morgan's gaze met Amelia's smugly. She would think twice before she spat on him again.

"Take her below," Austin ordered.

Amelia's eyes widened as the two seamen proceeded to drag her away. What? Examination?

Would she have to open her mouth? Did an examination hurt? She'd never had an examination. What was a maidenhead?

Turning back to Lanigan, Austin apologized. "I'm sorry you had to witness that bit of unpleasantness. She is a bit high-strung, but her mind is completely intact, and as you can see, her beauty is unsurpassed."

Lanigan watched as one of the mates picked up the fiery-haired temptress, hefting her roughly over his shoulder to haul her below.

Turning, the men started back to the captain's quarters to finalize the transaction.

"You will be our guest to Louisiana?" Brown inquired. "I can provide you with excellent quarters ... and many hours of pleasant diversion."

"No, as soon as the woman is ready we'll be leaving." Morgan hoped his luck could hold out that long. If just one man on board had met the notorious Lanigan, his hoax would be over.

"Then could I interest you in any of the other women?" Austin tempted. "As it happens, I have acquired an unusually lovely bounty this trip."

"Only the one this time."

"I understand, but there is one you must see before you leave." Austin held up his hand good-naturedly. "I know you only want the one, but Mahalia is a most exquisite Oriental creature. She is young, virginal," he lied, "and sure to bring a most handsome price. I would never forgive myself if I hadn't offered her to you first, and—of course, should you be taken with her beauty, as all who have seen her have been—considering you've already purchased the one loveliness from me, we can work out some sort of . . ."

"Bargain deal?"

Austin smiled. "Yes." He had that sly look again.

The bastard, Morgan thought as they entered the dimly lit passageway.

"This is a vocal bunch," Austin told him when the familiar sounds of weeping met them. Personally, he hoped to persuade Lanigan to take the whole squalling batch.

Morgan preferred not to put a face to the misery. He was powerless to rescue these women, and he didn't want them on his conscience when he left.

"The one is all I wish to purchase," he stated again.

"Now, now, don't be in such a hurry." Austin opened the door before them without knocking. "We have visitors, ladies!"

The women, startled, drew deeper into their filthy bunks.

Austin motioned to a young, dark-skinned girl with large, almond-shaped eyes. "Mahalia, come here, dear."

Whimpering, Mahalia scooted closer to Ria.

"Don't be shy," Brown cooed, extending his hand. "Mr. Lanigan wants to meet you."

Shaking her head, Mahalia burrowed deeper into Ria's side.

"Now, now, dear." Stepping to the bunk, Austin jerked her roughly to her feet. Her frail body was helpless against his brute strength.

Amelia, who had been tossed in the corner, still gagged and bound, lifted her feet and banged them against the floor in heated protest of the girl's rough treatment.

"See," Austin praised, ignoring the commotion going on in the corner. "Not an inch of fat on this one." He pinched the olive skin between Mahalia's waist and thigh between his thumb and forefinger like a prize turkey.

"And this hair," Austin murmured, his fingers playing over her long tresses, "black as a raven's wing with the texture of fine silk."

Mahalia moaned as he wound her hair around his hand at the back of her head and tightened his grip cruelly. "And so young." His eyes raked her youthful body. "Oh, the pleasures she will bring to the bed of an insatiable man."

Trembling, Mahalia averted her head to hide the tears of humiliation streaking down her cheeks.

Rolling onto her back, Amelia pummeled the wall with her feet angrily.

"Just the one," Morgan said firmly. His gaze moved to Amelia whose eyes fastened onto his in cold disdain. If looks could kill, he clearly would be drawing his last breath.

Amelia had never felt such consummate hatred. It was bad enough that the captain of her dreams had deceived her, but how could he call himself a man and do what he was doing?

Drawing Mahalia's face closer to his, Austin smiled down at her. "You're sure? She is most exquisite."

"I'm sure." When Morgan turned to leave, a flash of movement in the darkest corner of the cramped room caught his eyes.

He saw a sudden light as a young woman struck a match with her thumbnail and lit the cigarette dangling indolently from her lips. Her gaze locked brazenly with his as she slowly removed the cigarette from her lips and held the match just below her face. The matchlight cast a flattering glow upon her strong cheekbones, her straight nose, her arched brows. Her lips puckered in a provocative pout just before she blew out the match. In the sudden darkness, her eyes held his for an instant before Morgan turned and strode through the door.

Thrusting Mahalia aside, Austin hurried to join him.

"The woman will be ready to leave within the hour," Brown promised.

"Austin, I find that I am suddenly unusually weary. If your invitation still stands, I believe I will accompany you to Louisiana."

"Well . . . yes! Of course, it stands," Austin replied, surprised but elated that Dov Lanigan would accept his hospitality.

"Is it possible to have a tub of hot water?"

"Of course, of course. Anything you want, Dov. Something to eat or a bottle of brandy, perhaps?"

"No, but you mentioned a woman?"

Austin grinned. "I'll have her brought to your cabin immediately."

"I would like to select her."

"Certainly." Austin thought of the young beauty Dov had agreed to purchase. Although Amelia would bring more as a virgin, Dov Lanigan had been known to occasionally sample the fruits of his labor. Her virginity would be a plus, but, after all, it would be money out of Lanigan's pocket, not his. "As soon as her examination is completed, I will send her to you."

"No," Morgan said. "I don't want the woman I'm purchasing."

"Oh?" That was puzzling since she was by far the most tempting. "Is there another you have in mind?" Austin thought of the Oriental. Of course, she would heat any man's blood.

"I want the one who was smoking."

"Elizabeth?" Austin's eyes widened. Strange choice—that one's looks were mediocre and she had a most unpleasant and surly temperament.

Morgan leaned forward, lowering his voice. "Let's just say I like my women rough."

Well, Elizabeth was that, Austin had to admit. "As you wish," he conceded as they parted at the stairwell. "I'll have her sent to you within the hour."

There was no accounting for taste. Bad or otherwise.

Chapter 7

"Go ahead, say it. I'm an incredible fool."

"I didn't say it."

"You were thinking it."

Balancing a thin paper between his fingers, Morgan rolled a cigarette. Running his tongue along the paper's edge, he sealed it, then handed it to her. As he struck the match, his eyes locked with hers.

Inhaling deeply, she waited for the tobacco to soothe her jangled nerves before speaking. "We're in real trouble, aren't we?"

"I think we can safely say that."

Pacing the small cabin, Elizabeth nervously brought the cigarette back to her mouth. "I don't know what happened. It wasn't that I was careless—one moment I was walking along, minding my own business, and the next moment I was overpowered by two burly thugs who dragged me to this diabolical hellhole. In the blink of an eye I found myself a prisoner of Austin Brown, a despicable bastard who plans to sell me into prostitution, no less."

"It does boggle the mind, doesn't it?" Morgan moved to a small side table to pour himself a glass of brandy hurriedly sent to his quarters by his genial host, Austin Brown. Morgan found "Dov Lanigan's" quarters as dismal as the rest of the ship. An eight by ten cubicle in the bowels of *The Black Widow*. He had to wonder if the disreputable privateer would find Brown's attempts at hospitality as pitifully insulting as he did.

Drawing on the cigarette, Elizabeth paced the cabin floor like a caged animal. "If this isn't something. What do we do now?"

Taking a thoughtful sip from his glass, Morgan pondered the situation that was anything but amusing.

"Morgan," Elizabeth turned, her eyes pleading with his for understanding. "I'm so sorry—"

"There's no need for apologies, Elizabeth. We've worked together long enough to know that neither of us would intentionally endanger the other. The circumstances are unfortunate, I can't deny that."

"What will we do?" Elizabeth trusted Morgan more than any agent she had worked with, but the situation was so grave she had to wonder how anyone could survive unharmed. "What can we do?"

"I'm not sure. It all happened so fast I haven't had time to devise a plan. If it wasn't for Brown's greed I wouldn't have known of your capture."

"I was never so relieved to see anyone in my whole life as I was when you walked into the room with Brown earlier," Elizabeth confessed. "Yet, if you didn't know I was here, *why* are you here?"

Morgan briefly explained about Amelia, and events leading up to her abduction.

"The featherbrain? You're here because of the *featherbrain?*"

"That isn't quite accurate. She isn't a featherbrain, Elizabeth."

"Morgan, the woman will get us killed! She's reckless and impulsive."

"She's young and impressionable," he contended.

"Pigheaded and brash!"

"Childlike and inexperienced," he dismissed.

Elizabeth ceased pacing long enough to challenge him. "Why are you defending her? If it wasn't for her stupidity you wouldn't be in this mess."

"Her 'stupidity' might well have saved your life. I wasn't aware of your circumstances. I came aboard to rescue Amelia after overhearing a conversation Brown was having in a local pub."

"So, the McDougal woman inadvertently led you to me," Elizabeth allowed. "But what about the mission? This could destroy all we've accomplished." They were so close to seizing Lanigan. So close!

"The mission is intact. From what Brown said, Lanigan is still in New Orleans."

"This is madness," she murmured. "If even one man aboard the ship has seen or met Dov Lanigan—"

"We'll have to hope no one has. Brown hasn't met him personally, nor has the captain."

Elizabeth angrily discarded the cigarette and ground it out on the floor of the cabin with her heel.

"Elizabeth," Morgan chided. "What will our host think of your treating his guest quarters with so little esteem."

"If I could get my hands on Austin Brown I'd pull his testicles out and stuff them in his ears."

"For the moment, I'd suggest you discard the thought, and play the helpless captive."

"What do you plan to do?"

Morgan answered as candidly as he could. "I'm not sure. I'll need some time to think about it."

"Is there anything that can be done?" There were over fifty men aboard ship, fifty men against the two of them. It seemed hopeless.

"There's always something to be done; I just don't know what it is at the moment."

Morgan didn't like to think what would happen if he couldn't come up with a plan in time to get Elizabeth and Amelia out of Brown's clutches.

"Play it smart, and do as Brown tells you. The trip to Louisiana will take days, provided the weather holds. By the time we reach New Orleans, I'll have a plan."

"And Amelia?"

"What about her?"

"Shouldn't she be told that we're working together?"

"No," Morgan said flatly. "She is not to know."

"Why not? If she knew that we're working together she might show more caution."

"No, the less she knows the better."

"Ah! Then you agree with me. She's a worrisome meddler!"

"Charmingly impetuous," he maintained.

"Why do you defend her? You barely know the woman."

Morgan reached out to halt her pacing. Taking her arm, he turned her around to face him. "We have enough trouble without inviting more. The girl can be dealt with, Elizabeth." His voice turned grave. "I don't need to warn you that Brown and his men are dangerous. This is not the time for backbiting and petty bickering—"

Shrugging his hand aside, Elizabeth resumed pacing. "You might feel some misplaced sense of responsibility for Amelia McDougal because you rescued her from a jail wagon, but I don't. If I find a means of escape, I will—"

"Nor is it time for heroics," Morgan warned. "These men have no scruples, Elizabeth. None. You would do well to remember it. If Amelia knows nothing about our association, she can't arouse suspicion among Brown and his crew."

"I assume by your sending for me tonight you

want Brown and the others to think we are lovers?"

"Yes."

"And Amelia?"

Morgan calmly took another sip of brandy. "There's no reason for her to assume any differently."

Elizabeth sank to the lumpy mattress, the day's events suddenly catching up with her. "I suppose you're right. It will make it easier for us to talk if everyone assumes that I'm your mistress for the duration of the voyage." A weary sigh escaped her. "I'm scared, Morgan. There was a time when life held no meaning for me, but it isn't that way any more. When the war's over, there are so many things I'd like to do—so much living to catch up on."

"If we keep our heads there will be plenty of life for the both of us," Morgan said quietly.

She glanced toward the bottle of brandy. "Pour me a drink, will you? I desperately need one."

Reaching for the bottle, Morgan lifted his brows to lighten her mood. "Shouldn't you be performing your duties as a mistress to keep all this on the up and up?"

She made a wry face at him. "Very funny. I'm glad you still have *your* sense of humor."

Pouring a second glass of brandy, Morgan's features sobered. "Better get yours back, Elizabeth. I have a feeling we're going to need it before this is over."

* * *

Morgan heard the door to his cabin open. It was early, dawn still an hour away.

The creak, though controlled, grew more conspicuous as the door eased slowly back on its hinges. Cracking his eyes open a fraction, he watched as Amelia tiptoed into the room, quietly closing the door behind her.

The next moment he felt a pistol barrel resting on his temple.

"You're upset," he observed dryly.

"You low-down weasel!" she hissed, leaning closer to his ear. "I'm going to blow your brains right out of your scheming, two-faced, ugly head."

"Would it be impossible to ask why?"

The barrel of the gun pressed tighter. "Do you know what an 'examination' is?" She had never been so humiliated in all her life!

"Only protecting my investment."

Cocking the pistol, she let her voice assume a note of grim finality. "If you have any last words, you'd better say them."

Rolling swiftly onto his side, he grabbed her arm, dislodging the gun and pinning her to the mattress.

"Where did you get this gun?"

"Wouldn't you like to know!" She had been taught how to get anything she wanted, including how to steal a lazy seaman's pistol as he snored through his watch.

"Listen to me!" Morgan ordered.

Struggling, Amelia tried to break his grip, but she found herself imprisoned by bands of steel.

"I'm not Lanigan. I just said I was in order to save your rotten hide again."

Slowing her struggle, her lips pursed suspiciously. "Then who are you?"

"Exactly who I said I am—Morgan Kane."

She eyed him warily. She wasn't sure she could trust a word he said. First, he was Captain Kane, then Dov Lanigan, and now he was back to being Captain Kane. Who did he want to be next—Christopher Columbus?

He pushed her deeper onto the bed. The feel of his rock hard body pressed against her breasts made the blood in her throat pump faster.

She inhaled deeply to clear her head. Suddenly, she thought she detected a scent. A woman's scent. She lifted her nose to his shoulder and sniffed. Pressing her nose to the fabric of his long johns, she sniffed again and again. Elizabeth's scent!

"What in the hell are you doing?"

Her hand shot out and slapped him hard. The crack sounded like a whiplash inside the small quarters.

He grabbed her free wrist angrily.

"Elizabeth spent the night with you, didn't she?" Amelia had been present when Austin had come to take Elizabeth away, and now she knew where Austin had taken Elizabeth.

"That's none of your business."

Her eyes narrowed with contempt. "You despicable, evil, depraved—"

Morgan cut her off. "Listen, and listen close. If we're going to get out of this alive, you are going to have to cooperate with me."

The gravity in his voice frightened her. What if he was actually Morgan Kane, and he was trying to help her?

"Who are you?"

"Morgan Kane."

Settling down, she momentarily abandoned her struggle, afraid not to believe him. "If you're not Dov Lanigan, then how did you know I was here?"

"I overheard Austin Brown bragging about his conquest to some other men in a pub."

Amelia groaned, embarrassed by her incredible stupidity. "What an imbecile I've been!" It seemed she was once more at his mercy. "What should I do? I don't want to be sold to some ol' man!"

"For now, I want you to continue the role of the victim," he advised.

"I am the victim!"

"You'll be a dead victim if you don't listen!"

She struggled to free herself, but his strength overpowered her again. Gradually, the fight drained out of her, and her head slumped wearily back against the pillow. "What do I have to do?"

"For the time being, nothing. Go about your business as if you were resigned to your fate."

"And what do you plan to do? If you aren't

Lanigan, how can you hope to continue this pretense?"

"You let me worry about that." He loosened his hold on her wrist. "By the time we reach New Orleans, I'll have a plan—but I need your word you won't do anything to give us away until we get there."

"What are you planning to do?"

"To get you and me off the ship with our necks still intact."

She wanted nothing more, but she didn't see how he could do it. These men were not youthful Comanche looking for an afternoon of diversion. They were mean and evil cutthroats.

"I told you, by the time we reach New Orleans, I'll have a plan." Rolling her to her side, Morgan drew her tightly against his chest.

Struggling, she tried to wiggle loose. "What do you think you're doing?"

"I plan to sleep another hour or two, and I don't intend to be awakened by a pistol at my head."

Her eyes widened as she felt the imprint of his manhood pressing against her thigh. She knew if she looked close enough his chest would be tanned and covered with thick, dark hair. The thought produced a most wicked feeling between the juncture of her thighs.

"I won't try to shoot you again."

"I know you won't."

When she wiggled, trying to sit up, she found

herself being pressed firmly back onto the bed by his right hand. "You're not going anywhere."

"I am too! I'm not sleeping in this bed with you!"

"Perhaps you would rather I take you back to Austin Brown and tell him you just tried to kill Dov Lanigan."

"You wouldn't dare!"

"Oh, but I would. I'm despicable, evil and depraved—your words, I believe, not mine."

"Then I would just have to tell Austin Brown that you're not Dov Lanigan, and that you're playing a trick on him!"

"Go ahead, that is, if you think you'll look good dangling from a yardarm . . ."

She'd look awful dangling from a yardarm!

"Just relax and go to sleep," he told her, weary of her immaturity. "If we're discovered I will contend that I sent for you." He rolled over. "That should duly impress Brown."

"Glutton," she hissed, thinking he had already slaked his thirst on one woman this evening. "And stop telling me what to do."

"Stop making it necessary."

Rolling onto her left side, Amelia turned her back on him. He wasn't going to get the best of her. She might not be able to do anything about these sleeping arrangements, but she didn't have to be nice about it. Not that she had been nice about anything—except for the brief period when they had first met—and she wouldn't have been nice to him then if she'd known the kind of man that he really was.

Feeling restless, she switched onto her back. For a long moment, she studied him from the corner of her eye. It was the first time she had ever been this close to a man. For a man, he smelled nice, nothing at all like Captain Garrison's foul stench.

She tried not to look at his eyelashes, but she couldn't help it. They were long and curly and completely inappropriate for a man with his foul disposition. They should belong to a more genteel, honorable man, a man who wouldn't think of putting a woman through an "examination" just to get even with her. Why, she just ought to reach over and poke around inside him like that vile doctor had done to her. Just see how he would like that.

"Whatever is going through your head, I strongly advise against it." Morgan was aware she was looking at him, but he was bone-tired of wrangling with Amelia McDougal and the headaches that inevitably came from dealing with her.

Yet, as she continued to stare at him, he began to lose his patience. The bunk was small, and her resulting proximity too close for comfort.

"Stop staring at me," he commanded. He wondered if the men who had grabbed her other sisters were suffering as much trouble as he.

"I can't," she mumbled.

"Force yourself."

Propping up on her elbow on the mattress, she rested her chin in her hand. "I'm sorry."

"Apology accepted. Go to sleep."

"No, you don't mean it. Besides, you shouldn't just accept my apology and not even know what it's for."

Morgan was too tired to delve into her flawed reasoning. "It doesn't matter. Just go to sleep."

"No, it does matter," she insisted. From now on, she was going to try to get along with him. After all, she reasoned, it was the least she could do for someone who was actually trying to help her.

"All right!" His patience was gone. They were wasting precious time when he could be sleeping. "What is your *point*?"

"I'm sorry for making such a scene and almost giving you away. I should have known that you weren't really Lanigan. Lanigan is a brave privateer—"

"He's a cutthroat just like the rest of these men."

Without thinking, she pressed her face closer, trying to make him accept her sincerity. "Well, maybe, but I should have guessed that you were here to save me from the absolutely terrible predicament I've gotten myself into again."

"All right."

"I apologize." She lay her hand softly against his cheek. For some reason, she had to break through his cool reserve to make him understand that she meant to change her course, to support him rather than attack him.

"All right."

"You forgive me?" It was important to her that

he be aware of this significant change in her feelings. Her fingers curved around the back of his neck as she looked deeply into his eyes, her face very close to his.

He edged farther away from the temptation of her young curvaceous body. Her delicate fingers playing with the hair at his nape were heating up places he would have preferred to remain stone-cold. Her lips were so close he had an insane desire to taste them. She seemed not to notice that the fullness of her breast was brushing his chest with the same rhythm of her fingers lacing through his hair. He was vaguely aware that his fingers twitched to cup the softness and that his lips were drifting toward hers.

His voice was harsher than intended when he spoke. "It doesn't matter if I forgive you or not. Now that I'm committed, it is my duty to protect you." He edged away from her, hoping she would take the hint.

Curling closer to him, she settled her head back onto the pillow, her eyes openly assessing him now. "But it does matter. I now believe that you only have my best interests at heart."

"You couldn't know that!" The thoughts going through his head had nothing to do with her best interests. Her vulnerability intimidated him more than her outrage.

"But I trust you. Aren't I supposed to?" Her eyes were wide and hopeful.

"You trust too easily," he told her gruffly.

She just didn't understand this man. Did he want her to trust him or not? He'd said he needed her cooperation, and in her mind she couldn't cooperate unless she trusted him. It was that simple. Why did he have to be so difficult all the time?

"Are you mad at me again?" she asked in an exasperated tone.

"No, I'm not mad at you again." He sounded remote and very tired.

"But you'd prefer that I be quiet and go to sleep."

"Yes." He sighed. She had finally caught on.

"Then say it nicely."

When he didn't answer, she explained it to him, the way she would to a child who wasn't very bright. "Now say nicely that you would like for me to be quiet—not shut up—but be quiet and go to sleep."

"Go to sleep."

"Uh-uh. Not until you say it nicely."

Heaving a disgruntled sigh, he began. "Please be quiet and go to sleep."

"Certainly." Snuggling closer, she lay her cheek on her folded hands and closed her eyes. "See, that wasn't so hard, was it?"

From now on, she and Morgan Kane were going to be friends. She was going to be on her best behavior, and before he saw her safely back to Mercy Flats, he was going to like her better than he liked any other woman—and that included that rotten ol' Elizabeth.

She was prepared to forgive him for last night's indiscretion. Anne-Marie had talked about a certain itch a man got and how sometimes they did things to appease themselves when they were otherwise fairly decent. That's how she was beginning to think of Morgan: fairly decent.

She didn't like the thought of Elizabeth sharing his bed—she didn't like the thought of any woman sharing his bed—but there really was nothing between him and herself at the moment.

But that could change ... if she decided she wanted it to, so he'd just better watch out. She could be a woman to be reckoned with, if she chose to be.

"Morgan," she murmured sleepily, suddenly feeling small and alone again.

"What now?"

Her hand found his in the darkness. "I'm awfully scared. I want to go home."

Chapter 8

Taking a deep breath of briny air, Amelia admired the glorious sunrise. The sky was a magnificent blue above the dazzling waters. She felt wonderful this morning, even though she hadn't slept at all last night. She was not accustomed to a man in her bed.

It hadn't been that bad, really, having a man in her bed. Truth was, she had enjoyed the feel of Morgan Kane's body lying next to hers. She had been even more aware of the hardness of his thigh and the warmth of his shoulder against hers.

For now, she would protect his ruse, even though she was skeptical of the outcome. She couldn't argue that her situation was less than desirable. If Anne-Marie were here, she'd say that for the time being she'd better do as Morgan Kane said—even if he was a man.

"It's a beautiful day, isn't it?"

Amelia looked up to see Pilar standing beside

her. It bothered her that the girl's eyes were so lifeless. Anyone so young should have sparkling eyes
and a bright smile, but Pilar had neither.

"It's a glorious day," Amelia agreed, refusing to
lose heart. "Where are the others?"

"Below."

The wind battered the long hair of both women
as they stood at the railing watching the sun rise in
the distance. If it weren't for the gravity of the situation, Amelia would feel almost happy. Her own
fears were diminished now that Morgan Kane was
aboard. She'd like to ease Pilar's anxiety, but she
couldn't without breaking a promise. Morgan had
sworn her to secrecy; the outcome of their circumstances might well depend on her discretion.

"The others should come up for fresh air,"
Amelia observed. She was developing a motherly
fondness for the young women although she was
no older than most of them.

Over the hours, she had discovered the girls'
names. They were Pilar, the girl with sorrowful
eyes; Ol' Elizabeth, who held herself aloof and
above the others; Auria, quiet and frightened;
Belicia, the girl she had found sobbing on her bunk
yesterday; Ria, who laughed a lot, though she had
no reason to; Mira, who smiled through her tears;
Bunny and Mahalia, dark-skinned; and Faith and
Hester.

Sighing, Pilar leaned closer to the railing to peer
at the crystal water. "I told them they should come
up, but they don't want to. They're scared."

"Scared. Of what?"

"Of the men." Pilar watched the waves slapping against the ship's hull. "They're afraid of what they might do."

"They won't do anything," Amelia scoffed. "We're too valuable to them."

"Maybe you are, but not the rest of us."

"Poppycock!" Amelia knew Pilar was referring to talk among the hands that her beauty was uncommon and so would bring more on the black market, but that was rubbish. Each girl had her own beauty—a beauty that men could not help but find desirable.

"If you're smart, you'll use that beauty to your best advantage," a new voice said.

Amelia and Pilar turned to discover that the other women had decided to join them on deck. Elizabeth had issued the brusque challenge.

"How should I do that?" Amelia asked.

"You'd be wise to use your beauty to full advantage," Elizabeth repeated.

Amelia stiffened. "I refuse to barter myself, if that's what you're suggesting."

Elizabeth laughed. "Then you're a fool."

Aware of the developing animosity between the two women, Ria quickly intervened. "I say we all stick together."

A murmur of agreement rose from the women. If they were to endure their barbarous state, they had to stick together.

Amelia's eyes locked in silent duel with Elizabeth's. "I agree," she murmured. She felt a bone of contention between this woman and herself, and she wasn't sure why.

"You both have taken leave of your senses," Faith interjected. "What difference does it make if we stick together or not? When we arrive in New Orleans, we're going to be sold like cattle."

The women again added their voices of despondency to Faith's.

"We can't think that way." Amelia knew that hope was their only weapon. Without it, they would be lost.

"How can we think otherwise?" Hester cried. "Don't you understand? We're going to be sold! Sold!" she repeated. "Like pigs at market!"

"I know it looks bad at the moment, but if we put our heads together we can come up with something," Amelia reasoned.

The women clearly did not relish such hope.

"To hear this one tell it, we should all be singing," Elizabeth mocked.

"And if you listen to *her*"—Amelia pointed at Elizabeth—"we might as well as slit our throats and have it over with."

Bunny's eyes widened with distress. "Oh, I wouldn't have the nerve to slit my own throat," she cried.

"That's only a figure of speech," Amelia consoled, giving the girl's shoulder a reassuring pat.

"Well, what should we do?" Mahalia asked. "It seems hopeless to me."

"Well, for one thing, we'll have to be polite to Dov Lanigan," Elizabeth voiced.

"Polite!" Amelia sputtered. It was on the tip of her tongue to tell Miss Prissy Elizabeth that her precious Dov Lanigan was not who he appeared to be. And even if he were, wild horses couldn't make her be "polite" to the *real* Dov Lanigan.

"Polite, my fanny. Dov Lanigan doesn't deserve our courtesy. He plans to sell us," Amelia reminded her.

"Maybe he does, and maybe he doesn't," Elizabeth returned, refusing to concede the point.

Amelia wanted to slap the smug look off Elizabeth's face. It was apparent that this shameless woman was clearly smitten with the notorious hooligan, Dov Lanigan, and she didn't have enough decency to care who knew it.

Drawing herself up straighter, Amelia stood her ground. "I say we band together, overcome the scum, and hang them one by one by their egotistical appendages!"

Every woman's eyes widened at that thought—except Elizabeth's. She thought the suggestion plausible, but she'd die before she agreed with the featherbrain. "And I say, we sit back, bide our time, and look for a reasonable means of escape," Elizabeth countered. "One that won't get us all killed."

Pilar added her two cents. "What if we can't find a reasonable means of escape?"

Elizabeth's chin firmed with determination. "We will."

"But we don't know that—" Amelia's eyes widened as Elizabeth shoved her up against the railing.

"Listen, and listen good, you silly twit. We bide our time until we can think of a reasonable means of escape." Elizabeth was so close that Amelia could see the flecks of gold rimming the pupils of her eyes. "And we *stay* on Lanigan's good side," she ordered.

Amelia's eyes flared resentfully. "Why are *you* so concerned about Lanigan?"

"Let's just say I think it's in our best interest." Elizabeth straightened, releasing her bruising hold. "For now, we make the best of our circumstances, and keep our heads."

"Our heads, Elizabeth, are not our immediate concern," Amelia reminded her as she irritably straightened her disheveled collar. Casting a glance in Lanigan's direction to discover him still in deep conversation with Austin, Elizabeth added quietly, "Just keep quiet and do what you're told."

"I'm going to escape the first opportunity I get," Amelia vowed. "Anyone who wants can go with me." Morgan had never implied that he would take the other women when they left, but she couldn't leave them behind at Elizabeth's mercy.

Turning on her heel, Amelia walked away, leaving the other women to wonder who they were to believe: Elizabeth or her.

* * *

The hours at sea passed slowly. When Amelia wasn't lying on her bunk staring at the ceiling, fighting her queasy stomach, she was on deck, staring at the miles of endless water. The sea fascinated her. She could stand for hours, watching the dolphins frolic in the water like playful children on a school holiday. She had never been on water before, and it was a new and exhilarating experience. Land had dominated her life, just dirty, dry, dusty ol' land. This change was uplifting and invigorating.

"Shouldn't you be asleep, Miss McDougal?" inquired a deep, masculine voice with the undercurrent there as usual, mocking and somewhat disapproving.

Expectancy fired Amelia's blood as Morgan approached. He had an unnerving effect on her, and she suspected he had a similar effect on the other women as well.

"I'm not sleepy."

A match flared, bathing Morgan's rugged features in the soft glow. The rich smell of tobacco floated to her as she stood on the forecastle deck, admiring the moon's pattern on the shimmering water. Overhead, the wind snapped through the sails as the sleek vessel sliced silently through the dark waters.

Drawing deeply of the tobacco scent, Amelia decided that she rather liked it.

"Are you worried?" he asked casually.

"Me?" She chuckled. "Heavens, no." At least if she were, he'd never know it.

Settling his weight against the spray rail, Morgan studied her as if something might be wrong with her. It had seemed that she had carefully avoided him all day.

"Most women in your situation would be."

"I'm not 'most women,' Captain—," she caught herself, "Mr. Lanigan."

They stood for a moment without speaking, listening to the waves strike the bow of the ship.

Before Amelia realized it, she was voicing her deepest thoughts. "Do you find Elizabeth pretty?"

"Elizabeth?" he replied vaguely.

Elizabeth? she mocked silently. He knew perfectly well who Elizabeth was. She knew what was going on between those two. "Yes, Elizabeth. Do you think she's pretty?"

"The woman with the topaz eyes?"

"The woman with the topaz eyes." Ha! They weren't topaz; they were just plain ol' straw-colored eyes—the color of an old, ugly bale of straw, not topaz, like some rare jewel or something.

His tone was noncommittal. "She's attractive."

Amelia deliberately kept her tone light. "Attractive?"

"Actually, I haven't noticed."

She turned on him. "Yes, you have!"

"No, I haven't," he reiterated with infuriating calmness.

"Then what is it? A case of mutual attraction?" Amelia had heard of such things—a man and a woman—their eyes meeting across the room—a feeling of destiny. The thought that fate had destined Morgan Kane for Elizabeth made Amelia sick. Not that she wanted him, but she didn't want Elizabeth to have him either.

Taking a draw off his cheroot, Morgan waited for her to complete her thoughts.

"That's it, isn't it?" she challenged.

"That's what?"

"Mutual attraction." Drawing her shawl closer, she struggled against the strange feelings suddenly battering her. Was it jealousy rearing its ugly head? Sister Lucille had warned her about the serpent's ugly ways, but why would it pick this time, and most especially, this man, to plague her? She didn't care who Captain Kane looked at with lust in his serpent eyes! She rigorously jerked her cloak tighter. Not in the least!

"'What were you and the other women so deep in conversation about earlier?" Morgan asked.

"Escape."

A dangerous light entered his eyes. "You are not to attempt escape on your own."

"I don't see you doing anything to help," she returned crisply. "We'll be in New Orleans soon, and you haven't done a single thing to get me out of this."

"You are not to do anything foolish," he repeated. "When the time is right, I will handle the matter."

"Well, thank you anyway, but I've decided to rely on my own devices." She picked an imaginary speck of lint from her sleeve. "Do you like my new cloak? I bought it with your money."

"Your devices are what got you into this in the first place," he warned, unwilling to be diverted.

"They've always worked for me in the past."

"They'll get you deflowered this time," he said bluntly. "Is that what you want?"

"No, I don't want to be 'deflowered'." Whatever that meant. She was too proud to ask the meaning. He was trying to change the subject by talking about silly flowers, and she wanted to talk about escape.

"Then you'd better do what I say."

"Then you'd better tell me what you're going to do." She still wasn't at all sure she could trust him. She'd seen the way he'd been hobnobbing with Austin Brown and his band of thugs.

"The less you know, the better," Morgan said. "Just do as I say." Morgan Kane could be accused of many things, but being a fool was not among them. Because of her impetuous tongue, the less Amelia knew, the better.

She turned to oppose him. "You mean I'm just to follow along like a gullible dolt. Is that what you want?"

"That's exactly what I mean."

"Well, maybe I won't do that."

"Well, maybe you'd better. When the time comes, I'll get you off the boat safely, if you follow my instructions."

"And the other women?"

"What about them?"

"Are you going to take them, too?"

"That isn't possible," he said sharply, as if he'd already given the subject considerable thought. "As much as I'd like to, I can't save them all. Assuming responsibility for eleven women is out of the question."

"You're only going to save me?"

He paused, as if hesitant about voicing his next thought. "You, and one other."

"Oh, let me guess who that will be," she said, sarcasm ringing in her tone.

Taking another draw on his cheroot, he gazed down at the water without comment.

When she could stand the suspense no longer, she erupted with the name that she'd come to despise. "Elizabeth," she spat.

"I'll make that decision when the time comes."

Envy reared its head again. She just ought to demand to know why—why ill-tempered Elizabeth would be chosen while someone like Pilar or Mahalia or Ria would be left to the cutthroats!

"It is Elizabeth, isn't it?" Her head swung away. "That's disgusting!"

His hand snaked out, snaring her arm. Her chin firmed as he drew her roughly against his chest.

A thrill of frightened anticipation filled her at

his nearness. "So," she taunted, "I suppose you're going to bully me again."

His smile was devilishly wicked. "Perhaps, or perhaps I'll only kiss you again. You do enjoy my kisses, don't you?" His grip tightened, reminding her of the first night on their journey.

Her eyes met his threateningly. "They turned my stomach."

He laughed, an arrogant, male action that infuriated her. "You know, I could take you below and take some of that spunk out of you. No one would attempt to stop me." His eyes held his own measure of challenge.

She didn't blink an eye. "You do, and I'll scream my head off. I'll shout to the rooftops who you really are, Captain Kane."

His smile was nothing short of sinister. "I don't think so. You talk big, but you know that I'm you're only hope of getting out of this one."

"You lay one finger on me, and I'll scream," she vowed. "They'll shoot you the moment they discover that you're not Dov Lanigan."

Chuckling, he lowered his head, his breath fanning her lips. "Ahh, but what a sweet death."

Her features hardened with determination. "Don't kiss me again. You do, and you'll be sorry."

"I don't think so. I think you like my kisses." His mouth captured hers with a boldness that seared her.

She deliberately bit down on his lower lip, hard,

so hard that he nearly sank to his knees as he emitted a painful groan.

"I told you not to kiss me."

"Dammit," he murmured, trying to get loose from her.

She felt an immediate pang of remorse. She'd only meant to make her point, not to hurt him. The way she had it figured was that if they were going to get along, he had to understand that she was not going to be bullied, not by him, not by any man.

He eyed her warily. "Don't ever try that again."

Her chin lifted a fraction. "Don't take what isn't offered."

He could respect her point of view. Taking a woman against her will was not his style. He was more accustomed to picking and choosing from generous offerings. Why then did this woman drive him beyond reason? Why did he feel compelled to challenge someone who'd become as troublesome as a nest of nervous wasps? He shook his head at the irony, the foolishness of it. "Perhaps you'd better make up your mind about what you want and what you don't want." His face came dangerously near, and whether she realized it or not, she swayed toward him. He exhaled slowly before he spoke. "Seems to me you say 'come here' when you mean 'go away' and 'go away' when you mean 'come closer'."

"I," she began breathlessly, "I meant you no harm. It's just that ... oh, I don't know!" She closed her eyes tightly to stem the tide of longing that she felt despite her will. Without thinking, acting only on impulse, her head tilted upward, her eyes remained closed, her body throbbed with anticipation of his kiss.

Feeling his breath quicken as it fanned her cheeks, she knew that his mouth hovered just inches away. She lifted her heels to close the gap to put an end to the unmerciful suspense.

A chuckle from somewhere deep inside him rumbled to the surface, piercing her rosy haze of anticipation. "When you figure it out, my dear, do let me know."

Her eyes flew open as he swung away and strode off. The swiftness of his departure washed a chill over her body that was thrumming with warm anticipation.

"You are horrible!" She gasped.

His laughter floated on the breeze. "Go to bed, little girl," he tossed over his shoulder, his voice rich with irony. "That's what I plan to do."

The women were hungry. Amelia was tortured by the thought that men could treat women this way. It tore at her heartstrings to hear Pilar and Auria crying themselves to sleep at night.

If a McDougal was nothing else, she was resourceful. If Austin Brown refused to feed the women properly, then she would. A meager ration of hardtack and water was provided each day, but it barely appeased the women's appetites. Still, they devoured the slight fare, ignoring the catcalls and constant haranguing of the crew.

Amelia ate her meals in stony silence, trying to control her swelling anger. Morgan Kane sat among the men, laughing jovially as he shared a hearty meal of fowl, crusty brown loaves of bread, and wine.

"There's so little," Hester complained as she licked the remaining crumbs from her fingers that evening. "That's the worst part."

Amelia's eyes fixed on the men as she chewed thoughtfully. "Don't worry, there'll be more."

"Please," Pilar whispered. "Don't do anything foolish. The portions are small, but it's enough to keep us alive."

"They deliberately make us watch them eat to torment us," Bunny murmured. Night after night they watched the men stuff themselves like gluttons.

When the men had drunk themselves into a blind stupor, most of them retired to their bunks for the night. Only Austin and Morgan remained on deck.

Nightly, Austin would encourage Morgan to exhibit his remarkable skills with a knife. He was good, Amelia would allow him that. She wondered how he'd become so proficient. Had his years in the service honed his skill? Not only was he skilled with a knife; he was a master of deception. He maintained his charade as Dov Lanigan effortlessly, it seemed.

She turned away, shuddering at the consequences if his plan were to fail.

The following morning when provisions were left at their door, Amelia observed the tray of hardtack and water dispassionately. Closing the door with her foot, she discarded the tray on the floor, then knelt beside her bunk and reached underneath, withdrawing a large gunnysack.

Bunny's eyes rounded as Amelia began pulling loaves of bread and whole cooked chickens from the bulging sack.

"Where did you get those?" Faith breathed.

"She's a little thief," Elizabeth said. Still, she moved closer, openly intrigued by the confiscated bounty.

Amelia smiled as she handed Belicia a loaf of bread. "That's right, I am, and a darned good one." Slowly, she pulled a gold watch from her pocket and let it dangle enticingly between her fingers. "Anyone want to know the time?"

"Oh, dear," Mahalia murmured. "You didn't—"

"Sure I did; and there's lots more where that came from."

"Oh, you shouldn't have." Pilar's eyes were as round as Bunny's as she watched Amelia stuff the watch back into her pocket, then tear a chicken into halves and hand a nice, plump piece to her. The meat looked wonderfully delicious and succulent.

"Amelia, you're going to get us all hanged,"

Elizabeth predicted. "I don't know why you can't just play by the rules like everyone else."

"Just eat, Elizabeth, and stop criticizing," Amelia muttered, jamming a hunk of bread into Elizabeth's hand as she continued to dole out the food.

The women devoured the meal hungrily, grateful for the unexpected feast, no matter how Amelia had gotten it.

Early the next morning, Amelia disappeared again, returning a while later with a replenished gunnysack. The women repeatedly voiced concerns that she would be caught and dealt with severely, but the food was heavenly. They had slept the night before without the anguish of hunger pangs.

By the third day, the women were stretched out in the cabin like fat, lazy cats. They had eaten their fill for over three days, and they had become sluggish from the orgy.

Faith belched, then rolled lethargically onto her back as she broke out in giggles. "If Austin Brown knew what was going on, he'd hang us all."

Amelia smiled. "How will he ever know?" Abigail and Anne-Marie had taught her to be very good at her craft. She'd had a lovely time the past three days, duping the crew right under their noses.

"You'll tell them," Elizabeth predicted.

"I will not," Amelia said defensively. "Wild horses couldn't drag it out of me." Discretion wasn't necessarily her strong suit, but when it mattered, she could keep a secret. She hadn't given away Morgan's identity, had she?

The women jumped, trying to scramble to their feet as the door to their cabin was suddenly flung open. Austin Brown loomed in the doorway, a ruthless smile fastened on his lips. "Good evening, ladies. I trust you're enjoying the voyage?"

No one bothered to answer him. They were accustomed to Austin's false charm, to say nothing about his scarcity of wit.

"Come now, ladies. Cat got your tongues?" He stepped inside, slamming the door behind him. It wasn't hard to see that he was in a foul temper.

As usual, his dress was impeccable. If Amelia hadn't known better, she'd say he looked like a real gentleman. It was hard to believe he was such a boil on the butt of society.

"My, my," Austin clucked as his eyes centered on the discarded mound of uneaten hardtack. "Are you ladies ill? You're not eating your dinner." He approached Pilar, and the timbre of his voice was so ominous that the girl covered her heart and averted her face.

"Perhaps our portions have been too large," Austin baited. "I must speak to the cook about this."

Amelia, sensing Pilar's growing anxiety, interceded. "Go away, Austin," she said crossly.

"Ahh, the fair rose speaks up for the pitiful weed. How touching."

A sob caught in Pilar's throat as color flooded

her face. Amelia's eyes glittered dangerously. He had no right to humiliate Pilar in front of the others. Wasn't it enough that he had reduced them all to mere slaves?

Centering the tip of his cane beneath Pilar's chin, Austin forced her to look up at him. "What is it, my dear? Do I make you uncomfortable?"

Pilar tried to look away, but the cane dug into the soft flesh under her jaw, imprisoning her.

Austin's eyes darkened dangerously. "Speak up, dear. Why aren't you eating?" The tip of his cane bore deeper. "You must keep your strength up—it wouldn't look good if you were to fall ill under my protection."

"Please," Pilar whimpered as her eyes filled.

"Please? Please what, my lovely?"

The others watched, powerless to prevent his cruelty.

Austin suddenly thrust his face close to Pilar's. "Is there something you want to tell me, Pilar?"

"No," she whispered.

"No?" The cane increased its pressure.

Amelia's hand darted out, sending the cane clattering noisily to the floor. "Stop it!"

Furious now, Austin jerked Amelia roughly to him, his face mottled with anger. "Perhaps there's something you want to say to me?"

Amelia faced him defiantly, her eyes shards of steel. "I wouldn't have to steal your ol' food if you'd feed us properly," she hissed.

Austin's face went momentarily blank as a groan escaped Elizabeth.

"Steal my food?" he repeated.

Shrugging out of his grasp, Amelia rubbed her arm as she glared at Elizabeth, who looked back at her, shaking her head in disbelief.

Well, what's the matter with me, Amelia thought. She knew she shouldn't have blabbed. She should have played the innocent, but he'd had Pilar in tears!

"What's this about food?" Austin blustered. His eyes narrowed suspiciously. "You've been stealing food!"

Amelia looked aghast. "No!"

"That's what you said!"

"I did not! I only said that if you weren't feeding us, we would probably have to steal food!"

His eyes snaked to the others, who simultaneously flashed him timid, albeit substantiating, smiles. Yes, their eyes lied, that's what she said, sure enough.

"Then what is all this twaddle about food!"

Amelia raised her palms innocently. "How should I know! You started it!"

"Forget the food!" Austin bellowed. "A watch belonging to one of my men is missing. Do any of you know anything about it?"

"Oh, that." Amelia was so relieved that he hadn't caught on about the food that she was glad to give back the ol' watch. Fishing in her pocket, she produced the stolen item. "Here."

128 Lori Copeland

Pocketing the watch, Austin scowled at her churlishly. "You keep your hands to yourself. If I catch you stealing again, I will personally administer your punishment. Do you understand me?"

"Yes, sir. I understand you."

He turned and left the cramped quarters, mopping his perspiring forehead with a handkerchief. "Women!" they heard him mutter angrily.

Amelia stuck her tongue out at his receding back.

"Well," Elizabeth goaded as the door slammed shut, "you've about done it this time."

Dropping down onto the bunk, Amelia grinned. "Austin Brown doesn't scare me." Elevating the wallet that she'd just lifted from the pompous ol' windbag's pocket, she admired the fine, intricate carvings in the leather. This had to have set him back a pretty penny. "I've yet to meet the man who can scare me."

Chapter 9

Moonlight streamed through the dirty porthole as Amelia crawled out of her bunk and quickly dressed. The day of deliverance had finally arrived. Morgan had a plan; she was to follow the plan implicitly, and they would escape unharmed. If she were to take matters into her own hands, Morgan warned her that he would assume no further responsibility.

Creeping silently through the dim corridor, she paused before a door and rapped softly.

Fog shrouded the clipper as eleven figures crept soundlessly above deck. Morgan had told her to stay below until he gave the signal, but Amelia didn't want to miss anything. She wanted to be ready if excitement broke out.

Straining to see through the murky haze, she tried to detect movement on the bank. There was none.

A foghorn sounded in the distance, signaling an approaching ship.

"See anything?" Ria pressed closer to Amelia's side, her body trembling with anticipation. The ship had reached New Orleans late the night before. The captain, a cautious sort, had moored the clipper a safe distance from the landing to avoid suspicion. The women were to be transported ashore under cover of darkness by rowboats.

"No, nothing."

"Maybe Mr. Kane changed his mind," Mahalia whispered. "Maybe the crew has caught on, and they've bound and gagged him." Late last night, with Morgan's permission, Amelia had explained to the women how he was only posing as Dov Lanigan. The women were surprised, but vowed to keep the confidence when Amelia included them all in the impending escape. She had not taken Elizabeth into her confidence. She didn't care what happened to Elizabeth.

"No," Amelia said firmly. "He wouldn't change his mind, and he isn't foolish enough to get caught." Morgan Kane, aggravating as he was, was a man of his word.

Amelia's eyes found Elizabeth's and challenged them. Did Elizabeth know Morgan's true identity, and how he planned to take her with him and leave the others behind? Amelia still burned when she thought about the injustice of it all. She'd lain awake most of the night trying to think of a way she could save the others; in the end she decided to just take them with her. There would be little Morgan could do at that point.

Oh, she wished Anne-Marie and Abigail were here now! They would think of something to stop these evil men.

Suddenly, the signal came to her. The low, melodious call of a songbird somewhere near the shore. Pressing against the railing, Amelia listened more intently. There it was again, stronger this time.

"That's it," she murmured.

The women drew closer, fear evident in their eyes.

"Stay close together," Amelia whispered. "If we're discovered, don't stop, run as hard as you can. Escape by whatever means you can." Jumping over the side of the ship might be scary, but probably not fatal for a strong swimmer.

The women's eyes located the two seamen trussed up tightly on the deck. Captain Kane had overpowered the morning watch packet rats as they dozed. The remainder of the dirty, uncouth, ignorant brutes of the crew were sleeping below in their bunks.

Pilar's voice sounded lost and small in the shrouded darkness. "I'm scared."

Drawing the girl to her, Amelia tried to comfort her. "It's all right," she whispered. "Try to be brave."

Elizabeth seized Amelia's arm and jerked her roughly aside. Amelia stiffened with resentment as she glared into Elizabeth's eyes and decided that this witch's eyes had to be as hard as her black heart.

"Are you crazy?" Elizabeth demanded. "We haven't got time for that!"

"Let go of me!" Amelia said crossly, shrugging out of her painful grasp. "She's frightened. Can't you see that?"

"I can see you're about to get us all killed." Elizabeth's eyes darted to the bank. "Tell the others to go back, that we'll return for them later."

"No! That would be lying!" They only had a brief time before the crew would discover the insurrection taking place.

"You're a fool!" Elizabeth spat contemptuously. "We can't save everyone. We have to save ourselves!"

The women paused as Morgan's signal sounded again, clearer, more insistent this time.

"Come on. We've got to go. Now!" Gripping Amelia's arm, Elizabeth shoved her along the railing.

Wrenching free from Elizabeth's bruising hold, Amelia stood her ground, refusing to be bullied. "I'm not going anywhere without the others."

"You little fool. You're to obey Captain Kane's orders!"

Amelia gasped. Elizabeth knew. She knew about the plan. Morgan had told her who he was! Amelia's heart sank, and she felt sick to her stomach. Morgan had confided in Elizabeth, the witch.

"Come on, you little fool." Elizabeth tried to force Amelia to follow her, but Amelia dug her heels in stubbornly. She would never leave the others behind to face their horrible fate. Never!

After pulling free of Elizabeth, Amelia ran back to the women huddled in the damp morning chill. She gathered them around her protectively and declared defiantly, "They're coming with us."

"They're not."

"They are."

When Elizabeth attempted to grab Amelia, a shoving match between them erupted. Tempers hit the flash point, and the two locked into a spirited hair-pulling fight.

In desperation, Auria, Faith, and Hester waded between the women to separate them.

"Stop it!" Hester whispered harshly. "You're going to get us all killed!"

Pilar pulled Amelia to her feet while Bunny got a firm hold on Elizabeth.

One of the unconscious packet rats moaned, beginning to come to.

"You two can settle this later." Ria grabbed Pilar's hand, motioning the others to follow her.

"Now look what you've done!" Elizabeth rolled to her feet, shooting Amelia a murderous glare. "Morgan can't take all of us!"

"Then you stay behind, Elizabeth!" Amelia sprang to her feet and left Elizabeth cussing beneath her breath.

Some of the women feared heights, and others trembled so hard their movements were bungling and slow, so it took longer than expected to lower their bodies down the rope.

As they dropped silently into the cold water, they gasped, keeping their heads low.

Pilar clung to Amelia's hand tightly, her eyes wide with fear as she fought to keep her head above water.

"Don't be afraid," Amelia whispered. "It's not far to the bank."

"I can't swim," Pilar gasped.

"What?"

Pilar's whisper was laced with panic. "I can't swim."

Amelia grasped Pilar's hand tighter and pulled her along behind her.

When they reached the bank, one by one the women collapsed, panting for breath.

Morgan appeared, parting the grass that grew thick along the small inlet. Surprise dominated his features when he saw eleven dripping wet women struggling for breath.

Amelia looked up at him crossly. "Don't say anything!" she hissed. "We're all here, and we can't go back."

"All of you?" Morgan's eyes grimly assessed the gaggle of soggy women.

Amelia scrambled to her feet, pushing her wet hair out of her eyes. "You're taking all of us, or none of us are going."

Elizabeth hurriedly swung around to establish a stance beside Morgan. "Speak for yourself."

Amelia's eyes filled with contempt. "You traitor!"

Elizabeth sneered. "What do you know?"

"I know something about loyalty that you obviously don't. Why, you know these women as well as I do, and yet you'd sell them downriver as quickly as those men back on the ship."

"You idiot, you've jeopardized everything."

"Maybe so, but I didn't betray my friends."

The women lunged for each other, going for the eyes. They hissed and scratched as they thrashed over the ground, grunting and pulling each other's hair.

Stepping closer to Morgan, Pilar apologized for their reprehensible behavior. "They don't get along."

"That's an understatement if I ever heard one." At that moment, Morgan didn't much like them either. He waded between the two, grasped each by the arm, and hefted them to their feet. Holding them apart, he glared at them. "I'm fed up with your behavior. It endangers all of us." He gave them both a quick shake. "Stop it!"

"She started it!" Amelia accused.

"You were asking for it!" Elizabeth snarled.

"I don't care who started it. I'm stopping it!" Morgan tightened his hold as the women lunged at each other again.

"Please," Mahalia agonized, her eyes darting back to the ship. "They're going to hear us!"

Regaining her senses, Amelia realized that she

was foolish to throw caution to the wind, no matter how angry Elizabeth made her.

"Ladies," Morgan reasoned. "I can't take all of you with me." He wasn't certain where he planned to go himself! The area was swarming with war activity. A man traveling with eleven women was sure to draw attention.

Amelia stepped forward to shield the women. "We all go, or none of us go," she repeated.

"It would be suicide—"

"No!" Amelia interrupted. "We all go or none of us go." She paused, glancing at Elizabeth. "Unless you want to exclude her."

Elizabeth's eyes smoldered.

Suddenly a shout came from the ship as the alarm was sounded. Men poured onto the decks, pulling on clothes as they ran.

"Now look what you've done, Elizabeth!" Amelia accused.

"Me? You're the one who won't listen!"

Morgan swore as he realized there was nothing to do now but take them all and make a run for it. As he signaled for the women to follow him, the activity on ship grew more frenzied.

They scrambled away, side stepping a scurrying armadillo as it fled for safety in the underbrush.

"Maybe he's not coming back," Amelia announced dejectedly.

"He's coming back," Elizabeth replied with calm assurance.

Amelia's shoulders sunk lower. "You can't know that, Elizabeth."

For over two hours the women had waited, feeling cold, wet, and increasingly more discouraged. Morgan had promised to be back within the hour, and he hadn't returned. Had he deserted all of them? No one would blame him. Amelia knew that he hadn't been happy about bringing the other women along, but surely he wouldn't have just gone off and left them, would he? Her eyes turned resentfully on Elizabeth. Amelia wondered how Elizabeth could know whether he was coming back. Easy. Morgan, it seemed, had kept *her* well-informed so far.

Taking Elizabeth aside, Amelia kept her voice low. "Do you really think he's coming back?"

"He'll be back."

Amelia's eyes searched the wooded area, praying for a glimpse of the damnably handsome Yankee. "I'm not so certain."

"He'll be here."

"Why didn't he tell us where he was going?" Amelia fretted. He'd issued them an order not to go anywhere—as if they had anywhere to go,—then just left.

Elizabeth looked at her sharply. "He'll be back."

By the time Morgan returned, Amelia had all but given up hope. It was growing dark, and the women were faint with hunger.

"Where have you been?" Amelia exclaimed,

running to meet the captain as he approached the hidden clearing.

"You missed me?"

"Like an inflamed bunion."

Brushing past her, Morgan walked to the circle of women huddled against the blustery wind.

Elizabeth quickly moved to stand beside him. "I was starting to worry about you."

"Sorry. It took longer than I'd expected."

"Were you successful?"

Nodding, Morgan knelt on his haunches and began drawing a crude map in the loose dirt with his forefinger. "About five miles away, on the river, is *The Mississippi Lady*. The vessel is old but serviceable. The captain, a personal friend of mine, has agreed to transport you to Memphis." His tone took on a note of gravity. "You have two choices: you can split up and try to make it back to your families alone, or you can remain together and I'll do my best to see that you reach Memphis safely."

"How are you acquainted with this captain?" Amelia countered.

"Does it matter?"

"To me it does." What if he was another Austin Brown or someone equally worse?

"You have my word; he is reputable."

"What will we do once we reach Memphis?" Auria asked.

"There's a man I know there who will help you, once we get there—if we get there."

Pilar edged closer to Amelia, her young body visibly quaking.

"Will you be coming with us?" Amelia asked, looking squarely into Morgan's eyes.

"I will accompany you as far as Memphis. Once there, you'll be on your own." His eyes silently warned Amelia that she'd better get it right this time.

The women, shivering in the damp air, looked to one another for answers ... all except Elizabeth, who instead looked at Morgan. "I'm coming with you," she told him.

Turning back to the women, Amelia asked them softly, "What do you want to do? We could try to make it on our own." It would be difficult if not impossible. They had no money or knowledge of the area. "We could seek shelter with the church."

The women didn't know what to do. Most didn't have homes to go to; others admitted that they had long, distant journeys before their ordeal would be over. And with the war, the church shelters were in nearly as bad a shape as they were. Memphis or New Orleans—at this point, it didn't seem to make much difference.

"All right," Amelia said, speaking for all of them. She gathered Bunny and Belicia's hands to still their trembling. "We stay together."

Rising, Morgan nodded. "We'll need to move quickly. The captain wants to get underway immediately. No doubt, Brown will be right on our heels."

The small, bedraggled group set off once again to pursue an uncertain future, hoping that, at the very least, they would find warmth.

Chapter 10

A light mist was falling by the time the women reached the levee. Parting the thick undergrowth, Amelia looked at the tall steamboats tied side by side at the wharf.

The Mississippi Lady looked old, run-down, and depressing. The boat suited Amelia's mood perfectly.

Someone was playing a harmonica, while gangs of roustabouts loaded bales of cotton onto the decks of steamers headed downriver. Along the banks, men lifted trunks and carpetbags from horse-drawn wagons onto the low, main deck of a departing steamer.

The men's voices, singing in harmony, granted the only warmth to the unseasonably chilly air.

"Stay close together," Morgan warned.

He needn't have worried. He couldn't have scraped the women off his side with a bowie knife.

Motioning for Bunny to follow him, he started for the gangplank.

Bunny trembled with fear as she stepped into the lead, followed by Pilar, Hester, Faith, Ria, Mahalia, Belicia, Auria, Mira, Elizabeth, and Amelia. One by one, the women marched in a long row to the vessel, looking neither to their right nor left.

As they crossed the gangplank, Amelia held her breath against the stench of the hot oily engines. Her eyes took in the cargo and firewood strewn about on the old deck in a disorderly fashion. Hurrying around the other women, she fell into step with Morgan. "This boat doesn't look safe to me," she whispered, her eyes fixed anxiously upon the unprotected boiler on the main deck. If that thing blew up, they'd be flung clean into Houston.

"The boat is perfectly safe."

A distinguished, white-haired gentleman dressed in a blue jacket and wearing a captain's hat appeared on deck, a smile spreading across his amiable features. "Well, well. You were serious about having a passel of women, weren't you?"

Morgan made the hasty introductions. "Ladies, this is the captain of *The Mississippi Lady,* Will Shanor."

Captain Shanor, a man well into his twilight years, looked the girls over closely. They were a pitiable sight with cold, wet misery in their eyes. "Some of them are little more than children, Morgan."

"I know." Morgan didn't like the idea of transporting his young charges safely to Memphis any more than Will did. Trying to outfox Austin Brown long enough to get them all to safety wouldn't be easy. Morgan turned to Amelia, since she was nearest to him, and continued the introductions. "This is Amelia."

He paused, his eyes searching the group uncertainly.

"Pilar," said Pilar to fill the awkward silence. She helpfully filled in the rest of their names in turn, "And this is Auria, Belicia, Ria, Mira, Bunny, Mahalia, Hester, and Elizabeth."

The girls nodded, and Captain Will nodded back at them.

"Well, as I told Morgan, I mostly carry cargo." His eyes centered on the piles of cotton stacked high on the crowded lower deck. "I'm afraid I can offer you only the bare necessities."

Compared to the clipper, *The Mississippi Lady* was a floating palace. Amelia smiled their grateful acceptance. "Captain, we aren't in a position to be choosy."

"Well." If Will hadn't known Morgan since he'd been a baby bouncing on his mother's knee, he'd have had a choice in this matter. As it was, he didn't feel he could refuse. "I'll do all I can, but it won't be without a fair share of risk," he promised.

Morgan's eyes grimly beheld his charges. "We'd appreciate any help you can give us."

"My crew is old," Captain Will reminded him.

"But," a crafty smile touched the corners of his eyes now, "we can still outsmart anyone on the river."

"That's good to know," Morgan glanced over his shoulder, "because you can bet Austin Brown isn't far behind us."

"Then we'd better get underway. Most likely we don't have a minute to spare." Captain Shanor signaled to the pilot house, and a moment later the steamboat's warning bell clanged.

An old man, stooped and balding, lifted a Chinese gong, shouting, "All that aren't going get ashore!"

The Mississippi Lady's engines roared to life with a rhythmic *chaukety paw*, *chaukety paw*, *chaukety paw* as the gangplank was hastily drawn in.

A shout went up as plumes of black smoke powdered with sparks poured from the old paddle wheeler's stacks.

Amelia hung over the railing in anticipation, watching a rush of water appear between the hull and the shore as the old packet slowly turned to the stream, pointing its bow toward Memphis.

As the decks vibrated beneath her, she drew a long, shaky breath, wondering if she'd ever see her sisters or Mercy Flats again.

As Captain Will promised, the quarters were small. The women were assigned two to a cabin on the upper deck.

The Mississippi Lady, though far from spotless, was better than the clipper. The interior of the boat looked as if someone was attempting to keep it orderly, but didn't quite know how.

The women went immediately to their quarters, reeling from their exhausting day. They'd been underway only a short time when an interesting-looking gentleman, nearing ninety and wearing thick, bottled lenses, delivered food to their doors.

Tipping his frayed nautical cap, the old man displayed a row of overly large, protuberant teeth as he made his way from door to door. "Henry Muller's the name, and you'll be safe with us," he promised as he dished out plates, tin cups, and bountiful portions of the tasty fare.

The smell of the simple fare of biscuits, boiled beef, potatoes, and fried apples caused Amelia's stomach to lump with hunger.

"How far is it to Memphis?" She asked as she gratefully accepted the coffee he was pouring from a large black-and-white-splattered porcelain pot. By this time she was hungry enough to eat or drink anything anyone offered.

"Be a while," Henry conceded, "but the water's good!" He grinned. "Other than an occasional planter or sleeper, we shouldn't have any trouble."

"What's a planter or that other thing?" Amelia asked.

"A sleeper? Well, now, I can see you little girls have a lot to learn." Henry heaped a couple of extra biscuits on Amelia's plate. "I'm talking about snags in the river, trees, logs, driftwood—things like that."

Amelia took a sip of coffee, trying not to stare at him. She didn't want him to think she was looking at his teeth—she wasn't. It was just rather hard not to. They were so *big*.

"Is there some place we could wash our dresses?" Pilar asked. Hers had dried as stiff as a poker, making her feel miserable.

"Sure is! There's a big tub of rainwater just down the deck," he said, flashing another grin.

"Is there any soap?" Pilar asked hopefully.

"Made a fresh batch just this morning. I'll bring you all you need," Henry obliged.

After they'd eaten, the women gathered at the rain barrel to wash.

Henry provided several large bars of lye soap, which they used to scrub themselves, then their clothes.

Morgan sat in the wheelhouse with Captain Will watching the feminine goings-on below.

Shaking his head, Will smiled as he tapped tobacco into the bowl of his pipe. "Got yourself a handful, boy."

Morgan's gaze unwillingly fixed on Amelia, watching as she vigorously scrubbed her hair with a bar of soap. As she rinsed away the lather, the fiery highlights in the long strands glinted in the sun's fading rays. She slowly tossed her head and her tresses fanned out over creamy shoulders.

"That one's a real beauty," Captain commented.

"She's a real spitfire," Morgan grumbled. He resented the feelings Amelia McDougal provoked in him.

"Say you rescued her from a band of Comanche?" As they'd eaten, Morgan had told Will about the events of past few days.

"What was a lovely one like her doing in a jail wagon?"

Turning away, Morgan centered his interest on the passing scenery. "It's a puzzling story, Will."

As Morgan began to tell Will of the strange events leading up to this day, the captain turned his eyes toward Elizabeth. He hadn't been able to decide who Morgan had set his cap for—Elizabeth or Amelia—but it appeared that there was something going on between him and the two women. He had sensed it from the moment Morgan had stepped on board ship. Could be it was just his imagination, but he doubted it. He took a long draw off his pipe. No, he knew Morgan like the back of his hand, and something was going on.

This handsome son of Letty Kane had always attracted the women, no doubt about that. Will had watched the child grow from an impressionable young boy into a sensible, sought-after man. If he'd had his way, Morgan would have been his son. He'd begged to marry Letty, but like her son, she was an independent sort.

Will's eyes deepened as he drew on his pipe, half-way listening to Morgan's story. He was suddenly lost as he recalled that fascinating redhead. Letty was so beautiful that she could snatch a man's breath away, but stubborn as a mule, that one was. When she'd up and married Jim Kane, the local bad boy who operated the town ferry, her parents had disowned her. Big Jim was no good, they'd claimed, and they'd been right.

When Letty conceived Morgan, Big Jim took off, leaving the town without a ferry and Letty without a husband. Big Jim Kane was never heard of again.

Stubborn and proud, Letty had taken in washing and ironing to support herself and her infant son. Will had carried the torch for her until the day she'd died fifteen years ago.

At the time, Morgan had been fourteen, old enough to be on his own, or so he'd thought. He left for Washington Territory to work in the apple orchards owned by Letty's older brother, Silar, and his wife, Laura. Over the years, Morgan had always known where to find Will, and there hadn't a year gone by that they hadn't spent time together, even after the war began.

Will could admit that it wasn't the same as having a son of his own, but it was close.

He sighed as his thoughts returned to the present. "What are you going to do once you get them to Memphis?"

"I'm not sure. I was hoping you might have a suggestion."

"Eleven women?" Will shook his head. "Right now I can't think of a thing, except maybe take the youngest ones to the orphanage—and even at that they're a might old."

"That's one of the reasons why I only wanted to take two of them with me. The women's circumstances aren't the best, but if they'd been bought, at least they'd have a roof over their heads."

"You said some of them had been homeless when they were abducted?"

"Some were. Amelia said one or two of the younger ones have families to return to, but the older ones had been living on the street."

"That's a real shame."

It was more than a shame, Morgan thought, as his eyes returned to the women; it was a crime, one he felt powerless to do anything about.

"Once we reach Memphis, they'll be on their own. Because I assumed responsibility for Amelia, I've promised to see that she is returned to Mercy Flats, but the others will have to look after themselves. I don't like it, but circumstances leave me no other choice."

"Except for Elizabeth." Will looked on him kindly. Something was going on between those two, he'd bet a load of cargo on it.

"Elizabeth and I work together, Will. Nothing more."

"Work together, eh?" Will said as if he found

that amusing. "A woman in the service? Isn't that a little unusual?"

"There are some—and I don't need to remind you that this conversation is confidential."

"Oh, I know that. I've heard stories—but it seems a mighty risky business for a woman."

"Elizabeth's as smart as any man I've met. She's had some hard knocks in her life. She stays to herself, does her job, and doesn't take anything off anybody. She's the kind of woman I admire."

"That right? She married?"

"Not anymore."

"Uh-huh," Will mused thoughtfully.

"I know what it looks like, but Elizabeth and I are deliberately misleading the others about our relationship."

"Now, what's the point in that?" Aggravating a bunch of women didn't seem like Morgan's style.

"Because it's simpler that way." Morgan knew whatever he confided in Will would go no further. The same could not be said of Amelia. "We're on a mission, and until it's finished I don't want anyone to know of our connection."

Chuckling, Will drew on his pipe. "You have Amelia pretty well stirred up. Think that one's got a real crush on you, boy."

"There's absolutely nothing between Amelia and me. We barely know one another. I rescued her from a band of Comanche and I'm trying my damnedest to get her back to Mercy Flats with her scalp intact. That's the sum total of our involvement." Glancing away, Morgan interested himself in the passing scenery.

Will chuckled again. "If you say so." Will had witnessed more unlikely events than a young man falling head over heels in love with a pretty woman in the time it took to pick a sack of cotton.

"I say so."

"Still not ready to settle down yet?"

Morgan's eyes lifted to Will. "I haven't mentioned it, but once this mission is over, I'm going to be excused from service."

Will's white, bushy eyebrows lifted in surprise. "Is that a fact, son?"

"Yes, Silar is near death now. Laura can't work the orchards alone anymore. If we can believe the rumors that the war will be over soon, I will be free to leave. I've served my country, Will." Turning away, he finished softly. "Laura needs me more than ever now."

Will knew the deep affection Morgan felt for Silar and Laura. He loved them, and he would do anything he could to help. If the war were to continue, leaving the service would be a hard choice for the boy, but he'd come from hardy stock. He could be counted upon to do the right thing.

"Well, son, we can only take it one day at a time," Will offered. "That's all any of us can do."

"That's what I try to do, Will." And he'd been doing it well until he'd met Amelia McDougal. She'd sure jerked a knot in his strategy.

"But it wouldn't hurt to settle down in the meantime," Will added for posterity.

Rolling his eyes, Morgan got up to go in search of something more productive.

Chapter 11

Amelia was the first one up the next morning. She left Pilar still sleeping as she dressed and hurried up on deck.

Dawn was just streaking the sky. To her relief, the temperature was much warmer today. The old packet gently churned the muddy Mississippi as it made its way slowly upstream.

Taking a deep breath, Amelia smiled as she headed straight for the cook shack perched between the decks and the storeroom. She felt more optimistic this morning; and when she was optimistic, she was hungry.

The smell of coffee and frying bacon surrounded her as she climbed the steps to the galley.

She paused, looking around the railing to see if Morgan was on deck. He wasn't, and Elizabeth wasn't anywhere to be seen either. Were they together again, she wondered. They had both been on deck the night before.

Looking away, Amelia reminded herself that she didn't care if they were together—at least, she didn't care a lot. If he wanted to waste his time with Elizabeth, then it was his loss, not hers.

She pecked on the galley door and smiled when it opened to reveal an elderly woman. Everyone on this boat looked old!

"Hello," Amelia greeted her. "The bacon smelled so good, I thought I might snitch a piece."

The old woman looked tough as rocks. "You did, did you?" she said in a gravelly voice.

"Yes, ma'am." Amelia smiled again, hoping that the woman would reciprocate.

Leaving Amelia standing in the doorway, the old woman returned to the huge frying pan of sizzling bacon.

Without waiting for an invitation that obviously wasn't coming, Amelia entered the galley. "My name's Amelia. What's yours?"

After reaching for a slice of bacon draining on the sideboard, Amelia casually lifted herself onto the counter, making herself at home. She had spent hours in the Mission kitchen whiling away the time with the sisters. The nuns hadn't seemed to mind, and Amelia had had nothing better to do, so she'd talk for hours about anything and everything that had interested her—which had included anything and everything.

She was reaching for another slice of bacon when she jerked her hand back swiftly as the cook threatened to swat her with a wooden spoon.

"Got a whole boatload to feed, ya know."

"I know," Amelia replied sheepishly, "but it looks like you've got plenty."

The old woman shuffled to the counter and began to break eggs into a large bowl. "Name's Izzy. This here's my kitchen, and don't you forget it."

"Yes, ma'am, I won't. Want some help?"

"If I'd wanted help, I'd have asked you."

"Yes, ma'am." She eyed the bacon speculatively.

Throwing a pinch of salt in the pot of beans boiling on the stove, Izzy stared at her. "Don't you have nothin' better to occupy your time?"

"Not one thing." Sliding off the counter, she gave the old woman a gentle nudge aside. "Let me help."

The old woman shrugged, moving to the oven to check on a pan of biscuits.

"You're old, aren't you?" Amelia cracked an egg and frowned when she saw part of the shell drop into the bowl.

Izzy lifted the bacon out of the skillet with her right hand, her left hand resting on her aching hip. "Your mommy never teach you no manners?"

"I didn't mean any disrespect—it's just that you look pretty old." Amelia knew that she was often thought to be younger than she was, so what was the problem? She'd always wished that she'd looked older, and she imagined the old woman probably wished she looked younger. No one was ever really satisfied.

A smile threatened the old woman now. "Yes, I'm old."

"How old?"

This young'un seemed more inquisitive than disrespectful. "Just how old do you think?"

Amelia thought that this woman looked older than dirt, but she wasn't about to say so. Sister Agnes looked older than dirt, and she was seventy-two!

"Well, maybe . . . seventy-one?" she said instead.

Izzy dipped flour into the skillet to thicken the drippings for gravy.

She chuckled. "That's mighty kind of you."

"Older than seventy-one?" Amelia couldn't imagine such a thing. And still be standing!

"You're as old as you feel," the old woman replied brusquely.

"How old do you feel?"

Izzy had to admit most days she felt every day of her age—eighty-three. "You best get those eggs cracked. Folks around here want their breakfast on time."

Amelia hurried to crack the remaining eggs as Izzy stirred the gravy.

During breakfast, Amelia kept her eyes trained on Elizabeth, who sat beside Morgan, passing him biscuits and offering him gravy like she owned him.

Izzy was nice enough to mention that Amelia had helped with breakfast this morning. The rest of the crew commented on how nice that was of her, but Morgan didn't say so. He just buttered another biscuit and ate it.

Amelia chewed on a piece of bacon, studying the occupants of the long table. All of them, except Morgan and the girls, looked so old!

Izzy sat next to her husband, Niles, who was unbelievably old, but in good enough health to keep up with the rigors of operating a packet. There was another roustabout, Ryder somebody—Amelia didn't know his last name. Everyone just called him Ryder. "Ryder, can you get me this? Ryder, can you get me that?" Ryder always got whatever was asked of him, but sometimes it could take awhile.

Ryder reminded Amelia of a doddering turtle. He was slow, but he eventually got there.

When breakfast was over, Amelia helped Izzy and Niles clean off the long tables. Later, she offered to dry while Izzy washed.

Izzy didn't say much, but Amelia could tell that she appreciated her help. The other women had seemed hesitant about interfering with the crew's daily routine, but not Amelia. Before long, she and Izzy were chatting like old friends. Like the clerk at Galveston, the damp air had Izzy's lumbago riled up again. Amelia just felt awful about that after Izzy explained what lumbago was. Amelia decided it wasn't anything she'd want to have, riled or not.

When she finally left the galley, it was close to eight. The sun was full up, and birds were singing.

As she passed Elizabeth on the deck, she looked one way and Elizabeth looked the other.

Opening the door to her cabin, Amelia found Pilar sitting on the bed, hands crossed, staring out the window.

"Hi," Amelia said softly.

"Hi."

"What are you doing?"

"Nothing."

Amelia sat down to do nothing, too. Izzy had said it would take a few days to reach Memphis. Other, newer vessels could go faster, but *The Mississippi Lady* was old and cantankerous sometimes. Crossing her hands, Amelia studied the wall. It was going to be a long "few days."

"It was nice of you to help Izzy with breakfast," Pilar said.

"She's very old, and the damp weather has her lumbago fired up again," Amelia confided.

"Yes, everybody's old around here. I wonder why?"

"Izzy said they'd all been together for years now." Settling back on the bunk, Amelia recalled her earlier conversation with Izzy. "A long time ago, Captain Will used to be captain of a big passenger steamboat named *Lucky Lady*. Izzy and Niles worked together on the boat. A few years back, Captain Will decided he was getting too old to work so hard, so he bought *The Mississippi*

Lady and started to haul cargo instead of people.
Right off the bat, Izzy and Niles said they wanted
to come work for him. Well, Captain Will said he
didn't mind. In fact, he told them that was fine
with him; he'd be right glad to have them. Captain
Will's wife, Sunshine—isn't that a nice name, Sunshine? Well, Sunshine was sick, and Captain Will
thought maybe she would enjoy having another
woman aboard to keep her company.

"Now, Henry, he was already working on *The
Mississippi Lady* when Captain Will bought it.
Captain Will didn't really want Henry to stay on,
because, like the rest of them, he was getting on in
years and Captain Will figured he'd end up being
just another mouth to feed. But he said Henry
could stay if he wanted. Henry's wife's dead, you
know, and his daughter's married to this awful ol'
womanizing hardware salesman in Savannah. But
Henry says she seems happy enough.

"Anyway, Henry said he guessed he'd stay on if
Captain Will really meant it. Captain Will said he
wouldn't have said it if he didn't mean it.

"Then low and behold, it turned out that Ryder,
who had worked on *The Mississippi Lady*, too,
didn't have *any* family, so he said if Henry was going to stay, he guessed he would, too." Taking a
deep breath, Amelia glanced at Pilar. "That's why
everyone's so old."

Pilar looked back at her round-eyed. "How do
you know all that?"

"Izzy told me while we were washing dishes."

"Where is Captain Will's wife now?"

"She passed on last year."

"Oh."

"It made him very sad."

The two girls sat for a moment, trying to think of something further to pass the time.

"Where are the others?" Amelia asked.

Pilar frowned. "I don't know. After breakfast, I came straight back to my cabin. I didn't want to get in anybody's way."

They sat in silence a while longer.

"Did you see how Elizabeth was making such a fuss over Morgan this morning at the breakfast table?" Amelia asked in what she hoped was a neutral tone.

"Yes, but I don't think he's infatuated with her—I mean, not that way."

"Ha!"

Pilar tried to sound more worldly than she was. "Men will be men," she said.

"Yes, men will be men."

Amelia wasn't going to think about Elizabeth lying in bed next to Morgan, the way she had. She wasn't going to think about Elizabeth laying her hands on Morgan's bare chest, the way she had. Probably a lot of women had had their hands on Morgan's bare chest. And probably on a lot of other things, too, if she only knew it. And she wasn't going to dwell on the fact that Elizabeth was *anything* other than a case of raging insanity for a man like Morgan Kane—whatever kind of man he was. She didn't know what kind of man he was and she didn't know why she wished she did. She was so confused!

Getting up from the bunk, Amelia lifted her skirt, exposing her bare legs. "Tell me the truth. What's wrong with my legs?"

Pilar seemed puzzled by the question. "Your legs?"

"Yes, what's wrong with them?"

Turning to the right and then to her left, Amelia waited for the verdict.

"Well?"

"Nothing is wrong with your legs."

"I didn't think so." Sucking in a deep breath, Amelia thrust her chest forward. "What's wrong with these?"

Pilar frowned. "Those?"

"Yes . . . my bosoms." The sisters had referred to the girls' endowments as "peach buds," but Amelia had heard them called other things.

Pilar studied the items in question. Finally, she shook her head. "Nothing. They look fine to me."

"They look fine to me, too." Amelia hadn't considered them often, but they were all right. They weren't big like that old cow, Elizabeth's, but they weren't little either.

"Why are you worrying about your legs and your bosoms?" Pilar shook her head, confused.

Turning to the side, Amelia sucked in her stomach. "What about my waist? Is it too thick?"

"No, not at all."

"It was smaller before I ate," Amelia assured her. Four pieces of bacon and three biscuits, she could admit, had aggravated the situation.

Pilar nodded, but Amelia's waistline still didn't look bad to her.

"Is it as small as Elizabeth's?"

Pilar thought for a moment, trying to be helpful. "I'd say they're about the same."

Releasing her breath in a *whoosh*, Amelia dropped back onto the bunk. "Then why does he prefer her?"

"Who?"

"Morgan. Why does he prefer Elizabeth? Why does he always hang around Elizabeth? Why does he always look at Elizabeth!" She didn't know why it should bother her, but it did. It was like being picked second instead of first, and feeling robbed.

"Maybe he doesn't prefer her. I don't see him paying much attention to Elizabeth. Maybe you're just imagining that he does."

"I didn't imagine it when he sent for Elizabeth on the clipper." She seen it plain as day with her own eyes. That wretched Austin Brown had come for Elizabeth and announced to the world that "Dov Lanigan" was in need of female companionship. Well, she might be naive, but she knew what that meant.

"Well, no, you didn't imagine that, but maybe there were so many of us to choose from he just decided to take potluck."

"Potluck, Pilar? Potluck!"

Pilar's face looked like she didn't really believe that for a minute. He had asked for Elizabeth. Everyone seemed aware of that fact.

Pilar lowered her eyes with shame. "Does it matter?" she asked softly. "Maybe Elizabeth didn't want to go. After all, she's just as helpless in this matter as we are."

Sobering, Amelia pondered that observation. Was Morgan Kane the kind of man who would force himself on a woman? She couldn't imagine that he would. He had maintained a respectable distance with her, even when she had slept in his bed. Of course, there had been that kiss he'd imposed upon her. On the other hand, he'd only been trying to teach her a lesson.

"But maybe Elizabeth was a willing victim. Maybe she wanted to please Morgan Kane." Amelia hated to think it, but it was possible.

"Do you have feelings for Mr. Kane?" Pilar asked gently.

"No, of course not!"

Pilar looked up. "Are you certain?"

"Of course, I'm certain. Don't be silly." Amelia stood up, smoothing the wrinkles out of her dress. "I'm going fishing."

"Want me to come with you?"

"No, I need to think. I think best when I'm fishing by myself."

Pilar nodded. It appeared that Amelia had a powerful lot of thinking to do. For instance, why was the girl so preoccupied with thoughts of Morgan Kane? To Pilar, the handsome Yankee seemed somewhat decent, but after the string of worthless, heartless men on the clipper, she saw little reason to trust any one with anything as precious as one's heart.

Amelia found Henry on the deck dozing in the warm sun. They sat and visited for awhile until she inquired if he happened to have any worms. He said that he did and went to get them. When he returned, he was carrying a large fruit jar full of dirt inhabited by nice, fat river worms. After she talked him out of one of his cane poles and the jar of worms, she retired to the stern of the boat.

Selecting a comfortable seat, she stripped off her shoes and wriggled her toes, relishing the warmth of the sun.

She plucked a worm from the jar and carefully threaded it onto the hook, then cast her line some twenty feet behind the boat. She would have preferred that the boat was moored, but since it wasn't she'd have to do the best she could. Curling her legs under herself, she prepared to do some serious fishing and thinking.

She fished most of the morning, pondering all the while. By lunch time, she had failed to grasp any understanding of her puzzling new feelings toward men. However, she had caught six perch and two catfish.

When she presented her catch to Izzy, the old woman promised to fry them for supper.

After lunch, Amelia resumed her fishing and her thinking.

Amelia didn't even turn around when she heard a deep voice behind her. "The sun's getting hot. You'd better have Izzy lend you a bonnet." She knew who it was: Morgan Kane.

"I don't freckle easily," she replied casually as she picked through the fruit jar for another worm. After the way he'd acted toward Elizabeth that morning, she wasn't about to start cozying up to him now.

Removing his hat, Morgan stretched out on the stern and began peeling a turnip with a knife.

"Caught anything?"

"Six perch and two catfish," she answered briefly. She wiped worm juice on her skirt and tossed her line over the railing again.

"Been fishing all day?"

"Just about."

Morgan's mouth curved slightly. He was experienced enough to know when he was getting the cold shoulder. Leaning over, he extended a slice of the vegetable to her on the blade of the knife.

She eyed the offering suspiciously. "What's that?"

"Turnip. Eat it, it's good for you."

"I don't like turnips."

"Just try a small bite. You're going to die of scurvy if you don't start eating fruits and vegetables."

"I'm not dead yet." Lifting the slice of turnip off the blade, she brought it to her lips gingerly.

"Eat it," he encouraged as her reticence lingered. "It's not going to bite you."

Closing her eyes, she shoved the vegetable into her mouth, chewed quickly, and swallowed before she lost her nerve.

"That wasn't so bad, was it?"

It wasn't so bad, but she didn't want any more. "How far is Memphis?"

Morgan slipped a slice of turnip into his mouth. "Should arrive before week's end."

"Can't be soon enough for me." The air seemed much heavier with him around. It was an effort just to breathe deeply. She wished that his presence didn't have this effect on her.

"What are the others doing?"

"If you're referring to Elizabeth, I have no idea what she's doing." Her tone left little doubt that she didn't care what Elizabeth was doing.

Tipping his hat over his eyes, he grinned and stretched out more fully. "I don't recall mentioning Elizabeth."

She kept her eyes on her line, wishing he would go away. She couldn't think straight when he was so near.

"Something just took your bait."

"D-did not," she stammered. "That's just the current."

"Something just stole your bait," he repeated casually.

"Oh, for heaven's sake!" Just to show him, she pulled in her line and tried to ignore the smug look that lifted the corners of his mouth as she examined her stripped hook.

Grabbing the fruit jar, she dug around for another worm. Every time she snagged one, it managed to wriggle out of her grasp. She could feel the heat of Morgan's gaze. As her frustration mounted, she attempted to redirect his attention. "Austin Brown must be pretty mad at you," she huffed.

"I imagine he is."

"You outsmarting him like that and all."

"I imagine so."

She finally got her hook baited and stood to swing her line back into the water. It seemed useless to try to ignore him. With an exasperated sigh, she sat down beside him. Morgan wasn't the sort of man one could ignore for very long.

Her brow creased in a frown. "Do you think he'll really try to find us?"

"I know he will. Dov Lanigan has a great deal to lose in you."

She glanced over. She'd never thought much about how she looked, but the conversations lately had seemed to imply that she was prettier than usual. "Do you think I'm pretty?"

"You're all right."

"Prettier than Elizabeth?" The question was out of her mouth before she'd even been aware of the thought. She regretted asking, but when he didn't respond, she thought he might not have heard her. As the silence grew increasingly more awkward, Amelia felt she would explode if he didn't give her an answer. "Prettier than Elizabeth?" she repeated.

"What is this fixation you have about Elizabeth?" Annoyance vibrated in his voice.

Her tone took a personal turn. "I've seen the way she hovers around you."

He shrugged. "She's just friendly."

"She's about as friendly as a freshly castrated bull."

"The language you use," he chided.

"Well, it's the truth." She jerked her line, missing the catch. "Shoot," she muttered.

"I am well aware that you and Elizabeth do not care for each other," he told her as she dug through the worms.

Getting to her feet, she threw out her line, then sat down again. Suspicion gnawed at her nerves. "Has she been talking about me?" She wouldn't put it pass the witch. Criticizing her behind her back.

"Something got your bait again."

"Drat!" she exploded, frustrated by his evasions. To cover her feelings, she added, "At this rate, Henry will have to dig more worms when we reach the next landing."

She was silent for as long as she could stand it. When her strained whisper broke the silence, her next question seemed to stun him. "Did she please you?"

He opened one eye. "What?"

"Did she please you? You know, were you all hot and sweaty when it was over?" She still wasn't clear in her mind about how that worked, but she'd picked up the phrase by eavesdropping on the conversations of the other women.

Lifting the brim of his hat, he looked at her sternly. "Good Lord. You say exactly what's on your mind, don't you?"

She shrugged casually. "You can't learn anything if you don't ask."

He lifted his head and pinned her with a glare. "You shouldn't be thinking or asking such things."

"You shouldn't be doing such things." She squared her shoulders defensively. "You're not married."

He lay back again, adjusting his hat against the sun's unyielding rays. "How do you know what I do?"

"I know that you and Elizabeth spend a lot of time together. I know what that means. I'm not an imbecile."

When he didn't deny the charge, she felt such a rush of frustration that she grabbed the jar and dumped the remaining worms on top of his chest.

Jumping up, he slapped at the dirt and grubs strung down the front of his shirt. "Why in the hell did you do that?"

"For lying to me!"

"I have never lied to you."

"You were about to start."

Brushing the dirt off his chest, he lay back again.

"I want your opinion on something," she asked hurriedly before he could doze off.

His eyes opened slowly, wary of her now. "What?"

Getting to her feet, she gingerly lifted her dress, exposing the shapely length of her bare legs.

Morgan viewed the show, trying to keep a straight face. Not bad, he acknowledged silently. Unfortunately, not bad at all. He never knew what to expect from this woman. One minute she was dumping filth on him, the next she was offering him . . . what?

He couldn't read this latest ploy of hers, though part of him wanted to ignore her reasons and act on what he'd like to interpret as an interesting invitation.

Meeting his intent gaze, she deliberately baited him. "Do I please you?" She didn't know what had gotten into her, but it was suddenly imperative that she know whether or not she could please a man like Morgan Kane.

He closed his eyes. She was tempting all right, but he already had more trouble than he needed. "Put your dress down," he ordered.

Indignation colored her cheeks. How dare he ignore her! Centering the tip of her toe against the brim of his hat, she flipped it aside, sending it skittering across the deck.

He reached over and retrieved it in a tightly controlled movement. He was getting tired of this.

"I did that because you refuse to look at me."

"You're being childish. I never look at childish women."

Oh, he enraged her with his self-righteous, smug, holier-than-thou-attitude!

She sat down again and drew her knees up to her chin, clasping her hands together tightly. His rejection stung her deeply. How was she going to make him notice her? Maybe she could pretend to be more docile, more defenseless. She was good at pretending. Men liked dependent, helpless women, didn't they? That had to be it: her personality was just too strong for him. Like most men she'd observed, Morgan Kane liked women weak and submissive.

She got to her feet, clasped her hands, and tried a new approach. "Hey," she called softly.

"What?"

"Tell me something about yourself," she cooed demurely.

"What do you want to know?"

"I don't know," she said sweetly, and shrugged. "Anything." Morgan was the closest thing she had to security, and it had occurred to her that she knew nothing about him. Where was his home? Had he been conscripted or had he joined the service? "Tell me about the war. What's been going on lately."

"What's been going on lately?"

"Yes, you know." Her voice was gentle and re-assuring. "What's been happening? Is it going better for one side, or the other? I have been unable to keep abreast of current affairs of late."

There. That sounded priggish enough for anybody.

"I hear Lee and Grant are talking," he replied, "Well, now, that's good, isn't it?"

He fixed both eyes on her this time.

"What else?" she prompted.

"I don't know. The only thing I know for certain is that the war will be over for me as soon as I've finished my mission."

"What mission? What are you doing?"

He looked away "I'm sorry, that's confidential."

"Oh." *Docile, Amelia. Gentle, unassuming.*

"But I can tell you I'm going home soon." He sat up, running a hand through his crisp, dark hair. She watched, longing to do it for him.

Catching his eye, she hurriedly turned her profile ever so slightly, permitting him a better view of her delicate throat and her slender waist. "What's in Washington Territory?"

"My aunt and uncle, Silar and Laura Stevenson. They took me in when my mother passed away. Silar's health isn't good now, and he's no longer able to work his orchards. As soon as I'm finished here, I'll go back to help Laura."

"What sort of orchards?"

"Apples. Silar raises the finest Jonathan apples you've ever put in your mouth."

"Oh." Her face fell. Apples. Too bad it wasn't hogs.

"Is your father alive?"

A veiled look dropped over Morgan's features. "I don't have a father."

"I'm sorry. I don't either." She lifted her shoulders slightly, thrusting her bosom prominently outward. "My sisters and I were raised at the mission by the good sisters."

"How fortunate for you that there are women who dedicate their lives to selfless service." He gave no indication that he noticed how nicely she had developed.

Slowly, she casually lifted her hem, exposing her leg again as she pretended to check for insect bites. If he didn't notice her now, he never would—and he couldn't accuse her of acting childish. After all, she was being demure now. If he was still too blind to see that she was a full-blown woman, then there was just no hope for him.

Morgan's eyes fastened briefly on her leg before his glance eased away.

"That's where I'll be going," Amelia announced, forcing his eyes back to her.

"Where?" he asked.

"To the mission."

He nodded politely. "I'll do my best to see that you get back there safely, ma'am."

Getting to his feet, he settled his hat firmly on his head, then turned and walked away.

Letting her hem drop back into place, she watched him go, her lips curling in disgust.

Apples. He was going back to raise apples. How could you like a man who raised apples.

Chapter 12

After supper that evening, Amelia called a meeting in her room.

Elizabeth let it be known that she was attending to satisfy her curiosity, nothing more. Whatever Amelia was up to this time, Elizabeth wasn't interested in being in on it.

"I think Izzy, Niles, Henry, and Ryder are just too old to be waiting on us," Amelia began. "We won't reach Memphis for days yet, so I think we should shoulder some of their duties."

"I can clean," Pilar offered. "I've always been good at cleaning."

"And I can sew," Faith said. "I'm real good at crocheting and knitting, things like that!"

Amelia nodded, relieved that they were taking to the idea. "I don't know if there's any need for crocheting or knitting, but we'll ask."

"I can cook," Hester offered hesitantly. "I can make the best hotcakes you ever ate ... light as thistledown." Hester hadn't wanted to complain, but Izzy's hotcakes were heavy as lead.

"Hotcakes. That'll be good, Hester. Thank you."

"I can do the wash," Bunny volunteered. "At home, I always did all the wash for the family."

"Thank you, Bunny. That should help Izzy a lot."

The women all tended to their own needs, but the men didn't seem to turn a lick when it came to washing and cooking.

Bright and early the following morning, the women, with Amelia in the lead, marched to the wheelhouse to tell Captain Will of their plans.

"Well, that's mighty gracious of you," Will complimented them. Drawing on his pipe, he weighed their generous offer. They could make life considerably easier on Izzy and the others. Izzy was getting too old for the extra work suddenly thrust upon her by so many passengers. Only problem was, Will didn't know if Izzy knew it.

"Take over the cooking?" Izzy sank down on a chair when they told her, wiping the sweat from her brow with the hem of her apron. "How soon can you start?"

Amelia brightened. "You don't mind?"

"Mind? Lord, no! The sooner the better."

Henry, Niles, and Ryder had much the same reaction when they went to tell them.

Faith approached Henry with a shy smile and a gentle voice. "I'd be glad to do any repairs you might have. I can sew real good," she assured him.

Henry, who had done all the mending until now, nodded thoughtfully. "That's kind of you, girl." He went right off to return with the godawfulest pile of sewing she'd ever seen.

It was all set then. Hester would help Izzy in the galley; Faith would sew; and Pilar would clean. The others agreed to help wherever they were most needed. Everyone seemed happy with the new arrangements, except Elizabeth, who, it seemed, wouldn't have been happy if the good Lord had offered to appoint her his left hand.

Morgan watched the proceedings from a safe distance. He knew nothing about cooking and cleaning, and he didn't want to learn. If he could get these women to Memphis—particularly Amelia McDougal—without any further crises, he would have considered his contribution to that cause totally equitable.

Life aboard *The Mississippi Lady* was gentle. The river rolled along peacefully as the old boat slowly transported its unusual cargo to Memphis. At times, Amelia wondered if Austin Brown and his men were somewhere lurking around the next bend, but most of the time, she was so busy with her new duties, she didn't have time to worry about it.

Will Shanor was a kind man. The wizened old captain did what he could to make the old boat comfortable. One of the last things Sunshine Shanor had done was to dress *The Mississippi*

Lady up with a new set of curtains. She said she wouldn't rest knowing that the windows on Will's ship were so bare and ugly. The curtains she'd fashioned weren't much, just plain cotton print that could be taken down and washed, but they did a lot to brighten up the old vessel.

The new passengers on *The Mississippi Lady* gazed at the curtains and decided that the needed finishing touch was lace trim around the hems, nothing fancy, just something to make them even prettier. Perhaps the lace trim could be their contribution to the ship, a little something of themselves that would remain long after they had gone.

And lace was right up Faith's alley. She had taken her first needle in hand when she was six years old, and she had been sewing ever since.

Sewing was her special talent. She'd never been good at cooking or homemaking; but when it came to sewing, no one could beat her.

As the *The Mississippi Lady* churned along, Faith set her sights on a few yards of lace. Amelia still had a portion of the money Morgan had given her, so buying the lace would be no problem. The problem would be getting the men to stop long enough to purchase it.

"First town we stop at, I'll just slip away and buy it," Faith decided after supper that night.

"Until we reach Memphis, the captain isn't likely to stop for any reason except to take on wood," Pilar told her. "And that might not be at a town."

Many times they stopped mid-river to buy wood from a farmer who'd piled it along the banks. And the women knew without being told that Captain Will and Morgan would both think it was too hazardous to stop voluntarily just to buy some frivolous lace. Austin Brown was likely to be not far behind them, and Morgan wouldn't consider taking unnecessary risks that would allow Brown to catch up with them.

"Well, maybe he can be persuaded to make just a brief stop," Faith reasoned. "It couldn't take long to buy just a few yards of lace."

"The curtains look all right the way they are," Elizabeth said. "We're not going to be on this boat for more than a few days anyway."

"Maybe not, but Captain Will has been so nice to us that we just have to do something nice for him," Auria ventured. No one liked to buck Elizabeth, but sometimes one of them felt she just had to.

"I know how you feel," Bunny added, siding with Auria. "I can't do very many things, but I would like to do something to repay Captain Will for his kindness."

"Then that settles it." Amelia shot Elizabeth a you-better-not-throw-a-kink-in-it look. "If Faith wants to put lace on Captain Will's curtains, she can. Okay, Elizabeth?"

It wasn't okay, but Elizabeth nodded, deciding to let it ride until Captain Will and Morgan could take the wind out of their sails.

"Maybe we can talk Captain Will into stopping at the very next landing," Faith reasoned. "It wouldn't take but a few minutes to buy the lace, and the result would be well worth the small delay."

"Who will ask Captain Will?" Auria asked.

An unscheduled stop might be risky. Austin Brown could be ready to pounce on them at any moment. Approaching the captain with their request was evidently not a task that any of them relished.

"I'll ask him." Amelia didn't mind. She could ask anybody anything. If lace on the curtains would help repay Captain Will for his kindness, then of course she was happy to be their appointed spokeswoman.

Only Captain Will, as it turned out, didn't like the idea any better than Elizabeth had.

"I don't think that would be wise," he said when Amelia told him what they wanted to do.

"It wouldn't take long," she reasoned, "and it would make Faith feel good if she thought she was contributing something."

"Faith is not expected to contribute anything," Captain Will told her.

"Still, we'd feel better if we were doing something to earn our keep. It would certainly help us pass a few idle hours. If the ladies aren't busy, they tend to dwell on what happened to them—the abduction, you know."

The captain stroked his chin thoughtfully. "What does Morgan think of this idea?

Amelia sighed as she looked to the port side, glancing out between the paddles of the big wheel. "I haven't said anything to him about it."

"Don't you think he ought to be informed of this notion of yours?"

"Not my notion. Faith's."

"Still, don't you think he should know?"

"No." Amelia shrugged. "All Faith wants is just a little bit of lace."

"Still, it could be dangerous. We don't know where Austin Brown is."

"Oh, honestly, Captain! Faith'll be careful. She can be as quick and silent as a shadow."

Drawing on his pipe, the captain deliberated for a moment. He didn't want to upset these women. It was obvious that they'd endured unspeakable misery, and he knew that a creative project could give them an outlet for their pent-up emotions, but he wasn't comfortable with the slightest risk of letting any of them off the ship for any reason. He wouldn't be comfortable until they were all in Memphis, safely out of his hair.

"Please, Captain."

"No," Captain Will murmured as he shook his head. "As bad as I hate to, I'm going to have to refuse your request. I'll need to take on wood shortly, but I must insist that every last one of you remain aboard ship during that stop."

Morgan approached, nodding his agreement. He

had overheard the last of their conversation. "I firmly agree."

"But—"

"No buts, Amelia," he stated emphatically. "We've barely escaped Brown. We have no idea where he is, or if he'll try to abduct you women again. The answer is no. Faith and the others are not to leave this boat for any reason."

Her eyes snapped with indignation. "You're just an ol' stick-in-the-mud, Morgan Kane."

"Maybe I am, but someone has to *think* around here. I didn't ask to be saddled with eleven women, but now that I am, I believe their safety should take precedence over some damn silly lace for a set of curtains."

Amelia had rarely accepted no as a viable answer from anyone, and Morgan's rudeness made it even harder for her to swallow. "I can't believe you won't consider it! Even Austin Brown, tyrant that he is, could be sensitive to the needs of a woman. Why, look how he befriended me in Galveston when you had thrown me to the wolves—"

"The *needs* of a woman?" he cut in sarcastically, and she realized her blunder. "So you think Austin Brown was sensitive to the needs of a woman . . . Now I have heard it all." He shook his head. "Ask your friends, the ones he kidnapped, how sensitive Austin Brown was to their needs."

She slapped her sides in frustration. "You're putting words in my mouth, Morgan Kane!"

He lifted his brows. "Your words, Amelia, not mine."

"Oh, you! You're twisting everything I say so you can refuse to listen to reason. If Faith had asked you, you would have at least pretended to consider her request and you would have at the very least been polite when you refused it. But not me. Oh, no, not me!"

Morgan shifted uncomfortably. There was a fragment of truth in what she was saying. He suspected that if any one of the other women had posed the same request, he would have been firm but polite in his refusal. For a reason that escaped him, Amelia's stubbornness never failed to infuriate him. She haunted his dreams and tormented his days. "Just stop whining, will you?"

"Go ahead and admit the truth, if you're man enough." To her dismay, her eyes began to water, and she bit back scalding tears.

"How would you know the truth?" He turned away. This conversation was getting them nowhere, and he had a feeling it would be best to leave now.

Amelia took a deep breath as she watched him walk away. He would not rudely dismiss her this way. A suspicion had been festering and growing in the darkest part of her heart for days now. Every time she'd seen Morgan standing with Elizabeth, inclining his head toward hers, speaking in hushed tones, the suspicion had grown a little stronger. Now it had to come out or she would surely ex-

plode. "Truth is"—she squared her shoulders—
"you hate me!"

He scoffed at the absurdity of her thinking.
Women—who could understand them? He certainly couldn't. And certainly not this one.

Amelia watched his reaction, the look of repudi-
ation on his face, and it aggravated her. Why
couldn't she even make a point with him?

No matter what she tried to say to him, he
missed the point. She always felt compelled to defend herself. "Admit it, if you're man enough. You
hate me." She rambled on, the words tumbling out
as they spilled from her aching heart. "Ever since
the first night we spent together—you made it
clear that I wasn't good enough for you when you
pushed me down and kissed me, and the other
times, like the night I was in your cabin on *The
Black Widow,* you made me lie with you on your
bed and you held me down and ordered me to be
quiet—" She caught back a sob of frustration.

Captain Will's head whipped around.

Morgan's face flamed as he lifted his hand to
quiet her.

Amelia didn't notice the shock on Captain Will's
face, nor the flush of embarrassment on Morgan's
cheeks. She had no idea of the effect of her words
or the mistaken impression they gave the captain.

"Amelia, please," Morgan rebuked as he looked
at Captain Will helplessly. "She doesn't know what
she's saying."

Amelia's heart betrayed her as her tears spilled

over. Morgan didn't even have the decency to address her directly. Instead, he was looking plaintively at Captain Will. "See?" she demanded. "He doesn't care what *I* feel. All he ever wants is for me to quietly go along with whatever he says." She dropped her face into her hands, sobbing.

Captain Will looked upon her with deep concern as he reached his arm around her shuddering shoulders to give her a paternal squeeze. "Now, now," he soothed. He glanced reprovingly at Morgan, a man whom he'd admired without restraint.

"A man should be gentle with the fairer sex, son," the captain admonished.

A muscle at the corner of Morgan's eye jumped.

Amelia's voice was tiny as she stood with her face cradled against the captain's shoulder. "It's just some old lace. Faith could have bought it and been back before anyone even noticed she was gone. But here I am, trying to discuss it in a logical manner, and he won't even listen."

Morgan's jaw firmed with determination. "It's too dangerous, Amelia," he repeated. "I won't have Faith jeopardizing the safety of everyone for a scrap of lace."

She sobbed louder, and Morgan's eyes narrowed. She'd made a fool of him when she'd masqueraded as a nun, but he would not fall for the injured woman act again. "You can drop the drama, Amelia. The captain here might be momentarily impressed, but I can assure you that I am not."

Whirling, Amelia stalked off, determined that come hell, high water, *or* Morgan Kane, Faith was going to get that lace if Amelia had to get it herself.

Chapter 13

Izzy looked up as the screen door opened later that morning. Morgan led Amelia inside the small galley, motioning for her to sit down.

"What's wrong?" Izzy asked.

"Miss McDougal seems to be in dire need of something constructive to occupy her time."

"I thought of something worthwhile to occupy my time, but, if you'll remember, you voted it down!" Amelia folded her arms and squinted up at him.

"Teaching the women to shoot craps is hardly constructive," he replied.

Her chin jutted out. "Well, they wanted to learn."

"Nevertheless, I think your time is better spent here with Izzy learning something more beneficial."

"Can't think of anything I need done," Izzy said. She was sitting in the old rocker, peeling potatoes for lunch. The boat's old tomcat was curled around her feet, catching a late morning nap.

"Then maybe she can just keep you company for awhile," Morgan suggested, giving Amelia a sidelong glance.

Izzy nodded. "If that's what you want."

"That's what I want." Morgan turned and left the galley, leaving Amelia in Izzy's hair for awhile.

Izzy glanced up. "How'd you get in trouble this time?"

"I asked Captain Will if, when he stopped for wood, Faith could leave the boat to buy some lace to sew on the curtains to make them look prettier, but Morgan made him say no."

"Wouldn't be wise in view of the circumstances," Izzy agreed.

"What could it hurt? It wouldn't take a minute, and Faith was really disappointed."

"Yes, 'magine she was." Izzy had seen the way Faith took to her sewing.

Amelia watched as the potato peels curled around Izzy's knife in long spirals, dangling in front of the dozing cat's nose.

"Want me to help?"

"No, I'm about finished."

Sighing, Amelia's eyes traveled the small galley, looking for something that needed attention. There wasn't a thing. Chicken simmered on the stove, bread was baking in the oven, and it looked like Izzy had peeled enough potatoes to feed the entire Confederacy.

"You really wantin' something to do?"

Amelia sighed again. "Yes. Anything to make the time go faster."

"Well, don't know what to tell you. Hester's got things pretty well under control around here. Instead of keeping me company, why don't you go up and see if you can't carry on a conversation with Morgan without sparks flyin'?"

Izzy had seen the way Amelia's eyes followed the handsome young captain wherever he went.

"No, thank you. He just brought me here to get me out of his hair."

Izzy chuckled. "And a mighty attractive head of hair it is. Seems like you're missing your chance. Seems a nice man like Morgan Kane might just need a little female nudge—if you know what I mean."

"Oh, you don't know him, Izzy. He's not as nice as you think he is." She could tell Izzy a thing or two about Morgan Kane, about how he was all nicey-nice to their faces, but when their backs were turned, he was off doing things with Elizabeth that would shock Izzy right out of her boots. It had happened again last night. Elizabeth vanished after supper, and then, shortly afterwards, Morgan had disappeared, too. Amelia wasn't dumb. She knew what was gong on.

"Well," Izzy grunted as she got to her feet, trying to balance the heavy pan of potatoes on her knee. "All I know is he'd be a fine catch for someone. Captain Will says he comes from mighty good stock."

"Maybe so, but he's not interested in me."

Izzy washed the potatoes and set them on the stove to boil.

"Izzy?" Amelia glanced around the galley looking for the usual pies cooling on the shelf. There weren't any this morning. "Didn't Hester make pies today?"

"Told her not to. The captain's complainin' he's gaining weight again." Izzy reached into the wood box and got a few more sticks to throw into the stove.

Amelia's face fell. "No dessert?"

"Not today."

Sliding off the counter, Amelia moseyed around, peering into cabinets and cubbyholes. Izzy watched, a frown forming around the corners of her mouth. Finally, she asked, "Looking for something?"

"No." Amelia opened a jar of peaches and ate a piece. "Is it hard to bake a cake?"

"Nothin' hard about it. Why do you ask?"

"Oh, no reason." She dug out another peach half, tilted her head back, and let the juice drizzle down her throat. She had to learn to like those things.

"Didn't you get enough to eat at breakfast?"

Amelia glanced up. "Plenty. Why?"

"Just wondering."

Moving to the oven, Amelia checked on the

loaves of bread and Izzy told her it was time for
them to come out. Taking two large hot pads in her
hands, Amelia removed six crisp loaves from the
oven and set them out to cool. The bread smelled
so good, she pinched off a bite of the thick brown
crust and popped it into her mouth. It was so tasty,
she pinched off another bite and chewed on it
thoughtfully.

"Izzy, is it true that the way to a man's heart is
through his stomach?"

"That's what they say."

Cooking seemed an odd way to attract Morgan
Kane, but then it might be worth a try. Since she
couldn't hold a candle to Elizabeth in the worldly
department, perhaps a nice, tasty dish might be an
effective weapon.

"Izzy, I want to bake something."

"No need. Hester sees to the baking."

"But it's important. I want to bake . . ." She
looked around for something to create that would
be so irresistible even Morgan would be impressed.
Apple pie would be the first choice, since he
seemed to be partial to apples, but since there were
no apples, she settled for ". . . a cake."

"A cake?"

"Yes, a cake. I want to bake a cake."

"You ever baked a cake?"

"No, but I've watched Sister Agnes bake a hundred, at least." Amelia felt certain that Morgan believed that she was so young and foolish that she
wouldn't know how to do the simplest things.

Well, she'd show him. She'd bake him a cake that he'd never forget. "Where's the cake baking stuff?"

Izzy nodded toward the cupboard. "You'll find everything you need in there. Think I'll take a short nap before dinner. Watch the potatoes for me, will you?"

"Sure."

Izzy left shortly, closing the screen door behind her.

The pantry contained several well-organized jars of potential ingredients, all waiting to be transformed into a mouth-watering cake that would impress even the biggest skeptic, namely one Morgan I-want-to-murder-him-one-minute-and-I-would-die-for-just-one-serious-look-from-him Kane.

Tying an apron around her waist, she set to work. Selecting a large wooden bowl, she dumped ample amounts of flour and sugar from two of the largest jars. She wasn't sure if she had enough, so she dumped in another cup of each for good measure.

Moving to the water bucket, she ladled generous amounts of the liquid until the ingredients were thoroughly saturated.

Dipping into the lard bucket, she doled out a hefty chunk, then added salt and baking soda like she'd seen Sister Agnes do a hundred times.

Selecting five eggs, she cracked them one by one into the bowl. Peering at the concoction, she decided it didn't look right, so she added three

more. Then it looked like there were more eggs
than flour and sugar, so she added another cup of
sugar. Then there was more sugar than eggs and
lard, so she added another hefty cup of flour.

She glanced up when she felt a slight jarring
motion as the boat docked to take on wood.

Going back to her baking, she studied the mixture, then snapped her fingers. Searching through
the pantry, she located a bottle of vanilla, and sea-
soned the batter with a generous splash.

Taking a wooden spoon, she tried to stir the
gooey mixture, but it just knotted up into greasy,
odd-colored hunks.

Shaking her head pensively, she returned to the
water bucket for more liquid. By now, the mixture
was nearly overflowing the bowl.

Blending the concoction until it was frothy, she
realized she was going to have a big cake on her
hands. But that was all right. There were a lot of
people on hand to enjoy it.

Getting on her hands and knees, she searched
through the pantry for a pan big enough to hold the
mixture. She settled on a roaster, the only thing
large enough to hold it all.

Her eyes proudly measured her creation. Yes,
this was really going to impress Morgan.

Greasing the roaster with another hunk of lard,
she liberally sprinkled more flour into the bottom
and shook it around until the pan was lightly
coated.

Now all she had to do was get the roaster into the oven.

Pouring the batter into the roaster, she picked it up and moved gingerly to the stove. Setting the cake down on the stove top, she opened the oven door and studied the small area. It didn't look wide enough to hold the roaster.

Removing the chickens, she set them out to cool. After a few unsuccessful tries, she managed to wedge the roaster into the oven and close the door. She had no idea how long it would take to bake this size of a cake, but she supposed instinct would tell her when it was done.

After returning to the sink, she washed her hands, dried them, and then pulled up a stool to sit down and wait for the baking process to end.

Outside, she could hear activity on the landing. Men were loading wood aboard the boat, talking among themselves as they worked. In the distance, a man's voice lifted in anger.

Sliding off the stool, she walked to the sink to wash the pans she'd dirtied. Flour and sugar was everywhere, and Izzy kept a clean kitchen. Taking a peek in the oven, she saw that the cake was rising nicely.

She returned to the stool and sat down to wait again.

The minutes ticked by. The voices outside on the landing were louder now as the dispute between two men seemed to grow more heated. From what she could gather, they seemed to be arguing over a woman.

A shot rang out. The surprise of it sent Amelia toppling off the stool.

Clasping her hands over her mouth, she looked out the galley window, stifling a scream as she saw a man lying on his back on the landing, a crimson stain spreading across the front of his shirt.

"Well, will you look at that?" she murmured. Standing on her toes, she tried to get a closer look at all the commotion, but a crowd was gathering around the injured man, blocking her view.

"Drat." All this excitement going on, and she couldn't see a blessed thing!

Maybe the cake was done. If it was finished, she'd take it out and then slip over to the landing to see what in the world was going on.

Rushing back to the oven, she jerked it open again, frowning when she saw the cake deflate like a ruptured ball.

Well, it didn't matter. It would taste all right even if it wasn't pretty.

Hefting the pan out of the oven, she winced as she carried it to the table. It was not only flat, it was heavy. Flat and heavy and ugly. Big and ugly! If she had time, she'd sit down and cry, but she didn't. As it was, she was missing all the commotion outside.

Banging the roaster down on the counter, she flung hot pads aside and raced out the door.

A moment later, she was suddenly back again,

searching for something to write with. If Morgan returned to find her gone, he'd be mad as blue blazes. She figured she had to leave him a note. If she told him exactly where she was, he'd have no right to be upset with her.

After a lengthy search, she located a pencil stub in the bottom drawer of the pantry. Now, where should she leave the note so he wouldn't miss seeing it? Her eyes lit on the white tablecloth. He couldn't miss anything that big. Maybe he was already on the landing, and she wouldn't need to explain anything. Then again, maybe he wasn't. Maybe he was busy loading wood and didn't realize that something really exciting was going on. She'd better not take a chance.

Leaning over the table, she hurriedly wrote a note.

There, that ought to make him happy.

Racing out the door, she went to see what the shooting was all about.

Chapter 14

Morgan jerked open the door to the galley and looked inside. Black smoke was rolling from a pan of potatoes on the stove that had boiled dry. He grabbed for the hot pads, dragged the pot off the stove, and flung it into the sink.

As the smoke cleared, his eyes focused on the roaster sitting in the middle of the table. Stepping closer, his eyes quizzically searched the pan.

"What in the hell is that?" Leaning closer, he sniffed, trying to identify the aroma. When he couldn't, he lifted one end of the pan, surprised at its weight. Obviously it was something Izzy or Hester had baked, but he sure couldn't put a name to it.

Lowering the end of the pan back to the table, his eyes fell on the writing on the tablecloth.

Frowning, he leaned over to read the note.

There's been a shooting! Come to the landing quick!

> Cordially yours,
> Amelia McDougal.

P.S. Don't eat any cake. It's for supper.

Straightening, he swore. A shooting! Now what had she done? Turning on his heel, he strode through the galley, slamming the screen door behind him.

There was nothing like a shooting to liven things. Amelia hopped on one foot and then the other, trying to see over the heads in the crowd.

The injured man on the ground was rolling around, carrying on something awful as a doctor bent over him.

Spotting Henry, Amelia ran over to him. "What happened?"

"Female troubles," Henry told her with a toothy grin.

"They're fighting over a woman?"

Amelia stood on her toes, straining to see. She'd never seen anyone fight over a woman before.

"Yep, they sure are." Henry gave her another protruding grin. "Fightin' over one of them showboat women."

"A showboat?" Amelia's eyes pivoted to scan the landing. "There's a showboat here? I've never seen a showboat," she said softly. "Not ever."

"Right over there, big as you please." Henry

pointed to the landing where the magnificent, gaily lit spectacle was moored.

"A showboat," she murmured in awe. "A real, honest-to-goodness showboat!"

Grabbing Henry's hand, Amelia pulled him toward the big, glossy white paddle wheeler. Gilded lettering glinted in the afternoon sun. Intricate molding outlined the doorways. It was the most splendid sight she'd ever seen.

"Now hold on, girl. We've got to get back to *The Mississippi Lady* before she leaves without us," Henry warned, glancing back over his shoulder.

"She can't leave without us." Amelia pointed to the boats congregated around the landing. The shooting had caused so much attention, it had momentarily paralyzed river traffic.

"Captain Will's not gonna like this," Henry told her as his short legs pumped to keep up.

"I only want to see the showboat up close." Amelia pulled him along firmly. "Have you heard they have painted-up women and these really immoral men on showboats?"

"Yes, ma'am," Henry panted. "I've heard that."

"Hurry, Henry. Hurry, hurry!"

"Yes, ma'am—I'm hurrying." His bandy legs pumped faster.

The only force strong enough to repel Amelia at that moment was the solid wall she suddenly slammed into.

Bouncing a foot backward, her foot caught in

the hem of her dress and she toppled over, feeling momentarily dazed as her head reeled and she saw stars. The wall she'd run into spoke in a booming voice that sent her blood to pumping. "Who in the hell did you shoot?"

Peering groggily up at the voice, Amelia's shoulders relaxed when she saw that it was only Morgan. "Oh, good. You got my note."

"Who did you kill?"

"No one!" Climbing back to her feet, she confronted Morgan crossly. "Why do you always assume the worst about me?"

"The note said there had been a shooting," Morgan snapped.

"There was, but I didn't shoot anyone!"

His eyes swung to her wheezing accomplice. "Henry, what is going on here?"

"Well, sir, first I said—and then she said—and of course then I warned her—"

"Henry didn't do anything." Amelia glared at Morgan as she brushed the dirt off her hands and knees. "We were just going to see the showboat."

"You were told to stay aboard *The Mississippi Lady*."

"I was staying aboard *The Mississippi Lady* until I heard gunshots! Everyone else went to look, so I did, too."

"Didn't Captain Will explicitly tell you not to leave the boat?"

Their eyes locked in mute combat while a long

moment passed. The air was so tense that even Henry didn't dare breathe.

After a long staring contest, Amelia broke eye contact first when she glanced away and shrugged. "Shoot, I wasn't going to be gone long."

Henry finally caught his breath. "If you two don't mind, I'll just be going on back to the boat." He turned and left before they could object.

"What is all this about a shooting?" Morgan asked as they turned and fell quickly into step behind him.

"There was one—right over there." Amelia pointed to the crowd that was still gathered around the fallen man. "Two men were fighting over a woman, and one shot the other."

Morgan removed his hat and knocked the dust from it, then settled it back on his head wearily. "Couldn't you have included that in your note?"

"I did. I said plain as day 'there's been a shooting, come to the landing'—you didn't eat any of my cake, did you?" She shot him a glare.

He glanced over. "What cake?"

"The cake I baked."

"I didn't see any cake."

She didn't know how on God's green earth he could have missed that cake, but she wasn't going to labor the point. Apparently, he hadn't eaten any, so she'd be spared the humiliation of his knowing what a wretched cook she was.

"Morgan," she suddenly paused, laying a hand on his arm. "Couldn't we see the showboat?"

Morgan frowned. "Amelia, I would like to do that for you, but Captain Will wants to leave now."

"It'll only take a minute." Grabbing his hand, she pulled him along the path from which they'd come. She had never seen a showboat up close, and she might never have the chance to see one again.

Oh, the stories she'd have to tell Abigail and Anne-Marie. A real, honest to goodness, sin-ridden, immoral showboat!

"Oh, it's splendid." Amelia stood at the bank admiring the floating palace. The boat was old, but with its bright colored flags snapping in the breeze, it had an air of celebration about it.

Morgan watched as her face took on the glow of a small child's on Christmas morning. At times he was tempted to throttle her, but at moments like this one, he felt himself wanting to wrap his arms around her and swing her through the air.

She could exasperate him and arouse him all in the blink of a bewitching green eye. He had seen all of the world he cared to see. She, on the other hand, was just beginning to realize that a whole other world existed apart from the one she'd experienced with her sisters at the sheltered mission.

"Isn't it just beautiful?" she breathed. "Have you ever been aboard one?"

"Yes, a few times."

Amelia knew no lady should be seen stepping aboard a showboat, but oh, how she'd love to slip inside those grand rooms for a glimpse of that other life!

Morgan cupped his hand against the small breeze as he lit a cheroot. "It's not so wonderful."

"Men are lucky." Sighing, Amelia sat down on the ground, her eyes never straying from the showboat. "I've never done anything exciting like that. What's it like?"

"What's it like?" Morgan thought about the times he'd been aboard the riverboats. For days, prior to their arrival, colorful posters were pinned to trees, fences, and barns. "Showboat-a-comin' " echoed up and down the river as the spectacle pulled into town. A calliope played a popular melody as the floating theater arrived at small river towns in the morning.

The larger showboats often had a brass band that would make a big production of parading through the center of town, attracting a crowd. Actors, crew, everybody aboard traipsed about, enticing the audiences to the evening performance.

That night, the path to the showboat was marked by the fiery splendor of oil flares mounted on poles.

Once aboard, the audience was entertained by an orchestra until the curtain rose. From early spring until late autumn, the local residents were charmed by plays, vaudeville, and circus acts.

"It's a pleasant diversion," he said.

Clasping her hands together tightly, she looked

at him, her cheeks flushed with excitement. "What did you see?"

He chuckled when he thought about the performances he'd attended. "My first visit, the actors put on a play about a sickly-looking heroine who wandered from town to town, looking for a cure for her illness. The villain tried to deceive her by keeping her away from the cure. In the end, the hero arrived in the nick of time to save her."

Amelia grinned. "How?"

"With a magical remedy for her illness. When he gave her a spoonful of potion, she was immediately healed. The villain was foiled, and the heroine was returned to full glowing health. Then the curtain closed, and the captain stepped out, carrying a bottle of the magic elixir. 'Ladies and gentlemen,' he proclaimed"—Morgan spread his arms with a grand flourish, imitating the riverboat captain he'd watched—"'The miraculous medicine that has cured our lovely heroine. It can do the same for you!'"

"And people really bought some?" Her eyes glowed with excitement, trying to imagine it all.

"Fifty cents—three for a dollar!" he mocked.

"And was it really magical?"

"No," he admitted. "Many were taken in by the captain's promises for robust health, but alas, the magic elixir was nothing more than river water with color added after the mud had been drained out."

"Oh, but it still must have been wondrously exciting," she breathed. "To see all the people and hear the music. Did you ever see a real play?"

"Yes, a few."

"What? What did you see?"

"I saw *Bertha the Sewing Machine Girl*."

"Yes—oh, that must have been fun! *Bertha the Sewing Machine Girl*. What wonderful fun!"

"Actually, it was a melodrama that had all the women in the audience sobbing before it was over."

"And were there others?"

"Yes, there was *Ten Knights in a Bar Room*, and *East Lynne*," he told her.

"Oh, the life you've led. I envy you so much," she whispered. Her eyes returned to the colorful showboat. "Does it cost much to see one of these plays?"

"I think the usual charge is fifty cents."

"Fifty cents. Gosh, that's a lot."

"Not so much." His eyes gentled as he looked at her. "Maybe somebody will take you to see a play some day."

"Oh, I don't think so. I understand that no lady should be seen going aboard a showboat."

"Well," he said softly. "Perhaps if the lady is in the company of a reputable gentleman, she could get away with it."

Amelia longed for the day when a woman could do the same things that a man could. It hardly seemed right that the males got to have all the fun.

"Come along," Morgan urged gently. "Captain Will is waiting for us."

Sighing, Amelia lifted her hand, and he helped her to her feet. They began walking back to the boat.

"It's sad that there's so much good in the world and it can't be enjoyed because of all the evil," she said with a far away look in her eyes.

"For instance?" Morgan asked.

"Well, if it weren't for Austin Brown—the evil—then we could stay for awhile, and you could take me to one of the showboat performances— that would be the good. Maybe, somehow, we could all go—even Elizabeth," she added, feeling generous.

Morgan chuckled. "You would be willing to include 'ol' rotten' Elizabeth?"

Amelia wouldn't look at him now. "Only because I know you would want her along."

"I'm not sure I would take you, even if I could." Over the years, the respectability of a showboat had diminished, and many arrivals had been met by groups of armed citizens inviting the theater to keep moving.

"Still," she murmured, "it's sad that there are people like the Dov Lanigans and Austin Browns in this world to spoil everybody's fun."

They walked in silence a while before Morgan spoke again. "How is Austin Brown any different from you and your sisters?" His observation was made without malice, but it had no less impact.

"What?"

"How is what Austin Brown and his men do any different from what you and your sisters do?"

"Austin Brown is evil," Amelia said. "My sisters and I mean no harm. We've never hurt anyone. Everybody we've taken from could afford the loss."

"But still you were stealing."

"No, it isn't really stealing," she argued, "and everything we took was for the mission."

"Black is black," Morgan theorized.

His words stung her. She had never thought much about the ethics of the activities that she and her sisters engaged in. They were more like games to her—harmless larks, pranks really, nothing to do with evil.

"Do you think I'm evil?"

His features sobered. "Amelia, a person is judged by his integrity."

Oh, there he went again. He was always saying things she didn't understand.

"What is this 'integrity'?"

"It means a man—or a woman—doesn't cheat, or steal, or lie to gain what he or she wants."

"Well, how does she get what she wants then?"

His look was direct. "She comes by it honestly."

Neither spoke for a moment while Amelia tried to absorb the full meaning.

"How do you know so much about integrity?" she finally asked.

"My mother taught me about it."

"She must have been very wise." The sisters had taught her many things, and undoubtedly they had tried to show her integrity, but somehow it must not have taken.

"My mother was a good woman."

"Tell me about her." Amelia tilted her head up at him as they walked along. "Were the two of you close?"

"Very close. My father left before I was born. Mother was young, and times were hard. She took in washing and ironing to make ends meet." He smiled. "We were so poor, the church mice looked prosperous."

"Your mother never remarried?"

"I imagine she had ample opportunities, but she didn't."

"I bet she was pretty." With Morgan so handsome, his mother just had to be equally attractive.

"No. She was beautiful."

Amelia tried to imagine Morgan as a young boy, holding onto his beautiful mother's hand as they crossed a street.

"In a way, you remind me of Mother," he said.

Amelia paused, turning to look at him. "I look like your mother?" That must mean that he thought she was beautiful, too. Her heart nearly burst with happiness.

"No, you look nothing like Mother," he admitted. "But she was also a strong woman."

"Strong woman?" Amelia wasn't sure she wanted him to think of her as an Amazon.

Up ahead, they spotted a gypsy selling wares from her cart.

"A lovely flower for your lady?" The gypsy extended a single daisy for Morgan's inspection.

Pausing, Morgan examined the golden center and the pale, translucent petals closely. "Very pretty."

"Only a pittance, sir," the gypsy tempted. Her faded brown eyes rested on Amelia. "Small price for one so lovely."

"You're right, it is a small price." Reaching into his pocket, he extracted a coin. "Would you have any tobacco?"

"Ahh," the old woman's smile wreathed her whole face. "That I do. How much would you like?"

"Two sacks will do, thank you."

She handed him the two small pouches, and he paid her.

Amelia watched the exchange with a sinking heart. The tobacco, she felt sure, was a gift for Elizabeth. Morgan smoked nothing but cheroots.

"And two of those lovely apples," he added.

"Excellent choice, kind sir." Smiling, the gypsy woman polished the fat, round apples before handing them to him.

Turning, Morgan presented the daisy and one apple to her. "For the lovely lady."

"Thank you." Lifting the daisy to her nose, Amelia twirled it between her fingers letting the petals softly brush her skin.

"Read your fortune, sir?" the gypsy tempted.

"Not today, thank you." He paid the gypsy for the apples.

"Oh, please, Morgan." Amelia had never had her future told. The sisters were adamant against such things, calling it witchcraft and evil sorcery.

Bowing to her wishes, he turned back to the gypsy. "The lady would like to know her future."

"Ahh, t'would be my pleasure, kind sir."

The old woman lifted Amelia's hand, turned it over, and studied it thoughtfully. Her fingers lightly traced over the palm of her right hand. "Your life will be filled with much happiness," she murmured. "Sunshine and moonbeams and blue skies will follow you the rest of your days."

Amelia looked up at her, hope shimmering in her eyes. "Does it say if I'll marry?"

The old woman appeared amused. "Why would one so pretty worry about such things?"

"Oh, I'm not worried." She shrugged. "Just curious."

The gypsy leaned closer, her eyes pondering the lines in Amelia's hands. "Yes—you will marry, but it will take a strong man to hold your love."

"And children? Will I have little ones?"

The old woman's gaze searched her palm, and she nodded. "Umm, four, maybe five."

Amelia gasped. "Five!"

The gypsy nodded solemnly. "Ah yes, my child, you will be very fruitful."

"Fruitful!" That wasn't fruitful—that was a bumper crop.

Dazed, Amelia nodded. Five. Abigail and Anne Marie would just die when she told them!

The gypsy's eyes returned to Morgan. "And you, kind sir. May I see into your future?"

Morgan had little confidence in fortune tellers, but he good-humoredly extended his hand.

The old woman's wizened features grew more somber as she studied his palm. Lifting her eyes to him, she said softly, "Ahh, such a rosy future, once you find the one you love."

"And when will that be?" he asked tolerantly.

"I cannot say, sir, but it is near. Her love will bind you as tightly as the roots of the mighty oak."

"And will I have many children?" he asked with an amused quirk.

The old woman cackled wickedly as she pocketed his coin. "They will seem more than enough."

Turning away, Amelia and Morgan began walking again. The gypsy's words turned in Amelia's mind, intriguing her, as she bit into the apple. She suddenly wanted to really know about Morgan Kane.

"How did you get so good with a knife?" she asked.

"Mother taught me."

Her head turned sharply, thinking he must be teasing her again. "Oh, you!"

"It's true," he said when he saw her skepticism.

"She taught you to be proficient in throwing a knife?"

"She did." Morgan smiled as he remembered the many hours he had spent with his mother learning to be an expert marksman. A woman needed to know how to defend herself, and Letty Kane had been afraid of guns.

Over the years, she had become so good with a knife that any would-be antagonists had kept their distance. Many single men had brought her their washing, and a few had tried to be too persuasive with the beautiful young woman. When news had spread of her knack with a knife, men had been more careful to remember their manners.

She'd taught Morgan all she'd known and more. His expertise with a knife had saved his life more than once.

As they approached *The Mississippi Lady*, they could see Captain Will in the pilot house motioning for them to hurry aboard. The crowd at the dock was dispersing, and river traffic was moving again.

Crossing the gangplank, Morgan pulled Amelia protectively to the railing as Henry lifted the gangplank and the boat slowly swung upstream.

"Morgan," Amelia whispered, enjoying the feel of his arms around her. "Thank you for taking me to see the showboat." The past hour with him had been wonderful.

Gazing down at her, he smiled. "It was my pleasure."

Her heart was in her eyes now. "Do you honestly think I'm evil?"

Squeezing her waist, he wouldn't meet her gaze, but his tone didn't sound so judgmental. "Misguided, perhaps."

"But not evil?" The pranks she and her sisters had played weren't that bad, were they? She didn't want to believe that they could be as bad as Austin Brown and his men.

"Well," Morgan said quietly, "a person can always change, now can't she?"

A warm rush of hope spread through her. On impulse, she rose on her toes and kissed him lightly on the lips.

His eyes reflected a certain glint she had never seen before. Taking her by the waist, he moved her into the deep shadow of the stairway.

Their eyes met briefly in the darkness before he lowered his mouth to hers, kissing her gently, then running his tongue over the sweet fullness of her lips. She leaned against him, instinctively craving a closeness she couldn't fully understand. She tilted her face to his, her lips parted slightly, artlessly, awaiting each sensation he gave her, accepting, trusting, giving without restraint.

Whatever else she had done in her life, her lack of experience with men was apparent to him. Her trust in him struck a deep chord in Morgan. He kissed her forehead before moving his lips across her brow.

Amelia smiled up at him. His eyes softened as

he nibbled the corner of her mouth. Her breath caught in a gasp when his lips lowered to her neck, his tongue drawing lazy clockwise circles on her skin. Tingles of delight raced through her, and she moved nearer, hoping the moment would never end.

His fingertips stroked the curve of her back, urging her closer. Her ear was so near his heart, she could hear the powerful beating that must surely match her own.

With parted lips, she encouraged his kiss, letting him search and stroke until she thought she'd die from the sudden rush of feeling it brought her.

Closing her eyes tightly, she savored the sensations he drew from her very core.

The turmoil of the past months had taken their toll on him, and the innocence of her response, her willingness, nearly overpowered Morgan as he drew her tighter to him.

He held her for a moment, looking out at the churning, muddy waters of the Mississippi. He was losing his grip on reality, losing control, a fatal mistake in his business.

"Amelia," he said softly. How could this slip of a girl do this to him so quickly, so effortlessly?

"Hmm?" she murmured, still clinging to his shirtfront, still in the full, rosy rapture of the most romantic moments she'd ever experienced.

His back stiffened, and he firmly clasped her arms and pushed her away. "Look," he muttered,

"I apologize. . . . I didn't intend for this to happen." His voice grew harsh as he watched her bright features blanch. "I'm not going to tell you again. Stay out of trouble—do you understand?"

"No," she whispered raggedly, "I don't understand." He was rejecting her again, just when she thought they had reached a new understanding. Her beautiful new world filled with exquisite longing and delightful sensations was fading before her eyes. Why? What had she done wrong this time?

Her eyes searched his face for a clue, but all she could see were the doors they'd opened that day slamming shut, one by one.

"Look." He released his breath slowly. "Forget about this. I promise you it won't happen again."

Her eyes filled with hurt and humiliation as he gave her a final, dismissive look, and walked off.

Leaning against the railing, she hugged herself tightly, feeling slightly ill. What had she done wrong?

Gradually, the answer came to her. It was simple. She wasn't good enough for him. She'd had no idea how to please him. Her inexperience had betrayed her.

Suddenly, she saw a vision of Elizabeth, her lips curved in a knowing smile, her worldly eyes mocking. Elizabeth would have known what to do. Morgan would not have walked away from Elizabeth just now, full of regrets.

With a heavy heart, Amelia slowly emerged from her dark cocoon to seek the solitude of her lonely bunk.

Chapter 15

"What is it?" Amelia raced to the railing, straining to see what was causing all the excitement. The other women ran to join her. Another ship had suddenly pulled even with *The Mississippi Lady*. Amelia's pulse pounded in her throat as she anxiously watched the other boat.

"Are we racing?" Bunny asked. There was nothing more exciting than a race between two paddle steamers! Nothing more exciting, or dangerous. Tales of exploding steamboat boilers abounded, yet most captains took delight in racing.

"I hope not," Pilar called above the groaning of the engines.

"A race!" Amelia could barely contain her excitement. She'd never in her entire life ever seen a steamboat race, let alone been a part of one!

She rushed up to the pilot house and burst inside to find Morgan and Captain Will bustling about.

"Are we racing?" Amelia asked as she scurried

to peer out at the large paddle wheeler that was now gaining ground on *The Mississippi Lady.*

"Oh no," Captain Will stated calmly, "we're not racing." He looked over at Morgan, and they exchanged conspiratorial grins.

The boilers heated up. Black smoke and sparks belched from *The Mississippi Lady*'s tall stacks as she cut a wide path of boiling white froth through the water.

"Go below, Amelia!" Morgan shouted over the din as the pace continued to pick up.

Amelia, her brows puckered in a worried frown, didn't budge an inch. "Are you sure it isn't Austin Brown trying to trick us?" There had been no tangible evidence to indicate Brown was pursuing them, but everybody aboard knew that he wouldn't accept defeat so easily.

Morgan shook his head negatively. "It isn't Austin Brown. Now go below!"

The two steamboats shot down the river, keeping pace with each other. Amelia's pulse quickened as *The Mississippi Lady* began to quake and strain from stem to stern.

"Amelia!" Morgan roared.

"And miss all the fun?" she asked incredulously. *No, thank you!* She had a marvelous view of the excitement from right up here.

The two paddle wheelers struggled side by side, their scrape pipes expelling plumes of black smoke into the air.

Ryder and Henry frantically shoved wood into

the boilers, bumping into each other as they tried
to keep the fire fed.

"My back's killing me," Ryder complained.

"My feet are swollen so tight it'll take a crowbar
to get my boots off tonight," Henry grumbled.

"Did I tell you about the time I held the horns?"
Captain Will shouted as he deftly steered the boat
through the churning waters.

Morgan stepped over to steady Amelia as the
boat continued to gain speed.

"Did you retain the honor?" Morgan called
back.

"Sure did! Four years in a row!"

Amelia glanced quizzically over her shoulder at
Morgan. "The horns?" she asked.

Morgan bent his head, his breath warm against
her ear. "Holding the horns is a coveted award
among river pilots. The horns are a gilded rack of
deer horns, the symbol of the speed king. The captain who wins them mounts them like a trophy on
his pilot house or the most prominent place on his
ship."

Amelia bestowed an admiring grin on Captain
Will, and he winked at her. "Watch this, missy."

The old boat groaned under the building pressure as the two paddle wheelers came around a
bend.

Jumping up and down now, Amelia howled with
delight as Henry and Ryder pumped more wood
into the boiler.

"Yes!" Amelia clutched Morgan's arm. "We're pulling ahead!"

The decks of *The Mississippi Lady* vibrated as the stern slowly inched ahead of the other boat. Running full throttle now, white steam poured from the tops of the ships' scrape pipes. Boiling white froth faded into long white streaks as they cut through the muddy water.

Suddenly, the race was over as quickly as it had begun.

The Mississippi Lady shot ahead, taking the lead, as the other boat dropped abruptly behind.

Sounding a victory blast on the horn, Captain Will laughed merrily as *The Mississippi Lady* sailed on down the river.

With a shout, Amelia threw her arms around Morgan's neck and hugged him.

This was the most fun she'd had since she and her sisters had seeded the mission's well with wild onions!

"Wasn't that the most exciting thing you've ever done!" Amelia exclaimed as the women prepared for bed that night.

"Do you know how many people are killed by exploding boilers?" Elizabeth asked drolly.

"Oh, pooh," Amelia muttered. "The boiler didn't explode, did it? Captain Will wouldn't do anything to get us hurt."

"Captain Will is a man, isn't he?" Elizabeth stretched out on her bunk. "And a man can be

thoughtless when adventure calls." She deftly filled
a cigarette paper with tobacco as she murmured,
"Caught up by the prospect of a race, men have
been known to be downright reckless at times."

"Well, the boiler didn't blow up." Amelia
shrugged and looked away. "So let's talk about
something else." She glanced back again when she
heard a soft rustling sound as Elizabeth withdrew a
pouch of tobacco from her pocket.

Amelia's heart quickened when she recognized
the brown pouch with the red writing as one she
had seen Morgan purchase from the gypsy. Before
the question could form in Amelia's mind, before
she could weigh the wisdom of speaking it, the
words flew out of her mouth. "Where were you
last night?"

While everyone else had been eating, Morgan
and Elizabeth had conspicuously disappeared
again. Perhaps the tobacco Morgan had bought her
had inspired more than a few words of simple gratitude from Elizabeth.

A wave of jealousy knotted Amelia's stomach.
A small voice warned her to look away, to drop the
subject while she could still salvage her pride, but
a strong urge compelled her to stare accusingly
into Elizabeth's cool eyes.

Elizabeth broke eye contact to sprinkle tobacco onto a cigarette paper that she was holding
with steady fingers. With a practiced move, Elizabeth locked her teeth onto the drawstring and
tugged the pouch closed with one hand. Amelia's

eyes widened as she gazed at the same drawstring that Morgan had twirled aimlessly between his fingers.

Elizabeth casually rolled the cigarette and placed
it between her lips, full lips that quirked at the corners in a mocking smile. Unwillingly, Amelia
stared at Elizabeth's mouth. Had Morgan been
kissing those lips last night? She imagined Morgan
and Elizabeth embracing and kissing in the dark
corner beneath the stairway, the same dark corner
where Morgan had kissed her not long ago. She
suffered such a thrust of pain in her chest that for
a long moment she couldn't draw a breath.

"None of your business where I was." Elizabeth
raised an eyebrow as she struck a match. Everyone
in the room watched her hold the flame to her cigarette and draw on it until the tip glowed a bright
red.

The tension grew until the room felt suffocating
with humidity and smoke. Faith shot to her feet to
stand between Amelia and Elizabeth. With a noisy
snap, she shook out the dress she'd been mending
for Izzy. "Well, how do you think it looks?"

"Did you do something to the collar?" Auria
asked awkwardly. Casual conversation seemed difficult when Amelia and Elizabeth were both present.

"A little." Faith held the dress up for inspection.
"Like it?"

"It's very nice," Belicia praised. "You do such

intricate work. Have you thought of sewing for money?"

"Oh, no!" Faith protested. "I'm not good enough to sew for money."

"But you are," Pilar insisted. "I've never met a person who could sew such tiny, even stitches. They're practically invisible. With your skill, you should be making wedding dresses and beautiful gowns."

Faith fairly glowed from all the praise.

"Everyone here has a special ability," Ria said, being careful not to draw attention away from Faith. She nodded at the women around the room. "Each of you knows how to do something better than anyone else here."

"Everyone?" Mahalia questioned.

Ria nodded firmly. "Everyone."

As a lark, they decided to discover what special talents each one possessed.

"Faith can sew like a wizard," Amelia began. "And Hester can cook even better than Izzy." Which was saying a lot. Izzy's pies could make an angel weep.

"I'm good with numbers," Pilar admitted. When her father ran off with a woman young enough to be his daughter, her mother had turned to liquor for comfort. It was left up to Pilar to manage what meager funds were available to the family of ten. Many a time she'd had to stretch a dollar to make two.

"Maybe you and Faith can start your own dress-making business someday," Amelia said.

Faith and Pilar clapped their hands with delight.

"Wouldn't that be wonderful!" Faith exclaimed. "Think of it, our own business."

Pilar nodded. "Of course, and we could name it Sew and Sews and spell it s-e-w instead of s-o." They all laughed at her play on words. "I can do the sewing and Pilar can be the bookkeeper."

"Bunny can do miracles with ridding our dresses of stains," Amelia reminded them.

Bunny nodded. "If I had an iron, I believe I could make them look like new!"

"I can whittle," Belicia announced. "Give me a piece of wood, and I'll fashion any likeness you want."

"Really?" Amelia asked. She couldn't imagine doing anything like that.

"I can make hats. Why, if I had the proper materials, I could make the most beautiful hat you ever saw," Auria exclaimed.

"Honestly?" Mahalia exclaimed.

"Honestly. I entered a contest one time at my grandmother's church, and I won first prize!"

The women's enthusiasm grew as the list of their accomplishments increased. Finally, Elizabeth, who'd contributed little to their conversations, joined in. "I can whistle while eating crackers."

The girls' heads swiveled in unison to gape at her.

Taking a slow drag off her cigarette, she mocked, "What's the matter? Haven't you ever met a woman who could eat crackers and whistle at the same time?"

Amelia shook her head. She had never even met a man who could do that.

"Well, now you have."

"Prove it." Amelia wasn't about to just take Elizabeth's word for it. Eating crackers and whistling. At the same time? She didn't think so.

Elizabeth rolled off the bunk and sat up. "Get me some crackers."

Amelia left the room and was back in record time with a handful of soda crackers. The women clustered around Elizabeth's bunk.

"Okay, Elizabeth. Prove it." Amelia knew that Elizabeth couldn't, certain that she was just showing off again.

Elizabeth methodically stacked four crackers on top of one another and then bit into them, her eyes locked defiantly with Amelia's.

"She can't do it," Amelia assured the others. "She's just bragging, as usual."

Elizabeth ate the four crackers, chewing slowly, then polished off four more.

"Whistle," Amelia spurred.

"What do you want me to whistle?"

"Anything!" Pilar echoed in a rare challenge.

"Okay." Elizabeth began to whistle "Dixie" spiritedly.

"Gosh," Amelia breathed, fascinated by the

spray of crumbs spewing from Elizabeth's mouth. The woman was flat-out whistling all right after eating *eight* crackers.

"That's really good," Faith commended, in complete awe of this enviable feat.

"I told you I could do it."

Elizabeth, satisfied she'd shown them, settled back to finish her smoke.

Amelia returned to her bunk and sat down, looking around for something to do. She tried whistling "Dixie" under her breath, but gave up when she saw the others looking at her strangely.

"I've got an idea," she announced before the thought was fully formed in her mind. "Let's practice kissing."

The others looked up.

"You know—kissing. Is anyone good at it? With the exception of you, Elizabeth." Amelia gave Elizabeth a swift nod of dismissal.

Elizabeth leaned back in her bunk, seemingly uninterested.

The women exchanged hesitant looks.

"Anyone?" Amelia prodded.

Shrugging, Ria admitted softly, "Once a boy told me I could kiss pretty good."

"Well, there you are," Amelia enthused. "Now you can be the one to teach us."

The women looked at one another in puzzlement.

Amelia rolled her eyes. "Of course, we're going to practice on our hands, silly." Lifting the back of her hand to her mouth, Amelia kissed it loudly to prove her point.

The others watched for a moment, then reluctantly followed suit.

"This is, without a doubt, the stupidest thing I have ever witnessed," Elizabeth said, after watching them rehearse their kissing techniques for a few minutes. "What's the point? There are no men around—at least men you'd want to kiss."

Amelia looked at her accusingly. What did she consider Morgan? A horsefly?

Amelia assumed a condescending air. "Maybe not now." *Or for us,* Amelia thought. "But there will be, someday. And we should know how to kiss when the time comes."

Disgusted, Elizabeth turned away, reaching for her tobacco pouch again. "You have a brain the size of a gnat." What if someone caught them kissing their own hands? How demoralizing, humiliating, utterly embarrassing that would be. As Elizabeth would tell anyone, she was not a woman who blushed easily, but this was too much.

"How would you know, Elizabeth? You've never seen my brain," Amelia goaded.

"As if that's at the top of my wish list."

Amelia lay back on her bunk. "You act as if you know everything, Elizabeth. Besides that, you're cranky. And bossy. Cranky and bossy, that's you, Elizabeth."

"Maybe I know more about men than you think I do."

"And then, maybe you don't."

"Maybe I know more than you think I do." Elizabeth snorted derisively. "Especially about men."

The last taunt was more than Amelia could bear. "Maybe we're not like you, Elizabeth." The innuendo was clear. Amelia wasn't proud of herself for pointing it out, but it was true. They weren't like Elizabeth, especially when it came to men.

"No, you aren't at all like me. I was married once."

The silence in the room was suddenly deafening.

"Married!" Amelia found her voice first. "You were not!"

"Yes, I was."

Amelia's eyes widened with sudden understanding. *Well, no wonder Morgan prefers her!* She knew everything there was to know when it came to pleasing a man.

"Oh?" Amelia grew wary. It wouldn't be above Elizabeth to lie to them. "Well, if that's true, where's your husband then?"

Pain briefly crossed Elizabeth's face. "Never mind."

"Oh, no you don't," Amelia countered. "You can't just tell us you were married, and then brush it off with a 'never mind'. If you are married, where's your husband?"

"I'm no longer married," Elizabeth acknowledged.

"Why not?" Amelia glanced at the others. If
they weren't going to call Elizabeth's hand on this,
then she would. "Were you so rotten and mean he
ran off and left you?"

Nervous giggles broke out among the others.

"My husband is dead."

Elizabeth's tone was so grave that Amelia was
tempted to believe her. Then she reminded herself
that Elizabeth was an expert at deception. She'd
like nothing better than to make her look like a
fool.

"Well, I'm sorry, you should have told us," she
mocked.

"It isn't anything I care to talk about."

Amelia raised her brows at the others. Elizabeth
could certainly lay it on thick.

"Elizabeth," Pilar chided. "Death is very sad.
You shouldn't tease about such things."

"I'm not teasing. My husband is dead."

For a moment, no one could think of a single
thing to say. Finally, Amelia broke the strained silence. "Now, Elizabeth, is this really true? Were
you really married and your husband died?"

"My husband is dead," she repeated, more softly
now.

The mood in the room changed. Rising from her
bunk, Amelia crossed the room to kneel beside
Elizabeth. "Elizabeth—"

Elizabeth sat up, shrugging her hand aside. "I don't want your pity."

Amelia was silent for a moment. She glanced at the others, then back to Elizabeth. "Well . . . it would be all right if you wanted to talk about it."

It felt strange being nice to Elizabeth—not bad, but strange. Amelia examined her conscience and decided that she could be decent to Elizabeth, providing she was telling the truth.

When Elizabeth didn't answer, Amelia's suspicions that they were being played for fools were strengthened again.

As she turned to go back to her bunk, Elizabeth said softly, "We had been married five months when the war started. Marcus didn't believe in bloodshed. Our church prohibited his taking another man's life, so when he was asked to fight, he declined, holding to his beliefs. The men of our community were angered by his refusal. After that, we were considered outcasts."

Suddenly, years of bitterness and resentment came tumbling out of Elizabeth, word on top of word, as if by voicing them she would be cleansed of the terrible ache she had lived with for too long.

"We farmed twenty acres outside of town, so we were busy most of the time. We were so young and in love that what went on with the rest of the world didn't matter to us." Her eyes filled with love at the memory. "We were so happy.

Marcus worked the fields, and I tended the house."

A tear rolled from the corner of her eye, and she self-consciously wiped it aside.

"It was raining the day it happened. Marcus was reading a farm journal, and I had just taken a raisin pie out of the oven." She paused, remembering how much Marcus had loved raisin pie. "When we heard the horses, we thought it was a neighbor coming to visit, although that would have been unusual. Folks didn't much care for anyone who wasn't willing to fight for their cause."

Her features hardened, looking more like the Elizabeth they all knew. "Some men—members of a vigilante group—met me at the door. I asked them what they wanted, and they cursed me, saying that Marcus was spineless for not fighting. They called him a coward and a disgrace to his brotherhood. When Marcus came to the door to see who was there, they shoved me aside and dragged him out to the barn and hanged him there."

Pilar gasped softly.

"I tried to stop them—I pleaded and cried, but they wouldn't listen. After Marcus was dead, they torched the house and the outbuildings." Her voice turned flat and lifeless. "And then they took turns having their way with me.

"When they left," Elizabeth whispered, "I cut Marcus' body down and buried him. I stayed in what was left of the cabin for three days, not knowing what to do or where to turn. It was cold at night, and it rained during the days. Finally, a neighbor to the east saw the smoke and came to investigate. When he learned what had happened, he and his wife took pity on me and let me stay with them until I could find a place to go."

"What about your parents?" Ria asked quietly. "Couldn't you have gone to them?"

Elizabeth shook her head. "My father died before I was born. Mother was young and scared, and didn't know what to do. She left me with my grandmother until she could settle with a cousin who lived in Virginia. She promised to send for me, but she never did. Grandma Pierson died when I was fourteen. I had no one but Marcus."

"And his parents?" Amelia asked.

Elizabeth shook her head. "There was only his father, who was in such poor health I couldn't go to him and tell him about Marcus. The shock would have killed him."

Sliding off her cot, Belicia came to kneel beside her. "I'm so sorry, Elizabeth. We had no idea."

"A few weeks later, I discovered I was pregnant. . . ." Elizabeth paused, trying to collect her emotions.

"Was it Marcus's baby?" someone whispered.

"No. The baby was a result—" She paused, swallowing. "When I was four months along, I lost the child, and nearly died myself."

"Oh, Elizabeth," Amelia lay her hand on Elizabeth's arm. She'd had no idea what Elizabeth had gone through. She would never have been so mean to her if she told her of this before.

Elizabeth lifted her head defiantly. "I don't need your sympathy. I'm a survivor. Grieve for the men who did this to Marcus. Ask that their souls will burn forever in hell." Wiping the tears from her eyes, she straightened, her face showing none of her recent emotion. "Besides, I'm not the only one here who hasn't lived a fairy tale life."

A few nodded, recalling the abuse they had suffered at the hands of others.

Pilar reached for Elizabeth's tobacco pouch to roll a cigarette for her. She guessed if the things that had happened to Elizabeth had happened to her, she'd smoke, too. "I'll fix you a smoke, Elizabeth."

A hint of warmth entered Elizabeth's eyes as Bunny helped wipe away her lingering tears. "Thank you, Pilar—Bunny."

"You're welcome—and if you ever need anything else, you can come to me. I'll help you," Bunny vowed.

Clearing her throat, Amelia added softly, "You can have the friendship of all of us—if you want us."

The eyes of the two women met in silent understanding. Things would be easier between them now. They both knew it.

Reaching for Bunny's hand, Faith smiled. "Well,

the one nice thing about all this is that we're sort of like a family now."

The others murmured their poignant agreement.

Their paths were sure to take opposite directions, but from this moment on they would always be together in spirit.

Chapter 16

Amelia was up before the sun the next morning. Grabbing her fishing pole, she ran up on deck to get in a few hours fishing before breakfast. The old engine had been *kerplunk*ing along smoothly for over an hour before she noticed a strange noise.

Setting her pole aside, she ventured below to the main deck, where she found Morgan and Captain Will bent over the old boiler, shaking their heads and muttering to each other.

"Is something wrong?" Amelia asked, trying to see over Morgan's shoulder.

"Trouble with the pressure lines," Captain Will murmured. The race yesterday had taken its toll on the old boat.

Amelia stepped closer, peering into the boiler. "Can't you fix it?"

"Yes, but it means an unscheduled stop," Captain Will told her.

"Which does not give you license to leave this boat," Morgan reminded her.

The two men rolled up their sleeves and were soon immersed in repairing the boiler.

A few of the women dropped by to view the goings-on, but in general, life aboard *The Mississippi Lady* proceeded at a normal pace.

The boat struggled to the next landing where Captain Will moored it.

Amelia went back to fishing, but her heart wasn't in it. As the day wore on, her mind lazily thought about the lace Faith wanted for the curtains.

Dinnertime came and went. Izzy and Hester took Morgan and Captain Will their plates because they seemed too busy to eat with the others.

The sun climbed higher in the sky. Amelia slipped off her shoes and pushed up the sleeves of her dress. It was getting warm and muggy now.

After another hour passed, it became too hot to fish. Abandoning her pole, Amelia went to the water bucket for a cool drink.

Lifting her head, she blotted the drops of water above her upper lip on her sleeve as her eyes focused on the old boiler. The men looked completely absorbed in trying to repair it now.

She let the dipper drop back into the bucket, then sidled along the railing, to edge her way toward the bow of the boat.

Bunny was there, hanging out the wash. "Hi,"

she mumbled around the clothespins wedged between her front teeth.

"Hi," Amelia returned casually.

"Thought you were fishing."

Amelia helped Bunny pin another shirt to the line strung between two wooden beams.

"I am. I got thirsty and came down for a drink of water."

After pinning the last piece to the line, Bunny leaned back, stretching to get the kinks out of her shoulders. "Awfully hot, isn't it?"

Amelia nodded as she glanced about warily.

When Bunny returned to her washboard, Amelia slipped around to the left side of the boat.

The landing where they were moored was small. Amelia could see a livery, a small church, a schoolhouse, and a general store.

Her eyes centered on the general store. It couldn't be two hundred feet from the landing.

Returning to the stern, Amelia looked around the corner again, assuring herself that the men were still up to their elbows in sweat and grease. Maybe Faith wasn't quick enough to purchase the lace without getting caught, but she was.

As she traveled back to the bow, her eyes measured the distance between the boat and the general store again. She could be off and back before Morgan even missed her.

Ryder, Niles, and Henry were busy trying to help Morgan and the captain. Izzy was taking a nap, and the others would never tell on her.

Amelia's eyes darted to the general store, then back to scan the boat.

It would probably be hours before the men had that boiler fixed. She'd have plenty of time. Plenty.

Deciding to risk it, she raced up to her room, located the coins she had hidden beneath her bunk, then hurried back to the main deck.

When she saw that there was no one looking, she quickly walked down the gangplank. Her heart was pounding with fear that she would be stopped any moment by a commanding male who would threaten her within an inch of her life for disobeying him again.

After clearing the gangplank, she raced to a nearby willow and hid behind it to see if anyone had followed. When a few minutes had passed and no one shouted at her, she breathed a sigh of relief and rushed toward the general store.

Her spirits dampened as she entered the small mercantile and found it sparsely stocked. Its shelves offered only the bare necessities.

An elderly man dressed in a green and black plaid shirt glanced up from behind the counter. "Help you with something?"

"Lace," Amelia gasped, trying to catch her breath. "Want some lace."

The clerk frowned. "Don't know that I have any lace."

"You have to have some," she panted. She was risking Morgan's wrath for coming here in the first place, and this man was telling her he didn't have any lace?

Scratching his head, the clerk pondered for a minute. "Seems to me I've seen a bolt of lace around somewhere. Might be in the back room." He turned in that direction, then tilted his head and turned around again. "Of course, there could be some in the storeroom," he acknowledged.

"Go look," Amelia gasped.

He disappeared into the back room, and Amelia scampered back to look out the window. She could see the boat still moored to the landing. All looked calm.

Her eyes darted to the storeroom and back to the window. The storekeeper wasn't moving very quickly. Why didn't he hurry? She didn't have all day. Her pulse was drumming at her temples.

Another few minutes passed before the clerk returned, carrying a partially empty ribbon bolt. "Don't look like there's much on here," he admitted.

Amelia shoved a coin at him. "I'll take it anyway."

As he made change, the clerk looked her over. "You're new around here, aren't you?"

Amelia glanced anxiously over her shoulder. "Just passing through." She shoved the change he handed her into her skirt pocket.

Snatching the bolt of lace, she hurried out the front door. As she stepped down, she discovered that in her haste to leave the boat she had forgotten to put on her shoes.

Gingerly side stepping rocks, she headed straight back to the boat clutching the lace to her breast. She'd made it! She heaved a sigh. Only a few more feet and she'd be at the gangplank. Even if Morgan did catch her now, she could always pretend that she was just innocently sitting on the gangplank cooling her feet in the water.

Uh oh, her conscience nagged. *That would be lying, and a person who lies is short on integrity.*

Integrity. From the moment Morgan had mentioned that darn word integrity, she had wanted some. When he'd explained it to her, integrity had sounded so pure, so elusive . . . so desirable.

Her spirits suddenly lifted. Well, she didn't have to lie to him. Just a few more feet and she'd be back on the boat, and he'd never have to know that she had even been gone.

Only a few more feet . . . a few more feet . . .

She screamed as a hand clamped onto her shoulder. Squeezing her eyes shut tightly, she waited for the explosion, knowing full well it would come.

"Didn't Morgan tell you to stay aboard," a voice demanded gruffly.

Recognizing Ryder's voice, her eyes flew open. Amelia felt faint with relief. It was only Ryder.

"Did you hear me, girl?"

"I heard you, Ryder. You scared a year's growth out of me." The censure in his voice didn't sound favorable, but at least Morgan hadn't caught her. She leaned over to pick up the lace she'd dropped.

When she started to hurry past him, Ryder reached out to stop her.

Grasping her shoulders, he turned her firmly around to face him. "This is gonna have to stop," he told her sternly.

"I was just buying some—"

"You were told to stay aboard." Ryder's tone firmed. "Each time you pull one of your shenanigans, you put the rest of us in jeopardy."

Amelia glanced nervously toward the boiler. "Does Morgan know?"

"I think I'm the only one who saw you."

She breathed another sigh of relief. "Good."

"No, it's not good." Ryder's eyes didn't hold a hint of compassion. "Just because Morgan didn't catch you, doesn't mean you got away with it."

"You're not going to tell him, are you?" They both could guess the unpleasant consequences of that.

"No, but I suspect you will."

Amelia's brows shot up. She expected that it would be a long time before that happened, if ever.

"One of the lives you've put in danger is mine, young lady. I figure since I've made it to seventy-five, I don't intend to let any young whippersnapper endanger what precious time I might have left."

Amelia had never heard him talk like that.

Taking her by the shoulders, Ryder steered her toward the boat, keeping her firmly in check.

They crossed the gangplank quickly without notice.

Ryder pointed her in the direction of her cabin. "Now, stay out of trouble. And I'm not going to remind you again."

As Amelia watched him walk away, she felt a sinking feeling in the pit of her stomach.

Now even *he* thought she had no integrity.

"How will you explain this lace?" Faith carefully stitched the material to the bottom of one curtain panel. It was lovely. Faith had been ecstatic when Amelia had given it to her; nevertheless, she seemed worried. It would be hard to explain how she had come by the lace without admitting that someone had left the boat.

Amelia lay on her bunk, staring up at the ceiling morosely. *Yes, how am I going to explain the lace?*

Maybe Morgan was right about her. Maybe she didn't have any integrity and she never would. The idea hit her hard. She didn't much care what other men thought of her, but she did care what Morgan thought. For some reason, his opinion mattered a lot more than it should. She cared so much it made her miserable. A woman could be well-trained in social graces; she could be a tidy housekeeper; she could have excellent potential for motherhood; however, Morgan would never fall in love with a woman who did not possess integrity.

To her dismay Amelia discovered there was something she wanted even more than integrity, and that was for Morgan Kane to like her.

Certainly, she had done nothing to inspire his admiration, or his love, but she knew it was what she wanted more than anything else, even more than returning to her sisters.

Every day she prayed they were well and happy, but given the choice, she would stay with Morgan—that is, if she had even the slightest shred of integrity, and if he were to ask. Both seemed as likely as turkeys wearing corsets.

"Captain Kane seems like a gentleman," Faith said quietly. "Perhaps if you both laid aside your past offenses, you could speak of this matter."

"No, Faith, he would be furious with me for going against his wishes." Suddenly, the lace didn't seem nearly as important to Amelia as Morgan's approval. Why hadn't she thought of that hours ago?

Sensing the turmoil going on inside her friend, Faith laid her hand on Amelia's shoulder comfortingly. "Go to him, tell him what you've done, and ask for his forgiveness. Then promise him that in the future you will try to act only in the best interests of all."

"I couldn't ever bow to a man's wishes," Amelia confessed. She had relied on her own devices for too long to change overnight. "I didn't even like men until I met Morgan."

Faith smiled as if she knew an inside joke that

Amelia didn't. "Yes, you can change ... if you want to, for the right man."

When Amelia's eyes turned watery Faith moved back to the curtains. She bit the thread in two, then held the curtain up for Amelia's inspection. The lace did make a difference. The curtains were actually beautiful now.

A few nights later, as Amelia climbed the steps to the pilot house, Faith's words were echoing in her mind. *You can change if you want to, and if it's for the right man.*

Well, maybe she could change. She could at least try, for Morgan's sake.

Lately, Amelia had taken to spending time with Captain Will in the evenings. She liked to sit on the lazy bench, visiting with him as he piloted the boat upstream. They would talk for hours about this and that, but the subject always seemed to get around to Morgan.

Captain Will told her stories about Morgan's childhood that made her laugh and wish she could have been there to have seen him. Before long, she began to feel as if she knew everything about Morgan Kane. Everything except his role in the war. Even Captain Will remained vague about that. It was important, Amelia was certain of that. A man like Morgan wouldn't do anything that wasn't important.

Tonight, as Amelia entered the pilot house, she froze when she saw Morgan sitting in Captain

Will's chair. She turned in her tracks and started to leave when his voice stopped her.

"Looking for Captain Will?"

"Yes ... I ... I thought I'd visit awhile."

Keeping his eyes on the river, Morgan said casually, "The captain is having a second piece of pie with Izzy tonight."

"Oh, my goodness." Amelia knew how Captain Will would hate himself in the morning for that.

"You can visit with me," Morgan invited.

"Oh, no, thank you ... I don't want to be a bother."

"Since when has that become a consideration?" With a smile, he patted the seat beside him. "You want to pilot the boat for awhile?"

"Pilot the boat?" Amelia was astounded. She couldn't think of anything more exciting.

Morgan scooted over making room for her on the seat.

Amelia perched on the edge of the chair, feeling terribly self-conscious sitting so near to him. Somehow being this close to him felt more exciting than the time when they had slept in the same bed ... because this time she knew she was in love with him.

"Here," he said, closing her hands over the handholds on the wheel, "get a firm grip."

Before she realized what was happening, he'd slid behind her, his powerful arms bracing hers, his sure hands wrapped over her fingers, his firm chest supporting her back.

He was so close that his breath tickled her ear. She could hardly breathe. She'd dreamed of being in his arms again, but now that it was occurring and so unexpectedly, she was stunned into silence.

Her knuckles turned white as she gripped the wheel tightly, trying to concentrate on steering the boat.

"Easy," he murmured, massaging her fingers. "Your hands will go numb. You don't have to always take me so literally."

She tried to swallow the lump in her throat. "But the current," she whispered, her voice husky, "is so strong. It keeps pulling at me. I can feel it through the wheel." The force was stronger than she'd ever imagined it could be.

"Hold steady," he said next to her ear, "but don't fight it so much. Like this. You work with the pull, assessing how much resistance you need to apply." His fingers guided the pressure of hers against the wood. "Give and take. That's the secret. If you fight it like you were, you'll wear out in no time."

"Yes, that's better," she murmured. "There's so much I don't know."

There was a smile in his voice. "It's not so hard to learn, when you want to."

His words reminded her of Faith's. *Not hard to change if you want to . . . for the right man.*

She sighed. "I guess I'm a slow learner. I want to change, but old habits . . . and I forget to think." It was hard to concentrate at all, feeling his

strength wrapped protectively around her, savoring
the measured beat of his heart behind her shoulder.

"You have to keep your mind on what you're
doing," he said with a deep chuckle of irony,
directed at himself as much as at her.

I wish I could. How she wished she could confide in him her deepest longings and her greatest
fears.

She felt a bump, perhaps through her fingers on
the wheel, or maybe through the soles of her shoes
on the planked floor. "What was that?"

"Probably a sleeper," he said, scanning ahead.

"A submerged log?" she asked.

"I see you've been doing your homework."

"Henry told us about 'sawyers' and 'sleepers'
the night we came aboard."

"Henry's spent his life on the river."

"Why is the water so muddy?" she asked.

Smiling, Morgan started to explain. "The
'muddy Mississippi,' she's flowing fast with a lot
of loose debris." He caught something out of the
corner of his eye and he turned to look back.

Two Indians in a canoe were now following the
boat.

Following his gaze over her shoulder, Amelia's
heart sprang to her throat when she saw the intrud-
ers. "What do they want?"

"Nothing, I suspect," he said calmly, glancing at
them as he scanned the waters below. "They're intrigued by a 'fire canoe.' "

"Fire canoe?"

"Yes, that's what they call a paddle wheeler. Because of the sparks coming from the stack, they assume that the boat is on fire."

His attention returned to her. They were in such close proximity, she could feel the heat of his gaze on her skin.

"You don't really want to hear me tell you why the Mississippi is muddy, do you?" He skimmed a lock of stray hair from her cheek. "Why don't you tell me what you've been up to?"

"Me? Nothing," she stammered.

Integrity, Amelia. Find some!

"Oh." The sound of his reply sounded ominous to her. Did he already know about the lace? Had Elizabeth informed him even while she had appeared to be in on the lark?

"Just . . . normal things." She eased forward to the edge of the seat, his presence overpoweringly male.

"Where are you going?" he teased, aware of her uneasiness.

"Nowhere." She felt her cheeks growing red from his unnerving perusal.

They were both silent for a moment as the boat plowed through the muddy waters. The Indians eventually turned away, paddling their canoe into the arm of the river.

Morgan enjoyed the silence between them, regarding it as shared contentment. Amelia, on the other hand, agonized, suspecting it was his quiet condemnation.

"All right." She released a long, tense breath. "I left the boat and bought the lace," she blurted out.

Surprise flickered briefly across Morgan's features. "When?"

"Yesterday while you were repairing the boiler. I'm sorry." She drew a deep breath. "I *really* am sorry. I know it was foolish and irresponsible and I promise I'll never do it again."

"Then you do realize how dangerous it was?" His eyes searched hers sternly. "You know you could be back in the hands of Austin Brown tonight, Amelia, and that would make me very unhappy."

"I know, and I truly regret what I did." She turned her gaze up to meet his. "Really, I'm sorry. That's why I told you." Tears pricked the back of her eyes. "Oh, Morgan, I want to have integrity. You're just going to have to teach me how."

Lifting his hand, he brushed another lock of hair from her cheek. "I'd say you're learning, Amelia McDougal. Telling me the truth instead of fabricating some big, whopping story is a good start."

"Oh, Morgan." A dam burst somewhere inside her. "There are so many things I want you to teach me."

His eyes grew tender. "Tell me what you want me to teach you, Amelia."

"I'm not sure . . ." There were so many things she didn't know. "I'm so dumb about everything!"

Drawing her head to his shoulder, he held her for a moment. In many ways, she was a child inside a woman's body crying to be released. It made for one hell of a dilemma.

"I'm not sure I'm the one to teach you these things," he said softly. "If we were to give in to this attraction, well, I'm not sure it would work. I have my responsibilities, and you have your sisters." She had told him once about the blood pact she and her sisters had made—how they would stay together no matter what.

"I remember the pact, but that was before," she reminded him. Nothing had been the same since she'd met him. Nothing would ever be again.

"I have commitments that aren't finished. My life is not my own, not yet." He wished he could confide his thoughts, but they had to remain private. "And to a lesser extent, I feel deeply indebted to Laura. She and Silar took me in when my mother died. Their orchards are in a remote part of Washington where it's possible to not see another person for weeks at a time." He looked at her, recalling her impetuous, outgoing nature. "A woman might not be happy living in that kind of environment."

Amelia wasn't listening to his reasoning. She'd only heard his words "if we were to give in to this attraction." Was he attracted to her, even though he turned to Elizabeth for his needs?

They had known each other so briefly, and yet he, too, couldn't deny that something magical had happened between them.

Leaning back against him, she rested her head

on his shoulder. Their faces were now scarcely inches apart. His gaze traveled from her eyes to her mouth. She could see the tightening around his eyes, feel the intensity of his thoughts as he looked at her.

Instinctively, she leaned closer and raised her mouth. It was more temptation than he could resist.

His lips found hers hungrily, without reserve. Once again logic was swept away on a current of emotions.

She strained against him, sensing that when reason took over once more, he would never let himself be alone with her again, never touch her again, never kiss her again. So, she kissed him with all the pent-up longing in her heart.

When his lips parted hers this time, she took the initiative. This time she explored and probed in ways she hardly understood, letting new urges be her guide.

He groaned as the kiss deepened and shifted his hips against hers, locking them tightly together. Like the way he'd shown her to hold the wheel, she followed his lead and his advice: give and take.

His breathing grew rapid, his kisses more urgent, until they felt a thud, stronger this time, against the hull of the ship.

Pulling his lips from hers, he tried to focus his gaze at the water. He suddenly sat up, turning the wheel, hand over hand.

"Damn!"

Amelia pulled her hands out of his way and let them drop helplessly onto her lap. Squeezing her shoulders together, she tried to pull her elbows in tightly so he could work from behind her.

He fought the wheel for long moments until at last he held it steady again. Only then, did he release a long breath that resembled a groan.

"What happened?" she asked in a small voice, feeling dazed from the sudden passion and the unexpected alarm.

After a moment, he heaved a weary sigh. "It appears we drifted off course. At the rate we were going, we would probably have hit the bank, torn a hole in our side, broken up fast in this current, and probably have sunk into the muddy waters of the Mississippi—in short, what usually happens when we're alone together." Once again, the reproach in his voice sounded like it was meant entirely for her. "I should have stuck to just explaining why the Mississippi is muddy."

Chapter 17

"Not much longer, now." That's what Izzy told her each time Amelia asked how much longer to Memphis.

Standing at the railing, feeling the wind in her hair, Amelia thought about Morgan. She hadn't wanted last night to end.

How easy it would have been to have given herself body and soul to him. The time was drawing near when they would part, and the thought brought a dull ache to her soul. They had barely met, and now he would be lost to her forever. She needed more time to explore her feelings, but time was running out.

She tried to imagine Morgan in Washington, running the orchards for Laura. That wasn't hard to do. Instinct told her that a man like Morgan didn't need a variety of women, hard drink, or gambling to find fulfillment. With the exception of Elizabeth, she had never seen him so much as look at the other women with a wandering eye.

By the time they reached Memphis, he might ask Elizabeth to marry him. Amelia had to face the possibility. It didn't matter that he had kissed her twice and seemed to enjoy it; you could never tell about a man.

Amelia wanted to cry out at the injustice, but her heart told her that Elizabeth, for all her faults, deserved to be happy, too. Losing her husband and child had demanded its toll.

Amelia knew in her heart that she had done nothing to win Morgan's love. He thought of her as a foolish, willful child. Well, with so little time left, she had to prove that she wasn't as thoughtless as he feared.

"Good morning," a deep voice said behind her.

Amelia stiffened as Morgan joined her at the rail. Low-hanging clouds in the west promised imminent rain.

"Good morning," she murmured.

"Sleep well?"

"Not really." She had tossed and turned, trying to form her decision, until Pilar had lost patience with her, asking her to please settle down or leave the cabin.

Tipping her face upward, he smiled at her tenderly. "I didn't either."

"Morgan, I have something to say."

"Is there a time when you don't?"

"Don't say no until you've heard me through."

Avoiding his gaze, she stared out on the water. "I want to leave the boat at the next landing."

Sighing, he leaned against the rail. "Amelia, we've been through this time and time again—"

"It's really me that Austin Brown wants."

Morgan was silent for a long moment. Finally he looked up to meet her eyes. "You know that he's following us now?"

She nodded. For the past few hours she had been aware of the boat hovering a safe distance behind *The Mississippi Lady.*

"Do the others know?"

"No, I've said nothing to them about the boat. They're worried enough as it is."

"They haven't noticed?"

"No, if they have they haven't said anything."

When all was said and done, Austin cared nothing about the other women. His financial interest lay with Amelia. She knew that, and she was ready to accept responsibility. For the first time in her life, she was going to consider someone else's welfare above her own.

"Captain Will is certain he can outrun Brown's vessel," Morgan said quietly.

"I don't want him to outrun him. I want off at the next landing, where I will willingly go with Austin Brown."

Morgan turned away with impatience. "What sort of nonsense are you talking now?"

Lifting her eyes from the water, she searched his. "Austin doesn't want the other women. They will only bring him a small pittance. He doesn't want you, because you've made a fool out of him in front of his men, and he'd just as soon avoid the opportunity for you to do so a second time. He wants me, and I'm willing to go with him."

"Are you aware of what that would mean?"

She turned back to the water as her hands tightened around the railing painfully. "I'm not so naive that I don't know what will happen to me."

"Then you will understand why I couldn't possibly accept your offer, no matter how generously noble."

"But you *must*. If I go with Austin, then you can see the others safely to Memphis. Austin Brown will no longer be breathing down your neck, and you can complete your mission, and return to Washington as you planned."

"And what about you?" he asked.

"I would—I don't know what will happen to me," she admitted. "It doesn't matter. Just promise that you'll send word to my sisters in Mercy Flats, telling them what has occurred."

Leaning back against the railing, Morgan crossed his arms, a smile hovering near the corners of his mouth. "Amelia McDougal, offering to be the sacrificial lamb."

She nodded, more frightened than she'd ever been in her entire life, but knowing it was the only way to keep the others from harm's way.

She braced herself, holding on to the railing tightly. "Now you can answer," she whispered.

"Now?"

"Yes."

"Right now?"

"Yes," she said tightly. "*Right* now."

"Not a chance in hell."

Her head whipped around angrily. "It isn't your decision to make! I'll ask the others—it's their lives—"

"Forget it." His tone was so ominous it turned her insides to mush. "They'll tell you exactly what I'll tell you. We're all in this together, little 'lamb.' There isn't a man, woman, or cat aboard that would willingly see you walk off this ship and surrender to Austin Brown."

Turning, he walked away in search of his fishing pole.

"You can at least *ask*," she shouted after him heatedly.

Lifting his hand, he casually dismissed her shout. "No—but thanks for thinking of us."

For the remainder of the day, Amelia avoided him. She wasn't sure why; she just knew she couldn't face him after he had refused her help.

Periodically throughout the long day she stood at the back of the boat, watching Austin Brown draw closer. The others appeared not to notice, going about their business quietly.

After supper that evening, Bunny came running from the bow of the boat, her cheeks flushed with excitement. "Come see! There's a huge boat coming toward us carrying *hundreds* of people. Come on!"

Everyone stopped what they were doing and ran to the front of the boat to see what all the excitement was about.

"Lord A'mighty," Niles murmured. "Where in the world are all those people going?"

Amelia asked the same question when Morgan appeared at the rail to stand beside her.

Morgan's eyes followed the steamer as it made its way slowly upstream. "I can't imagine."

Someone aboard the other boat, the *Sultana*, started shouting, cupping his hands to his mouth, trying to be heard above the clatter of engines.

"What?" Henry shouted back when they couldn't make out what he was saying?

"Over—war—have you heard the war is over!"

"Eh?" Niles cupped his hand to his ear trying to hear above the engines.

"War—over!"

Amelia turned to Morgan, breaking into a smile. "The war is over—that's what he said. The war's over!"

Hope sprang to Morgan's eyes as he leaned over the railing, shouting. "The war's over?"

Waving and jumping up and down, the caller shouted back. "Lee surrendered to Grant! War's over!"

"When?"

"On the ninth—Appomattox! Lee surrendered to Grant!"

"The ninth," Morgan murmured. "What month is this? April?"

Amelia nodded. "April." It hardly seemed possible but nearly a month had passed since Morgan had rescued her from the jail wagon.

Bedlam broke out aboard *The Mississippi Lady* as everyone celebrated the wonderful news. The war was over! Praise God!

Jumping up and down, the women cried and hugged each other, saying they could hardly believe it. Even Elizabeth was seen lifting the hem of her dress to wipe away tears of joy.

As the *Sultana* pulled even with *The Mississippi Lady*, the mood turned somber.

Hundreds of discharged, ragtag soldiers leaned wearily against the rail, staring back at them with lifeless eyes.

The man who had been doing all the shouting leaned over the railing and shouted again, "Have you not heard? Lincoln is dead!"

"Dead?" Morgan called back. "When?"

"Week and a half ago—Ford's theater—shot in the head! The funeral train is taking his body as we speak to Springfield, Illinois—"

President Lincoln was dead. The war was over and a man of gentle spirit, a man who had made himself needlessly accessible at times, a man who was unswerving in his goal of restoring and preserving the Union, President Abraham Lincoln, was dead. It was almost more than they could absorb at one time.

"Where are you going?" Morgan called.

"There's two thousand troops aboard returning from prison camps," the man shouted back, "in addition to some two hundred civilians."

Twenty-two hundred people aboard that boat. Morgan's features tightened as the ship moved slowly by them.

"Isn't that an awful lot of people?" Amelia murmured, still trying to sort out everything she had just heard.

"Sure seems like it is," Morgan returned somberly.

Running up to Morgan, Mahalia hugged him tightly around the neck, nearly taking him to his knees in her jubilance.

"Thank you, oh, thank you for saving us!" It was the first time any of the women had openly expressed gratitude, but the joyous occasion opened their hearts.

Hester came to join Bunny, and pretty soon Morgan had women hanging all over him, showering him with their gratitude.

All except Amelia.

She stood back, smiling at the exhibition, but feeling unable to join in.

Morgan's eyes found her above all the commotion, and somehow her gaze told him more than she ever could have.

Did she feel grateful to him?

Grateful yes, but even more so, she adored him.

Not for what he had done, but for who he was.

For the first time in her life, she knew the full measure of love.

Chapter 18

Morgan reached out and caught Amelia by the arm as she tried to side step him the following afternoon. "You can't keep avoiding me."

Refusing to look at him, she struggled out of his hold and turned to walk away, but he stopped her.

"Do you want to talk about it? Has something I've said or done offended you?" Their brief exchange when they'd learned that the war was over had gone well enough, but it was obvious that she was deliberately avoiding him again.

She drew a deep breath. "No, I just don't want to talk to you."

Her admission didn't surprise him. He knew that his distorted relationship with Elizabeth was partially to blame, yet her reticence went deeper. At times, he told himself that it was better this way. At other times, he didn't deny that it had come to matter to him what she thought.

Matter to him? A strange choice of words, he

mused, as he watched her walk away. However, any other words he might use to describe his feelings for her sounded even more disturbing to him.

As they took on wood that morning, the news that had been so joyous only hours ago had turned grim.

In the dead of the night, the *Sultana*, carrying two thousand troops and two hundred civilians, had blown up, her whole battery of boilers exploding.

The boat had been only a few miles north of Memphis when the tragedy had occurred. Because the river was nearly fifty miles wide at that point, rescue had been being severely hampered. Word was spreading that the disaster scene was a gruesome sight.

For weeks afterward, men would tell stories of the shores being strewn with stark, mangled bodies lodged in the crotches of trees and caught in the undergrowth of willows and cottonwoods.

After all were accounted for, nearly a thousand persons perished, proving this to be one of the greatest steamboat catastrophes ever. The news cast a pall over the occupants of *The Mississippi Lady*.

Dark, threatening clouds had hung overhead all day. Toward evening, the storm finally broke.

Amelia was in the galley with Hester and Izzy when the first roll of thunder sounded in the distance. Izzy looked up, concern wrinkling her brow.

"Better batten down the hatches, girls."

While Izzy locked the cupboards, Amelia and Hester put away everything that was breakable.

Morgan appeared in the doorway, glancing around for Amelia. "It looks like heavy weather moving in. Take the proper precautions."

Lightning forked the sky, followed by the crackling sound of thunder. The storm was closer now, moving in fast.

Faith ran to help Bunny gather in the wash, while Niles and Ryder secured the boat.

The wind started to blow, sending chairs skittering across the deck. Auria ran to rescue them, shouting for Mahalia to corral the other women and get below.

Jagged lightning streaked the sky followed by peals of explosive thunder.

The men on the boat donned oil slickers, shouting to hear one another above the rising wind.

"But I can't swim," Pilar exclaimed as Amelia hurried her along the deck. "What if the boat capsizes?"

"It's too big, it won't! You won't have to swim!"

"But what if it does and I do?"

"Then I'll be right there beside you," Amelia promised, "just like when we had to escape *The Black Widow*."

"But it wasn't storming then!"

"Hurry, Pilar! Hurry!"

All hell broke loose as the storm vented its full

fury. *The Mississippi Lady* rocked back and forth as sheets of rain pelted the old boat.

The women huddled in the cabins, listening with mounting terror as rain lashed the portholes. The boat shook and creaked back and forth in the heavy waves as lightning and thunder came on the heels of each other now.

When she couldn't stand it any longer, Amelia slipped away, returning to the pilot house where both Morgan and Captain Will were fighting the wheel.

"Where are the others?" Captain Will shouted.

"Below."

"Better get us all together. It's gonna be a bad one!" If he had to give the order to abandon ship, they'd need to stay together.

Morgan fought the wheel, spinning it to a sharp right to keep it in the channel. "Amelia."

"Yes?"

His eyes left the river long enough to find hers. "Be careful!"

She saluted him. "Aye, aye, sir!"

Minutes later, a drenched Amelia ran up and down the row of cabins banging on the doors. "Captain Will wants us all in the pilot house!" she shouted.

Ria and Bunny were the first through their door, following close on Amelia's heels.

The other women poured out of their cabins and held onto each other as they made their way along the slippery walkway. Rain blinded Amelia, who grasped Pilar's hand tightly and led the way.

As they reached the galley, a violent gust of wind nearly blew her off her feet.

Screaming, Pilar clutched tightly to Amelia's skirt as the two women fought to retain their footing. Thunder crashed overhead, and the boat rolled on the heavy waves. Above, in the pilot house, Amelia could hear Morgan shouting to her.

"We're coming!" she shouted back.

A fierce gust shattered the row of galley windows as the women scrambled up the steps.

Gasping, Pilar grabbed for Amelia and pointed to the curtains—the beautiful lace curtains, being whipped to pieces in the wind.

"We can't do anything about them," Amelia called. "We have to get to the pilot house!"

"No, Faith worked so hard!" Breaking away, Pilar ran back to the galley steps and began to climb them.

"Pilar, no!" Amelia shouted. The wind and rain were ferocious now, battering the old boat violently.

Pilar climbed to the galley and burst inside. Snatching the curtains from the windows, she screamed as the boat lurched sideways.

Following her up the steps, Amelia slipped, slashing her knee open as she tried to get Pilar.

Bursting into the galley, she jerked down the last curtain, but the old boat was rocking back and forth so violently, it was impossible to keep her footing.

"Leave them," Amelia shouted, trying to pull Pilar to her feet. "Faith can make more later!"

"No! They're the only thing that Captain Will has that Sunshine made!"

The two women battled the wind to save the curtains. Hail began to fall, tiny spheres at first, and then vicious ice pellets rained from above. The sky turned a peculiar brackish color as Amelia lost her balance again and skidded across the floor of the galley.

Crawling back to Pilar, she latched onto the hem of her skirt, trying to pull her away from the broken glass.

"We have to go, Pilar! Leave the curtains!"

Both women screamed now when another heavy wave hit the boat, tipping it sideways.

They clung together, and Amelia's heart sank as another powerful wave swamped the boat. They were going to drown if they didn't get to higher ground.

Locking hands with Pilar, Amelia started to crawl, prepared to drag her to safety. Pulling Pilar out of the galley, Amelia dragged her down the steps as the storm raged.

Muddy waters lashed the decks with vengeance as Amelia began inching her way to the pilot house steps, dragging Pilar behind her. By all that was holy, she wasn't going to give Morgan another thing to worry about. He and Captain Will had enough trouble trying to keep the boat afloat. She'd promised Morgan that she'd be careful, and she intended to keep her word if it killed her!

When she realized what she was thinking, she squealed, lifting her face to the storm to let out a gleeful shout. By golly, she did have it! She didn't know where or when she'd gotten it, but she had it now! Integrity. How sweet it was!

Her joy was short-lived as she felt wave after wave crash against the sides of the boat. Water and hail were coming from every direction as the two women struggled up the steps, trying to hold on to each other.

"Don't let go of me!" Pilar screamed, becoming hysterical now.

"I won't—" Amelia bit her lip, tightening her hold. "I'll hold you!"

Wind and lightning pounded the boat while another wave surged. Suddenly the two women were catapulted through the air and over the railing.

As Amelia hit the water, the breath was momentarily knocked out of her.

Waves crashed over her head. The muddy Mississippi had become a dark, churning demon as thunder and lightning rolled across the sky.

From high atop the boat, Morgan helplessly watched the events taking place below him. Even as he shouted to Amelia, he realized she couldn't hear him.

Bursting from the pilot house, he felt a wave of

panic. Racing to the lower deck, he shouted her name.

In the water, Amelia called for Pilar, straining to catch a gulp of air. "Pilar! Pilar!"

A wave engulfed her, taking her under once again. Surfacing, she spat out a mouthful of dirty water. She couldn't see anything but black, rolling water. Hail beat down amid bursts of thunderous explosions.

As lightning split the sky, Amelia suddenly saw a boat in the distance.

The Mississippi Lady! she thought joyously. "Here!" she shouted, waving. "Over here!"

Looking around, she cried out for Pilar again, struggling to swim against the swift current. It was useless. She was a good swimmer, but the water's pull was too strong.

Her head slipped under again.

The boat drew closer, trying to angle alongside the figure thrashing about in the water.

"Can you swim to the boat?" She heard a voice call.

Wiping the water out of her eyes, Amelia tried to focus. Where was the boat? Where was the voice coming from? Pilar. Dear God, where was Pilar? Pilar couldn't swim!

"Over here!" the voice shouted.

"Morgan?" Was it Morgan's voice calling to her? Had he seen her go overboard? Hope sprang to life within her, and she began to thrash through the water, trying to get to him.

"Morgan?" she shouted.

"Over here! Swim to the boat!"

Blindly, she struck out in the direction of his voice, fighting the wind and the rain.

"That's good," the voice encouraged. "Just a few feet more!"

Gasping for breath, Amelia swam harder. She'd swum often with her sisters, Abigail and Anne-Marie, but they had never attempted to swim in conditions like this!

"Where are you?" she gasped.

"You're close, very close!"

Amelia reached out, grasping at thin air. "Where? Where? I can't see you!"

"Just a few feet more!" The commanding voice urged. "Come on, you can do it!"

With every ounce of strength left in her, Amelia battled the elements. Twice, heavy waves swamped her, but she surfaced with a new vengeance.

"Pilar! Pilar!" she called, her voice weaker now.

"She's aboard!" the voice shouted back.

Relief flooded Amelia. Thank you, God, oh, thank you, God! I'll never do anything bad again! Pilar is safe. They both would be saved.

Reaching out again, she prayed there would be a hand to meet her.

This time, there was.

Strong fingers gripped her arm, lending her the strength she needed to push through the last few feet to the boat.

She wanted to cry out when she felt his hand

closed over hers. For all their differences, he cared. He cared whether she lived or died. She understood that he had thought enough of her to risk his life to save hers. *Oh, Morgan, you care,* she thought, as she was pulled from the water.

A blanket was thrown around her shoulders as she wiped the muddy water from her eyes, gasping for breath.

"Oh, Morgan—" Her voice died an instant death as her eyes began to focus.

It wasn't Morgan standing before her; it was Austin Brown.

A leering, triumphant Austin Brown.

With a wicked smile, he raked a lecherous look down her trembling body. "Hello, lovey. It seems we meet again."

Chapter 19

Amelia stared into Austin's sinister black eyes. *No, not now,* she agonized. Not now when she was trying so hard to prove to Morgan that she wasn't a careless child.

Trailing a long, bony finger down her muddied cheek, Austin's lips curled with contempt. "Surely you didn't think you and that reckless, misguided young Union officer could outwit me, did you?"

Amelia's eyes searched her surroundings. "Pilar—where's Pilar?"

His brows lifted questioningly. "Pilar? Why, I don't believe I've seen your friend recently." He threw his head back and laughed at his own great joke. Then, just as quickly, his eyes turned dangerously cold. "The fish should be feasting on her just about now, dear one."

Flying at him, Amelia struck out, pummeling him angrily. He had lied to her! He had made her believe that Pilar was safely aboard. For that reason, she had stopped searching for her in the water.

Enraged, she struck at him over and over, but he only laughed harder. "You little fool! You and Kane thought you were so clever," he sneered. "You thought you could escape me."

Grasping her roughly by the shoulders, he shook her until her teeth rattled.

"Fool!" he shouted above the rain and the thunder. "Silly, mindless fool! No one escapes Austin Brown!"

A shot rang out and blood spurted from Austin's shoulder. Stunned, he momentarily released his hold on Amelia.

Whirling, Amelia broke from him and ran toward the railing as a hail of gunfire sprayed the boat.

"Seize her!" Austin shouted.

Men sprang forward to grab her, but she scrambled over the railing of *The Maiden Belle* and dove back into the churning water.

Gunshots peppered the air over Amelia's head as she thrashed about, her eyes searching for *The Mississippi Lady*.

"Here!" Faith's voice came to her through the din of rain and gunfire. "Over here!"

Swimming toward the voice, Amelia felt herself becoming disoriented. Thunder and lightning raged overhead.

"Here! No! You're going the wrong way!" Faith

shouted. Amelia could hear the others calling out, urging her on.

"Dadblast it, girl, look where you're going!" Ryder shouted. "Over here!"

Ria's voice joined in. "Follow the sounds of our voices!"

Shots volleyed over Amelia's head as the occupants of the two boats fired on one another.

Diving beneath the water, Amelia swam as hard as she could. Her head pounded and she thought her lungs would burst, but she swam on.

Surfacing periodically, she took deep gulps of air as her eyes frantically searched the turbulent waters.

A flare suddenly illuminated the sky, and she cried out with relief when she saw *The Mississippi Lady* only a few feet in front of her. With a desperate effort, she reached out and felt a hand grab hers—an incredibly strong hand that pulled her safely aboard.

This time it was Morgan's arms that enfolded her, holding her tightly as she clung to him.

"You are putting gray hairs on my head," he whispered gruffly.

Lifting her mouth to his, she succumbed to his kiss as shots whizzed over their heads.

"Oh, Amelia." Bunny rushed up to hug her as Morgan turned away and began firing on Austin's boat again.

The women ducked behind the galley, taking shelter as Morgan, Captain Will, Henry, Niles, and

Ryder kept up a steady rain of bullets directed at Austin Brown's boat.

"Girl, you had us worried sick," Hester told her as the women huddled together tightly.

"I'm fine—but Pilar—" Amelia broke off in a sob as her heart broke at the thought of losing Pilar. She had trusted Amelia to save her, and Amelia had let her down.

"What's wrong with me?"

Amelia looked over to see Pilar grinning back at her as she tried to get warm beneath the blanket Elizabeth was holding.

Climbing over Ria, Amelia threw her arms around Pilar's neck, and the two women hugged.

"I thought—"

"I know—I thought you were, too!"

Captain Will rushed by, heading back to the pilot house. "Hang on, ladies, we're going to have to make a run for it!"

Thunder rent the sky as Captain Will took his place at the wheel. As the others continued firing, the captain began the race of his life.

Crouching low, Amelia made her way up to the wheelhouse.

"What can we do to help?" she asked as she entered, quickly closing the door behind her.

The men had their hands full. Captain Will swung the boat around preparing to make a run.

"Lighten it up!" Captain Will shouted, and the men below began pitching cotton bales over the side.

The women ran to help, aware that Captain Will was sacrificing precious cargo for their safety.

Two by two, the women hauled bales of heavy hay to the railing, then pitched them over.

Spotting Morgan, Amelia broke away and ran to where he was shoving wood into the old boiler. Niles and Henry worked feverishly at his side. The old boat began to pick up speed as the fire was stoked hotter.

Amelia stood back so that she wouldn't be in the way. "Can I help?"

"Go to the kitchen and get all the bacon sides you can find!" Morgan shouted.

Wheeling, Amelia ran to do as he asked, wondering why he wanted bacon at a time like this.

"Sure would like to have a peck of pitch and pine knots right about now," Niles hollered. In a race like this, all was fair, even though using highly combustible fuel such as bacon sides, pitch, and pine knots wasn't necessarily the safest thing to do.

The two boats whipped along in the storm with Austin Brown and his men in hot pursuit of *The Mississippi Lady*.

With cargo disposed of, the women ran to help feed the boilers. Pilar and Hester hurried to relieve Amelia of her load as she returned from the galley with an armload of bacon sides.

Working as a team, the women broke up chairs and crates and anything they could find to fuel the boiler.

Black smoke and sparks belched from the paddle wheeler's tall stacks as the two boats raced neck and neck.

Peeling out of his shirt, Morgan tossed it aside. Sweat ran in heavy rivulets down his muscular back, bringing on a sheen that accentuated every ridge and valley of his powerful chest and back. For a moment, Amelia stood and stared. Workers at the mission had never removed their shirts. No matter how hot it had gotten, out of respect for the nuns, men had remained fully clothed, despite their discomfort.

She had viewed a bare-chested man only on rare occasions, but never had she imagined that any man could look as wonderful as Morgan Kane did at that moment. She itched to touch his strong back, feel his warmth beneath her fingers. The very thought heightened her breathing, arousing longings not unlike those that Morgan had excited in her with stolen kisses.

When Morgan saw the way her eyes lingered on his chest, he grinned, momentarily easing the situation. "I suppose you 'never in your life had so much excitement,' " he mimicked, echoing her now familiar phrase.

"No, and I hope I never will again!" she assured him, feeling a flush of embarrassment that she'd been caught gazing at him with unconcealed interest.

Frowning, she stepped aside as Elizabeth approached.

Morgan tossed Elizabeth his rifle and bent to shove more bacon into the boiler.

Amelia stepped away, feeling helpless. There was nothing she could do. Elizabeth seemed as natural with a rifle in her hands as Izzy did holding a mixing bowl.

Aware of Amelia's consternation, Elizabeth suddenly lowered the rifle and motioned for her to come to her.

Hurrying to Elizabeth's side, Amelia accepted the rifle, grasping it tightly, as Elizabeth positioned it on her shoulder. Elizabeth shouted above the din, "This thing will kick like a wild mule."

"I don't mind!" Amelia had never shot a rifle before, but she was eager to do anything she could to help defeat Austin Brown.

Standing behind her, Elizabeth steadied the rifle, saying firmly, "Easy now. Squeeze the trigger real slow-like."

Amelia took aim and squeezed. The gun exploded, rocking her backward on her feet, but the feeling it gave her was exhilarating.

"Again," Elizabeth encouraged, and Amelia fired off a second round.

The two ducked as the volley was returned, peppering the deck of the boat. The men aboard *The Mississippi Lady* were doing everything short of tying down the safety valve, which was too dangerous to consider. No one wanted to be reckless enough to explode the boiler.

Amelia straighten and fired again. "You know,

Elizabeth. You're not so bad," she said thoughtfully after she squeezed off another round. Lately, she'd almost come to like her.

"Well," Elizabeth picked up another box of cartridges and prepared to reload. "You take some gettin' used to, but once a person clears that hurdle, you're not so bad either."

"Faster!" Austin shouted. "You fools! They're getting away!"

The crew shoved wood into the boiler, sweat rolling down their backs. Austin, clasping his bloody shoulder, paced the deck amid the thunder and lightning, his eyes searching the stormy night. His prey was within reach if these fools would only hurry!

"Faster!"

"We're doing the best we can!" one of the men shouted back.

White steam boiled from the scrape pipes as the boat cut through the turbulent water.

"Tie down the safety valve!" Austin shouted.

"But boss—"

"Tie down the damn valve!"

The pace remained frantic aboard *The Mississippi Lady.* The women worked alongside the men, piling more fuel into the old boiler. They knew all too well that at any moment the boiler could blow, killing them all, but they worked on at a feverish pace.

Wiping the sweat from her eyes, Amelia handed Morgan another pile of kindling. "The last of the galley benches," she shouted.

The two boats snaked around another bend in the river.

Elizabeth and Morgan worked side by side, she supporting his every move. Glancing up, Elizabeth caught Amelia staring at them, and her hands slowed.

The young fool was staring at them with her heart in her eyes.

Touching Morgan's arm, Elizabeth motioned toward Amelia.

Glancing up, Morgan's eyes found Amelia's. For only a moment, they stared at each other as the two boats sped through the stormy night.

Exchanging a quick look with Elizabeth, Morgan sighed, laying aside the last of the kindling. "Amelia," he called, motioning her to approach.

Walking toward him, her eyes locked with his. Her heart hammered against her ribs painfully. Was he going to confirm her worst fears that as soon as this was all over—provided they weren't all killed—he and Elizabeth would go to Washington? In the midst of all this chaos, did he intend to add more? Elizabeth would warm his bed and have his children and live on that damned ol' apple farm Morgan was so certain no woman wanted.

Amelia knew that wouldn't be the worst thing that could happen to him; only the worst thing that could happen to her.

Elizabeth had known love once, and Amelia didn't begrudge her finding it again. She just wished she had found it with someone other than Morgan Kane.

When she reached Morgan's side, he briefly enfolded her in his arms. Though he was dirty and smelled of oil and sweat, Amelia didn't mind in the least.

"There's something that Elizabeth and I want to tell you," he said firmly.

"No." Amelia shook her head. "You don't have to tell me," she whispered desperately. "I know."

"You know so little," Elizabeth said, but not unkindly. She laid her hand on the girl's arm, wondering if she herself had ever been that innocent.

"It's all right, Elizabeth." The two women looked at each other, their eyes mirroring mutual respect.

"What's all right, you silly twit?" Elizabeth demanded in an almost affectionate tone.

It hurt Amelia to answer, but she knew that she had to. "It's all right that you love Morgan. I can understand why you would love him." Her eyes confirmed that she did, too.

"I don't love Morgan," Elizabeth scoffed, sending Morgan a quick grin. "I'm fond of the big lout, but I'm not in love with him."

Amelia's eyes darted to Morgan, her heart going out to him. "Oh, Morgan, she doesn't mean that!" Surely, Elizabeth's candor had hurt his feelings! Who could *not* love this man?

"Amelia." Morgan gently pulled her to him again and held her for a moment. "There is nothing between Elizabeth and me except work."

"Work?" Well, they needn't think she was a blind fool!

"Yes, work," Elizabeth agreed. "Morgan and I are working for the Union. We've been tracking Dov Lanigan for the past six months. When we met in Galveston, we had no idea that events would unfold the way they have."

Morgan picked up the story. "Dov Lanigan was due in Galveston about the time you and I got there. For some reason, Lanigan was delayed, but Elizabeth and I agreed we had no choice but to wait him out. Elizabeth was abducted the same night you were. Fortunately, for me, you were both taken to *The Black Widow*, and you know the rest."

"Then you're not a Union officer?"

Morgan smiled. "Of course, I'm an officer— Elizabeth and I serve the Union, but, let's say, in a more discreet fashion."

"Then why didn't you tell me?" Amelia fumed, angry that they had let her agonize for so long. "The way you two have been acting toward each other, I . . ."

"We didn't tell you because you can't keep a secret even if your life depends on it," Elizabeth said bluntly.

"I could—" Amelia caught herself and nodded sheepishly as she finished, "not." She was glad that they hadn't told her. Even she could concede that her impetuous tongue *would* probably have given them all away. "Then you and Morgan aren't lovers?"

Morgan and Elizabeth smiled at each other. "No, the times you saw us disappear together were only business meetings," Morgan said. "We've been trying to figure out what to do with the others once we reach Memphis."

Amelia's eyes returned to the boat carrying Austin Brown and his scurrilous crew.

"And now it looks as if none of us are going to make it," she whispered.

Morgan bent down and picked up the last of the kindling and shoved it into the boiler. "Well, we'll give it our damnedest."

The two boats kept slicing through the water, their big paddle wheels churning the muddy water into white froth.

The women gathered from all ends of the boat and huddled together as they awaited the outcome of the race. The crew of *The Mississippi Lady* was nearly out of wood. Niles, Ryder, and Henry slumped on the railing, their strength ebbing.

Above in the pilot house, Captain Will fought the wheel, but even he knew that they couldn't hold on much longer. His eyes watched the white steam pouring from the scrape stacks, aware that they couldn't keep up the pace forever. The old boiler was pushed to the limit and beyond.

Moving to stand in the shelter of Morgan's arms, Amelia wanted to cry, not for herself, because here in Morgan's arms she would die happy, but for Abigail and Anne-Marie who would never know what had happened to her. They would wait for her for the rest of their lives, never knowing that she had lost her life trying to outrun Austin Brown and his villainous crew who'd wanted to sell her into prostitution and had ultimately caused her death during a steamboat race on the Mississippi river.

She frowned. Chances were, they'd never believe it if they did happen to conjure up such an unlikely scenario.

Suddenly, there was a thunderous explosion, followed by another. Flying wreckage, scalding water, escaping steam, and cries of distress filled the air as Amelia felt herself being lifted up and flung back into the churning waters.

There were just some days when it didn't pay to get up.

Bobbing back to the surface, Amelia fought the heavy waves, her eyes searching the littered waters. "Morgan!" she screamed.

"Over here!"

As her eyes began to clear, she saw Izzy and Niles clinging together to a piece of floating wood. In the distance, she heard Faith and Hester encouraging Ryder to swim to shore.

Bunny and Mahalia latched onto Henry and Pilar while the others swam against the swift current.

"Is everyone accounted for?" someone shouted.

One by one, each began to call out his or her own name: Niles, Izzy, Ryder, Henry, Hester, Faith,

Mahalia, Bunny, Mira, Ria, Belicia, Auria, Pilar, Elizabeth, Morgan, Captain Will, and Amelia. They were all accounted for.

Grabbing onto anything that floated, they made their way to the bank, collapsing there as they gulped air.

Debris blanketed the muddy Mississippi.

Struggling to sit up, Amelia expected to see Austin Brown sweeping down upon them any minute. Her eyes widened when she saw a piece of wood with the name *The Maiden Belle* on it float by. Her face broke into a weary smile.

"Morgan!" she shouted. She scrambled to her feet and rushed over to kneel beside him. Not only had *The Mississippi Lady* blown up, but Austin's boat, *The Maiden Belle*, had exploded, too.

Pandemonium broke out as the crew of *The Mississippi Lady* rejoiced.

Holding onto each other, Morgan and Amelia watched the last of *The Maiden Belle* sink slowly into the middle of the Mississippi, with no survivors.

It was over. It was finally over! Amelia was going home.

Chapter 20

Two weeks later a sizable entourage of wagons topped the hill overlooking Mercy Flats.

It was all there, just as Amelia had remembered.

Sighing, she looked over her shoulder and smiled. "We're home."

Of course, her sisters and the nuns would be happy to see her, and she wasn't alone. When it had been time to part, the women had discovered that they couldn't. For the past few weeks, their affection for one another had grown into real caring.

"Come to Mercy Flats," Amelia had encouraged them.

"But what will we do?" Pilar asked. "From what you've said, the sisters are old and have too many responsibilities as it is." Pilar longed to have a home—a real home—but she wouldn't let herself dream it was possible.

The voices of Bunny, Auria, Ria, and Mahalia

had joined in support. How could they burden the sisters with yet more mouths to feed?

"Don't you see?" Amelia explained. "The sisters are old, and they desperately need healthy, young hands like yours to continue their work. Think of the orphans and what it would mean to them if you were to carry on the sisters' work when they're gone."

If nothing else, Amelia's adventure had proven one thing to her. She didn't like reckless adventure any more. She'd prefer to live a nice, sane life from now on, one void of excitement—at least, continuous excitement.

Once she explained how she felt to Abigail and Anne-Marie, they'd agree that it was time for them to change their ways. Ever since she'd had the talk with Morgan about integrity, she knew that his was the kind of life she wanted. She wanted to keep her newfound integrity, and she wanted Morgan.

She knew now that she wanted a husband, a man she could share her life with. Maybe Abigail and Anne-Marie wanted nothing to do with men, but they hadn't met Morgan yet. She suddenly felt possessive. And while Morgan was wonderful, they'd better not like him overly much.

"I don't understand," Faith said. "Are you suggesting that we might be of help to the mission?"

"Of course, you can be of help." Amelia reached for Mahalia's hand. "Why, with the talents you each are blessed with, you can keep the mission going for many, many years."

"Do you honestly think so?" Auria breathed, afraid to hope for such a miracle. It was a wonderful dream. They could all stay together, perhaps even marry and raise families in Mercy Flats.

So it was decided. Come hell or high water—and they'd been through both—the women wouldn't separate. When Amelia returned to Mercy Flats, she would bring fourteen extra souls with her. Fifteen, if Elizabeth agreed to come.

Sixteen, if Amelia's heart had its way.

"You're the one I would miss the most," Amelia told Elizabeth the night before they left Memphis. "No one can be as ornery as you, and I'd have no one to have a meaningful argument with. Please say you'll come with us."

"There's too many now," Elizabeth maintained. Niles, Izzy, Henry, Ryder, and Captain Will had no place to go now that *The Mississippi Lady* was gone, so they, too, had decided to finish the remainder of their lives in Mercy Flats, in service to the mission.

"Oh, shoot, one more won't hurt." Taking Elizabeth by the shoulders, Amelia made her look at her. "Where will you go? The war's over, and you have no one—you said so yourself."

"I don't need anyone."

Amelia's eyes narrowed. "Everyone needs someone."

"There you go, being bossy again." Elizabeth tried to look mad, but she couldn't. She wanted to go to Mercy Flats as much as the others, but she felt she just didn't have a right to intrude. However, if the sisters truly needed help . . .

Amelia made the decision for her. "You're going!"

And so seventeen pairs of eyes looked down on the town that was to be their new start in life. It wasn't much—the Mission San Miguel and a few adobe buildings sitting under the blazing sun, but it looked good to them.

The big hurdles were behind Amelia. Only the biggest one remained.

Turning to Morgan, she asked quietly, "May I have a word with you in private, please?"

Removing his hat, Morgan wiped his forehead with his shirt sleeve before settling it back on his head. He knew that he had been unusually quiet during the trip. Transporting the large group by rail and then by buckboard to Mercy Flats had not been easy, but it was the questions in his mind that were giving him the most trouble.

Marriage had always been a consideration for him. He had even gone so far as to picture what his bride would be like—responsible, academic, beyond social reproach. She would be the cornerstone of his life.

Amelia McDougal fit none of his criteria for a wife, yet he was drawn to her. So strongly drawn that, at times, he wondered if his feelings went even deeper. Deep enough that it had cost him the past few nights' sleep. She would be home soon.

Could he walk away from her and never look back? He wasn't sure.

After climbing down from the buckboard, he followed her to a small clearing a short distance from the other wagons.

Locking her hands to her waist, Amelia began to pace, not sure where to begin. She had given her subject significant thought—in fact, that's all she had thought about lately. She was aware that Morgan was a man who would prefer conformity in a woman, but she was what she was. If she were meek, she would lose him, and she couldn't lose him.

"Morgan," she began.

"Yes."

"I want you to know that I plan to purchase books on Washington Territory and read every last one of them, even if it takes me years." She wasn't much on reading, but that would change. She clasped her hands together tightly as her pacing picked up tempo.

Morgan watched her walk, wondering what her mind had concocted this time. "That's interesting."

"Yes, many books," she murmured. "All on Washington Territory, and I swear I'll study them carefully."

"You planning on visiting Washington?" His tone was casual, but she was encouraged to continue by the hint of interest she detected in his voice.

"Well, it's possible—I don't know if you've noticed, but I've been eating a lot of apples lately."

"Yes, that has come to my attention."

"I find they're quite tasty, actually."

"I noticed you seem to lean toward the tarter ones—Jonathans, I believe?"

"Yes, Jonathans are my personal favorite."

"Well, they're certainly better for you than all that bacon."

"Yes—I've been thinking about coming to Washington," she mused. "If you want me to."

Removing his hat, he dusted it on the knees of his denims. "If I want you to," he repeated. He didn't recall that this subject had ever come up.

She paused, turning to look at him. "Now, I'm aware that Elizabeth—even though you both say you're not attracted to each other—would make you a better wife."

Surprise flickered briefly across his features.

"But I could love you more," she contended. "Now, I've been thinking. You have to return to Washington to run the orchards for Silar and Laura, and as big as they are, you really do need my help—or someone's help," she retreated a step. She looked back at him. "Wouldn't you agree?" She plunged on, afraid to face the risk of letting him answer. "I mean, four hands are better than two, besides which, if you're ever going to have children, you should start soon, or you'll be too old to enjoy them. Agreed?"

He nodded, beginning to get the drift. "Agreed."

"And as far as I can tell, you don't have anyone in particular at this point that you want to marry. Am I right?"

"You're right—not yet."

"So, why don't we do this." She started to pace again. "My sisters and I had made a blood pact to always stay together, but I can get out of it."

"You can get out of a blood pact?"

"Sure! When I tell them about you, and how you saved my life and how you need a good, dependable, *strong* wife"—she emphasized the word *strong*—"to help you pick apples, they'll understand."

"You're sure about that?"

She nodded solemnly. "Sure! I'm positive. They're very understanding people."

Running his hand through his hair, he glanced at the wagons, hoping no one was eavesdropping.

"After we get the others settled, I'll have a nice little chat with my sisters, then we can leave for Washington right away. I know you've already been delayed longer than you planned," she conceded. "But we can be on our way very shortly." She looked back at him hopefully. "Agreed?"

True, it was a backdoor marriage proposal, if there ever was one, and she knew that he should be the one asking her, but she wasn't one to hold to tradition. Asking him to marry her flat out seemed too pushy, so this was the only way she could see to do it.

"Agreed?" she prompted again. Damnation! He

just had to agree. Now that he'd come into her life, she couldn't bear to think of being without him.

Turning away, Morgan tried to keep from smiling. When he turned back, he did so with a straight face. "I want to be sure I understand what you're saying. You are proposing marriage. To me?"

She nodded. "Yes, but only because I know that you would never ask me."

"And how do you know that?"

"Well." She thought for a moment. "We've only known each other a short while."

"Yes."

"And we've had no time alone," she reasoned. She blushed as she corrected herself, "Well, very little time together. So you really couldn't have fallen in love with me, not the way I have you. But," she maintained, "although I tend to be rather impetuous at times—I always know what I want—at least, almost always, and in this instance I'm certain I do—want you," she clarified.

He conceded the point. "Go on."

"And I have been a considerable burden to you," she admitted, "so I understand why you wouldn't have thought of marriage—I mean, marriage between you and me. But you see, I can simplify things because I *know* how I am when everything is normal, and I know that if I set my mind to it, I could make you a fine wife—maybe not as good as Elizabeth . . . because, well, Elizabeth has been married before, and she knows how things are done—you know—" Her words faltered.

"No, I'm afraid I don't. Tell me."

"Well." This was embarrassing, but if they were going to be married, she supposed they'd have to get around to the subject sooner or later.

"Elizabeth knows . . . about the bed thing."

"The bed thing?"

"Yes, you know, that thing a man and woman do together after they're married?"

"Oh, *that* bed thing," he clarified.

"Yes, that bed thing. You know, Morgan, I've thought a lot about that lately."

"The bed thing?"

"Yes, the bed thing. Now mind you, I've never done anything even remotely close to that . . ." It was hard for Amelia to imagine doing something like that with a man at all, but she could, if the man was Morgan. "But I actually find myself looking forward to the experience with you," she finished.

"Really, now."

"Really." She glanced at him uneasily. "You don't mind, do you? I mean, my thinking things like that about you?"

"No," he offered graciously. "I don't mind."

"Well," she continued. "What about me? Are you looking forward to . . . you know . . . doing that thing with me?"

Scratching his head, he wasn't sure how to answer her. It wasn't that the thought hadn't entered his mind. It had, many times, but he wasn't sure she should know it.

"Well?"

"Well, what?"

"Well, will you marry me and will you teach me to do that . . . thing, you know?"

His eyes ran over her lazily. "I can assure you if we marry, we will do that thing often."

"Oh." She smiled, loving him even more for his understanding. "That will be nice." Her pulse hammered at the thought.

His eyes drifted from her lovely face down to her firm, ripe curves. His heartbeat quickened. "Yes, I imagine it will be."

"Morgan." Her voice suddenly sounded small and uncertain again. "What . . . what if something has happened to Abigail and Anne-Marie?" Amelia hadn't let herself dwell on that possibility, but she had to face it now. Her frightened eyes turned toward the cemetery where her parents were buried. It looked empty this morning. Only the colorful flowers blooming around the old tombstones gave her hope that life went on, no matter what bad things happened.

He reached out to take her hand. "Whatever awaits you down there, I'll be with you." In that moment he knew the answer he had been searching for for days. He had felt this way for some time now.

Lifting her eyes, she looked at him. "I'm scared," she whispered.

"I am, too," he said softly. He took her hand and held it.

They looked at each other, and the same love that was in her eyes was mirrored back from his.

"Does this mean that you'll accept my proposal?" She was afraid to hope or believe that he could ever be really hers.

"No," he replied thoughtfully, "however, I've been doing some thinking on my own, and I've come to the conclusion that you would do me a great honor if you would accept mine."

Their relationship had grown faster than he'd expected, but eventually, he'd decided that in a real partnership, length didn't matter, only depth. And his love for Amelia McDougal knew no bounds.

Her eyes filled with joy. "Do you mean it?" she whispered. "You're actually asking me to marry you?"

He smiled, aware that it was meant to be this way all along. "I think it's only proper when a man loves a woman, he should ask her to marry him. Agreed?"

"Oh, agreed!" She threw her arms around his neck ecstatically. "We may not have known each other very long, but I think you'll really like me. *Really* like me, once you get to know me," she promised.

He smiled, wondering how he could love her more. "I can't tell you how much I'm looking forward to that."

Their lips met in a long, hungry kiss that promised deeper pleasures yet to be discovered. With a groan, Morgan took her mouth again, devouring her lips in an ardent kiss. Amelia thought she would burst from the joy of being in his embrace once again.

Applause sounded from the wagons, and they broke apart, their gazes reluctant to leave each other's.

"Shall we go meet your new sisters-in-law?" she asked at last.

He extended his arm. "It would be my pleasure, Miss McDougal."

Arm in arm they walked back to the wagon. She wasn't afraid anymore. With Morgan by her side, she could face anything.

"You might as well come away from the window." Abigail watched as Anne-Marie lifted the curtain again to look out. If she'd looked out once, she'd looked out a hundred times this morning. "He'll be back."

Her sister let the curtain drop back into place dispiritedly. "I wish I believed that as much as you do."

"He'll be back, just as Amelia will be here any day now." Abigail contentedly stitched the hem of a new shirt she was making for Daniel. She had to guess at the size. He'd probably grown a mile since she'd left him last month. Only this morning, a letter had arrived from the Mother Superior telling her how well he was doing. She had written that Daniel was growing like ragweed and was looking forward to the arrival of his new parents.

Resting the shirt on her lap, Abigail thought about Daniel's handsome, strong father—her new husband, Barrett Drake.

At first, she had been worried that her sisters had met with ill fate, but barely a week after her arrival back at the mission, Anne-Marie had returned. Now, only Amelia remained absent. But Amelia was late for everything, so there was no cause for alarm. She'd be back as surely as Anne-Marie had returned safely.

Leaning against the windowsill, Anne-Marie wondered what Creed was doing. She'd thought about the stolen hours they'd shared at the mission before he'd returned to his duties. The war was over now, and there'd be nothing to prevent him from marrying Berry Woman. Nothing except the love he'd had for her.

"Were you surprised?" Abigail bit the thread in two and laid the needle aside. "You never said."

"About you and Barrett?"

Abigail's marriage had taken place shortly after Anne-Marie's return. Anne-Marie had thought that they should wait for Amelia, but she understood Barrett's desire to spend a few days with his young bride before he returned to be discharged from the service.

"No, I would marry Creed as quickly, if he were to ask."

"He will."

Turning away from the window, Anne-Marie flecked an imaginary piece of dust from a porcelain figure sitting on the table in front of the window. "Maybe."

"No maybe about it. He's in love with you." Abby's eyes softened. "It's written all over his face."

Anne-Marie desperately wished she had seen it on his face. She'd seen only a sense of duty in his eyes.

When a Crow gives his word, he keeps it. Lord knows, she'd heard that enough to begin to believe it.

"Still, Creed Walker is a man in love, and a man in love can fight it all he wants, but eventually, it will get the best of him," Abigail predicted. She stood up to stretch. "I can't understand what's keeping Amelia. She should be here by now."

Neither sister thought otherwise. The McDougals were survivors. They would be reunited, but it was strange that Amelia was taking so long.

"How do you think she'll take to the news?" Anne-Marie murmured.

"About Barrett and Creed?"

"About Barrett," Anne-Marie corrected softly. Barrett was a sure thing; Creed wasn't yet.

"I don't know."

"There is that pact we made!" Anne-Marie had gravitated to the window again, and Abigail joined her there.

"You know," Abigail murmured in awe, "I would have never in a hundred years thought that

I would meet a man that I would fall so desperately in love with."

A sad smile touched the corners of Anne-Marie's mouth. "I know."

Wrapping her arms around her sister's waist, Abigail hugged her. "I hate to see you so sad. He'll be back—I promise—he'll be back."

Tears welled to Anne-Marie's eyes and would have spilled over if not for the sudden distraction in the courtyard.

Abigail lifted the curtain to look out. "What in heaven's name is going on?" Four buckboards had pulled into the courtyard, stirring up the guineas who were making a terrible racket.

"Amelia!" Grinning, Abigail dropped the curtain back in place and gave Anne-Marie another hug. "See, I told you she'd be back!"

Running out to the courtyard, Abigail and Anne-Marie greeted Amelia with a round of hugs and exuberant kisses.

"What took you so long?" Abigail exclaimed. "We were about to come looking for you!"

"Well, you'll just never believe what's happened," Amelia said breathlessly. "You see, this man, Morgan Kane, rescued me, and we rode to Galveston, and he gave me some money to buy passage on the ship back to Mercy Flats, but I foolishly decided that I wasn't going to do what he wanted me to do, so I went shopping, and before I knew it, I had shopped too long to buy my passage on the ship back to Mercy Flats. I wandered around and I bumped into this man who I thought was a wonderful, generous person, but it turned out he was nothing but a scurrilous, evil man, and before I knew it, I was abducted and thrown on a ship named *The Black Widow*, and this horrible man named Austin Brown was going to sell me into prostitution, but then I got away from him and onto this old riverboat called *The Mississippi Lady*, whose crew were all as old as Sister Agnes!"

Abigail's eyes rounded. "No!"

"Yes. And then we were heading for Memphis where Captain Will and Morgan thought they could get us all to safety, but then the boat broke down, and I left the boat to buy some lace and got in trouble again. Then, lo and behold, just a few miles from Memphis, a huge storm came up and I was thrown overboard and I thought I could hear Morgan calling for me to take his hand, but it wasn't Morgan. It was that bastard—"

"Amelia!" Anne-Marie scolded.

"Well, that's what he was," Amelia contended. "It was that bastard, Austin Brown, and he pulled me aboard his boat *The Maiden Belle*, but then Morgan took aim and let him have it with a Sharps rifle, and then all at once, everyone was shooting at each other and Captain Will said he'd have to make a run for it, which we did, but then the boilers on *The Mississippi Lady* overheated because we were throwing everything from bacon slices to kitchen benches in it, and all of a sudden, there was this horrendous explosion, and I was thrown out into the water again. Everyone started calling out their names, and I started crying because I was so happy no one was hurt, but then we still thought Austin Brown was after us. About that time, we noticed a piece of wood floating by with the name *The Maiden Belle* painted on it, and we knew that Austin's boat had been blown up, too, so everyone was rejoicing that it was over—not that we were happy that anyone was dead, but actually, we were, since everybody aboard Austin Brown's boat was evil. Very, *very* evil. Then, it took us a few days to arrange for train tickets and wagons for everyone." She took a deep breath. "*Then,* we had to talk hard to get everyone to agree to come back with us, and I had to explain to them that the mission really needed them because none of them had anyplace to go anyway, so they might as well come back with me. Captain Will, Ryder, and Henry, you know, are alone now, and then, of course, there's Izzy and Niles. They're really old, but you'll just love them, I promise. Then there's Pilar, Auria, Belicia, Ria, Mira, Bunny, Mahalia, Hester, Faith, and, last but certainly not least, Elizabeth." Amelia reached out to take Elizabeth's hand. "We used to not get along, but we're doing better now." She took another deep breath. "Anyway, that's why I'm late."

The scary thing about the McDougal sisters was that they understood what the other ones were saying. Always.

Turning to Anne-Marie, Abigail smiled. "*See,* I told you it was something simple like that."

The nuns came out to investigate the racket, and the reunion was complete. The mission was filled with sounds of laughter and happiness as introductions were made all around.

Sister Agnes took an instant liking to Izzy, personally showing her and Niles around the mission. Sister Lucille took the others under her wing and saw to their immediate comforts.

That evening, everyone retired to rooms earlier than usual. The McDougal sisters were finally back in their own room, the one they'd shared since childhood. It was the first moment of privacy they'd had.

Pulling a brush through her hair, Amelia stared at her reflection in the mirror. She had changed during the past few weeks. Not only on the outside, but on the inside as well.

She blushed, recalling the embarrassing way she had proposed to Morgan that afternoon. Yet he had accepted. A smile touched her lips. He had accepted. She could still hardly believe it.

Lifting her finger, she touched her lips, his scent still lingering there. There had been barely time earlier for a brief stolen kiss in the dark foyer before retiring. She had yet to tell Abigail and Anne-Marie about him and the future they planned together. In all the excitement, he had been briefly introduced as the man who had been her rescuer.

"Abby," she mused thoughtfully. "Do you know anything about integrity?"

"Integrity?" Abby thought for a moment. "Is that something like honor?"

"Yes, something like that."

"I know a little." The past few weeks had taught Abby a lot about honor and commitment. Barrett had been instrumental in showing her right from wrong, as well as *teaching* her right from wrong.

"What about you, Anne-Marie? Do you know anything about integrity?"

"I know honor and integrity are good things among men." Creed Walker was the most honorable man she had ever known.

"Yes, integrity and honor are good." Laying her brush aside, Amelia turned to face her sisters. "From now on, I intend to be filled with honor and integrity."

Gathering around her feet, Abigail and Anne-Marie nodded. "Me, too," Abby admitted.

"I've given the matter considerable thought, and I agree," Anne-Marie said softly. The three sisters looked at each other. They'd all changed. They couldn't put a finger on it, but they *were* each different now.

"You know this means we can no longer do what we did," Anne-Marie said.

"That's okay with me," both Amelia and Abigail voiced.

"But without our help how will the mission survive?"

Amelia explained how the women she'd brought with her were truly gifted and how they would stay on and run the mission for the aging nuns. The mission would be in good hands. They could rest assured of that.

The three were silent for a moment, thinking.

"You know, there is the other matter of authorities," Anne-Marie said quietly. They were still wanted by the state of Texas for their crimes.

"I guess we could turn ourselves in," Abby said in a worried tone.

"No!" Amelia hadn't meant to sound so sharp, but she couldn't turn herself in. Not now that she had Morgan in her life.

Honor and integrity, they each wanted it, but their former lives hung around their necks like millstones.

"What we did was wrong," Anne-Marie repeated. "It doesn't matter that we felt we were right because we were doing it for a good cause. We were wrong, and we shouldn't have done it."

Abigail and Amelia both nodded in full agreement. "But how do we make amends?" Abby asked.

"I have a good deal of gold. Perhaps we could repay those we have wronged," Anne-Marie said. Her portion of the gold was sizable, but she wanted it go to the mission.

"We'll never be able to find everyone we've wronged," Amelia said, disappointed.

Yes, that would be impossible. Their Robin Hood–like crimes had encompassed a multitude of men.

"Actually," Anne-Marie mused, "the McDougal sisters, as we knew them, died that day in the jail wagon accident."

The thought was so grave, they had to ponder it for a moment.

Reaching for the hands of her sisters, Anne-Marie said softly, "I don't know what's happened to each of us since the day the Comanche attacked the wagon, but I know we've all changed."

During dinner that evening, they had marveled at the differences they saw in each other. They seemed older now, more mature and compassionate.

Undoubtedly, the authorities assumed that they'd been carried off by the Comanche and either killed or taken as brides. The empty jail wagon and the driver with an arrow through his heart would have sealed that conviction.

"I know what happened to me," Amelia whispered.

Abby and Anne-Marie gazed at her.

"I fell in love," Amelia admitted.

No one spoke for a moment as the words hung in the air.

"With a man," Amelia clarified. She waited for the horrifying looks that would surely be coming.

"With Morgan Kane," Anne-Marie supplied.

Amelia frowned. "How did you know that?"

Abigail looked at Anne-Marie, and they both grinned.

"Aren't you mad at me?" Amelia slid to her

knees to face them. "I mean—there is the blood
pact and all, but I love Morgan—no, I *adore* Morgan Kane, and I asked him to marry me this morning."

"Amelia!" Anne-Marie scolded. "You asked
him?"

"Yes, and then he turned around and asked me
back," she related proudly.

"You silly goose!" Abigail and Anne-Marie
hugged her in spite of her foolishness.

"Then you're not mad?" Amelia asked, hardly
daring to believe they wouldn't be.

"We're not mad." Grinning, Abigail held out her
left hand, displaying the plain gold band on her
third finger. "I was married two weeks ago to my
own rescuer, Barrett Drake. He's the most wonderful man in the whole, wide world."

Shrieks of joy broke out as Amelia and Abigail
hugged one another. "I can't believe it!"

"I can't either."

"A man! We each fell in love with a man!"

"But what men!"

Amelia's face suddenly sobered. "Then you've
already done . . . the bed thing?"

"Yes!"

She leaned closer. "Did you *like* it?"

Leaning even closer, Abigail whispered. "I *love*
it. Haven't you and Morgan . . . ?"

"No, we were hardly ever alone—but we're going to. A lot!"

Anne-Marie shared their excitement with a

smile, though her heart was breaking. *Creed*, she thought. *Oh, Creed, why couldn't it be us?*

When the excitement died down, the girls shared their adventures of the past weeks. Amelia described her adventures with Morgan and the women, Izzy, Niles, Ryder, Henry and Captain Will, vowing it was the most exciting thing she'd ever done—but she didn't want to ever do it again.

Abigail spoke of how Barrett had rescued her from the jail wagon, the flight from the Comanche, the trials and tribulations they'd had to endure on the trip back to the mission, Doyle Dobbs's marriage proposal, and, of course, baby Daniel.

Anne-Marie told about her rescuer, Creed Walker, and of John Quincy Adams, Storm Rider—Creed's Indian name—and Storm Rider's blood brother, Bold Eagle. Her voice softened as she spoke of Berry Woman, the young maiden Creed was pledged to marry, but who had been mauled by a bear and lay at this moment gravely wounded.

They all had a good laugh when she told them how she and Creed and Quincy had tricked Loyal Streeter out of the shipment of gold.

Reaching over, Abigail put her arm around Anne-Marie and held her for a moment. "He *will* be back," she whispered.

Amelia joined her, hugging her, too. "Yes, he will . . . who'll be back?"

"Anne-Marie fell in love with her rescuer, too."

"Creed Walker—Storm Rider? The Indian?"

"He's a very refined Indian," Anne-Marie defended crossly.

Amelia giggled, recalling the tall, incredibly handsome savage who had ridden off with her sister. "He's a very *handsome* Indian."

Anne-Marie's eyes filled with love. "He's wonderful, and I love him so much it hurts."

Abigail and Amelia nodded. They knew the feeling.

The girls talked long into the night, trying to analyze their new feelings toward men.

Barrett had been hesitant about remarrying because of his first wife, Abigail admitted. "But in the end, he realized that we were meant for each other."

"I can hardly wait to meet Daniel," Amelia exclaimed. Daniel was her first nephew. "And Barrett, of course. I know I will love them both.

"Morgan and I plan to be married as soon as possible," she confided. She went on to explain about Silar and Laura and how Morgan needed to return to the orchards in Washington as quickly as possible.

"Barrett will be back any day now, too." Abigail hugged her pillow thinking of how she'd be back in her passionate husband's arms very soon. "Then we'll be going to pick up Daniel and then on to Louisiana."

"Well, I wish you all happiness," Anne-Marie said. "Both Barrett and Morgan sound like wonderful men."

Scooting closer, Amelia took her hand. "What will you do if Creed doesn't come back?"

"Amelia," Abigail warned in a low undertone. "He'll be back."

"I know—but if he doesn't." Amelia knew now that not everything happened the way they wished it would.

"Then I will stay here and dedicate my life to the mission."

Abigail and Amelia looked at each other, wrinkling their noses.

"Honestly?" Amelia asked.

"Honestly."

The sisters hated the thought of being separated, but love was that way sometimes.

They understood that perfectly now.

Chapter 21

The sun was just setting behind the treetops as Morgan and Amelia exchanged vows.

It had been a beautiful day, one befitting this wedding.

The wedding party was large. From Pilar all the way to Elizabeth, the women were decked out in pretty calico dresses that Faith and Hester had lovingly sewn for the occasion.

Abigail and Amelia stood by their sister's side, two maids of honor. As with all things in Amelia's life, her wedding was unconventional. Father Luis, very old now, performed the ceremony, his voice faltering at times as he forgot what he was doing.

Because she wanted her parents to be there, Amelia had chosen to marry Morgan Kane beneath the spreading oak, near her parents' grave in Church Rock Cemetery. But it was far from an ending; it was a new beginning.

Morgan looked so handsome, it took her

breath away. He stood tall, strong, and handsome in his military uniform. The sun shot glints of gold in his dark hair, and his eyes danced with a twinkle that had been missing for the last several years.

Barrett had arrived the night before, and Abigail's cheeks were still flushed from the hours they had spent reacquainting themselves with each other.

"Do you, Morgan Franklin Kane, take this woman, Amelia—"

Anne-Marie closed her eyes, listening to the vows being exchanged, silently repeating them to Creed. *I take thee, Creed Walker, as my wedded husband, to love, honor, and—*

"Obey," a deep voice interrupted softly in her ear. "Remember that, woman."

Whirling, her eyes met Creed's, staring somberly back at her. He was wearing black pants, white shirt, and a black frock coat. He was dressed as a white man, and he'd returned to her as a man in love.

"Creed!" she whispered. They dropped back from the wedding party, speaking in hushed tones.

Drawing her to him, he kissed her like a man who'd lived in fear that he might never again hold the woman he loved in his arms.

Crushing her to him with one arm, he raked his fingers into her hair, and lifted her face close to his. Nuzzling her lips, he breathed in her delicate scent. This was the woman he would have walked across hot coals to see just once again. He loved her body and her spirit with everything within him.

She moaned with pleasure as his familiar touch made her forget where she was. The warmth of his hands sent a flash of heat through her, recalling the times he had made love to her. Gently, he traced the cherished shape of her face with his fingertips, the outline of her lips with his tongue, firing their senses.

When their lips finally parted, Anne-Marie drew back ever so slightly until her eyes met his. "Berry Woman . . . is she . . . ?" Was she dead? Was that why he had returned? She didn't want to be his second choice, but she would be if that was the only way she could have him.

"Berry Woman is in good health," he said quietly. "I returned because of my deep love for you."

They could hear the applause as Amelia and Morgan finished their vows and the groom kissed his bride.

"But you vowed to Bold Eagle—"

Creed's eyes met hers. "The pledge is broken."

"Broken? How?"

His gaze turned even more somber. "If I tell you, you will laugh."

"Laugh? No, tell me. You know that you can tell me anything. I won't laugh."

"You will."

"I won't. Tell me, Creed. What?" Her heart beat faster. *Why* was he here?

Clearing his throat, he looked past her, into the sun. "Berry Woman has married Plain Weasel."

Anne-Marie giggled, then despite her attempts to control it, she laughed out loud.

He looked straight ahead, unflinchingly. "You said you would not laugh."

"Plain Weasel and Berry Woman?" She grabbed her sides, laughing harder. It was a perfect match—she was just delirious with relief.

"It seems Plain Weasel was of great comfort to Berry Woman during her convalescence," Creed responded, somewhat defensively.

"Oh." Sobering, Ann Marie wiped the tears from her eyes. She glanced over her shoulder, relieved that they were not diverting attention from the bride and groom.

"Well, you must be crushed," she said graciously, hoping desperately that he was not.

"No, I cannot say that I am crushed."

She looked up, and they grinned at each other.

"Then Bold Eagle will have to deal with the fact that his sister has broken the pledge, not you."

"I have thought of this."

"You're not disappointed?" she asked, love shining in her eyes.

"Disappointed? *Disappointed?*" It was he who grinned this time. "I congratulated Plain Weasel and gave him fifteen blankets, ten horses, and

threw in my damn saddle, I was so disappointed."

"Oh, Creed!" Flying into his arms, she kissed
him, not caring at all that Sister Agnes and Sister
Lucille looked on with their mouths agape.

Squeezing her bottom, Creed said softly. "I love
you, Anne-Marie, and I've missed you so damn
much I could hardly bear it. I would have been
back regardless. I don't know how I would have
worked it, but I would have been back."

"I never thought you wouldn't, not for a moment." Not deep in her heart, she hadn't.

Squeezing her bottom again, Creed whispered
into her ear, "Want to go to bed with me or get
married first, Miss McDougal?"

"Both, Mr. Walker. Both." She cupped his
proud, handsome face in her hands, then pressed
her lips to his to erase any doubts he might have
about her eagerness for both of the choices he'd
offered.

Slipping her arm through his, Anne-Marie led
her man to Father Luis and the rest of the assem-
bled wedding party. No one would be too surprised
by another wedding: they were used to the
McDougal sisters by now.

And Lord knows, everyone would rest easier
now that they'd gotten *those* girls settled.

A soft wind gently lifted the curtains at the mission window as Amelia turned and presented her
back to her new husband. Anne-Marie and Abby

were just down the hall, safely tucked away with their husbands, Creed and Barrett.

Husband. The word still had a funny sound to it, but Amelia rather liked it.

Morgan patiently began to undo the tiny row of buttons on her wedding dress. "I have never understood women and their complicated finery," he complained.

"Yet a man wants his woman to look beautiful, doesn't he?" She tilted her head and smiled at him. "Well, am I beautiful?"

Lowering his head to her neck, he kissed it softly. "You are beyond beautiful, my love."

"You've never told me."

"Ah, how remiss of me." Turning her in his arms, his mouth found hers, telling her all she longed to know.

"Can't you hurry," she whispered, impatient to get on with it.

His own voice held just a touch of impatience now as he returned to the task of undressing her. "I'm hurrying. I can't get you out of this thing."

She sighed as his large fingers struggled to free the restrictive garment. "Did you see the way Creed looked at Anne-Marie when Father Luis pronounced them man and wife?"

The dress gave way, and his fingers released her undergarments, freeing her breasts to his waiting hands. His breath was warm against her cheek, a whisper so soft that it sent shivers racing down her spine. "It seems the McDougal sisters have their men completely captivated."

"Do I have you captivated, Morgan Kane?" she murmured.

Morgan savored her intoxicating scent as he drew her flush with him. "Do you even need to ask?"

"Morgan," she asked softly. "You don't think that I'm still that foolish, irresponsible girl you rescued from the jail wagon—"

His gentle kiss stilled her words, assuring her that he did not. "Even if you were, it wouldn't matter. I love you for who you are, Amelia," he told her when their lips parted momentarily. "The last thing I'd want is for you to lose your freshness and vitality for life."

She frowned, wrinkling her nose. "Don't worry. I'll probably go right on being young and foolish, but I promise to think more often when I'm about to leap."

"Now, come on, are you sure about that?" He grinned.

She nodded. "I know I'm not exactly the kind of woman that you had in mind to marry, but I have loved you from the moment you pulled me from the jail wagon and I fell on top of you."

"Well, I have to say I wasn't looking for love to fall right on top of me," he admitted, "but you certainly got my attention."

"Good—now I want *all* of your attention." She

picked up his left hand and placed a feathery kiss on the shiny gold band she had slipped onto his third finger a few hours earlier. "Agreed?"

"Oh, I don't know." He leaned back, his eyes running lazily over her winsome curves. "Why don't you convince me."

"You think I can't," she murmured as her hands began to take shameful liberties with him.

He chuckled as her fingers grew even more audacious. "Why, Amelia, who has been teaching you these things?"

She grinned wickedly. "I know more—lots more. Abigail told me."

His hand captured hers and stayed its place. Their eyes met in the growing twilight. "I love you."

"I love you," she whispered back. Slipping her arms around his waist, she lifted her mouth to meet his with a fevered eagerness that continually amazed them. "Hello, my darling husband," she whispered against his mouth.

"Hello, my love." His mouth moved to her shoulders, then down her bare arms, teasing, exploring the silkiness, then dipping lower again to taste the creamy swell of flesh he cupped in his hand.

Her fingers tangled into his mass of dark hair as she drew his head closer to her breast. The naked heat of their bodies fused them tightly to each other, and she could feel his branding heat, firm and ready to take what would now be forever his.

It only took a moment for him to shed his clothes, and they went hungrily back into each other's arms.

They stood in the darkness, listening to sounds from the courtyard, exchanging long, feverish kisses. The shifting lantern light coming from the window boldly revealed him as a most splendid man.

Their lips parted, and Amelia lifted a hand to his cheek. "I cannot bear to think what would have become of me if you had not happened along that day to rescue me."

He chuckled, drawing her closer. Spreading his hand along her bare rib, he tested the proof of his desire against her belly. "You would have met some other man, and I would have been the loser."

"Oh, you're wrong, Morgan. We both would have lost." Her lips brushed his, allowing the kiss to deepen until they were both drowning in it. He was all flesh and bone and steely muscle, and touching him made her weak with longing as they stood flesh to flesh, mouth to mouth. There was a sweet nagging ache growing in the pit of her stomach, and with the knowledge that he would soon appease it, her body grew limp with anticipation.

Moving slowly toward their marriage bed, her hands explored him as he whispered into her ear, sweet hoarse murmurings that only a man and woman in love can share. They drifted onto the downy softness that would be the cradle of their love.

"Oh, Amelia," he whispered as he gathered her slender fingertips into a gentle grasp and brought them to his mouth. His weight was heavy, but she welcomed its comfort. "I've waited so long for you."

She gazed up at him with all the love she had stored in her heart. "Then wait no longer, my love. . . ."

Their mouths touched again, this time hungering to consummate their vows. Their hands touched and explored and grew increasingly more impatient as desire became master.

Amelia had never dreamed there could be so much to discover about this man she loved, so many new sensations, so much pleasure. As their pleasure heightened to exquisite torture, Morgan whispered her name as if he understood and shared her thoughts.

Amelia wanted to both laugh and cry with joy as she whispered back her undying love.

Easing his weight from her slightly, his hands slowly undid the pins in her hair. The fragrant mass tumbled about the pillow as he caught it and buried his face for a moment, overcome by his love for her. Lifting his gaze, their eyes met again. This time Amelia could see in them a love that would be there for the rest of their lives.

Closing her eyes, she allowed the beauty of the moment to enfold her.

She was his now; today, tomorrow, and forever.

For more escapades of the McDougal sisters
look for these other novels
by bestselling author and
winner of *Romantic Times'* Career
Achievement Award for Love and Laughter:

Lori Copeland

Published by Fawcett Gold Medal Books.
Available in your local bookstore.